TREATING THE LOVE BUG

"What's wrong?" Paige said.

"I think we need to make love," Ross blurted.

Paige stared at the man. "Wh . . . what?" she said, her voice shaking more than it should.

He held out his arms. "I don't know about you, but I'm wildly uncomfortable at the moment, Ms. Hart."

"You think it's the disease?" she asked, stalling for time. Not that she would agree to this insanity in the end, but because her body was crying for her to do exactly that.

"Who knows?" he replied. "Who cares? I want you. From that kiss earlier, I'd say you aren't exactly disinterested."

"I think," she said, "we have to be careful not to jump into something we might regret."

He rubbed the back of his neck tiredly. "Of course. You're right."

She was ridiculously disappointed he hadn't put up more of a fight.

Get a grip, Paige. But she couldn't seem to, because now images of his hands on her, exploring her, just about stole her breath. "I suppose there are other . . . err . . . things we could do," she heard herself say, much to her horror.

He cocked his head as he looked at her with a twinkle in his eyes. "You mean, like necking?" He strolled closer and touched her cheek. "You mean, like playing baseball? I haven't done that since high school, but if I remember correctly, it was a lot of fun."

Other *Love Spell* books by Trish Jensen:
AGAINST HIS WILL

TRISH JENSEN

Stuck with You

LOVE SPELL   NEW YORK CITY

To Sandra Hill. You know why.

A LOVE SPELL BOOK®

September 2001

Published by

Dorchester Publishing Co., Inc.
276 Fifth Avenue
New York, NY 10001

If you purchased this book without a cover you should be aware that this book is stolen property. It was reported as "unsold and destroyed" to the publisher and neither the author nor the publisher has received any payment for this "stripped book."

Copyright © 2001 by Trish Jensen

All rights reserved. No part of this book may be reproduced or transmitted in any form or by any electronic or mechanical means, including photocopying, recording or by any information storage and retrieval system, without the written permission of the publisher, except where permitted by law.

ISBN 0-505-52422-8

The name "Love Spell" and its logo are trademarks of Dorchester Publishing Co., Inc.

Printed in the United States of America.

Visit us on the web at www.dorchesterpub.com.

ACKNOWLEDGMENTS

One old adage for authors is "Write what you know." Somehow that one slipped right on by me when I was plotting this book. I went into this venture knowing next to nothing about hospitals or medical procedures. My undying gratitude to Betty Bennett, who patiently answered my incessant and often outrageous questions without blinking an eye. And even though my brother is a lawyer, the extent of my legal knowledge is what I've learned watching Court TV. So, of course, I made the hero and heroine both lawyers. Thanks to my personal geek, Ross Bennett (whose name you might see once or twice throughout this book) for help with the legalese. And for allowing me to turn him into a snake lawyer. In both cases, any mistakes and/or fictional license are strictly mine.

Stuck with You

TIBETAN n: a native or inhabitant of Tibet

CONCUPISCENCE n: strong desire, _esp_: sexual desire

VIRUS n: the causative agent of an infectious disease

Prologue

"You are a snake."

"And you are a shrew."

She'd take great offense at that if it weren't so damnably true. "Your client is not getting Doodle."

"He bought and paid for Doodle."

"As a gift for Jasmine, and her name is all over the ownership papers."

"Jasmine stated unequivocally that she'd have preferred jewelry."

They separated long enough to sidestep the sea of reporters camping out at the courthouse to cover the sensational trial of mob boss Carmine "Boom Boom" Carbone—so nicknamed because of his penchant for blowing up his enemies with homemade bombs.

Once past the chaos outside the doors to Courtroom One, they resumed. "Jasmine changed her mind," she said. "She now loves Doodle and she's not giving him up."

"For crying out loud, he's already agreed to give her the house in Palm Beach and the cabin in Maine."

"She deserves those and more. Your client wouldn't have two nickels to rub together if it weren't for her father's investment in his stupid widget company."

"That stupid widget company is now a multibillion dollar venture because of my client's business savvy."

"Because of my client's father's influence."

"Good Lord," he muttered, rubbing the back of his neck. "Of all the courthouses in all the towns in all the world, you had to walk into mine. Why can't you stick to tax law?" He snorted. "Oh, right, your client is also your cousin."

"Second cousin; which is completely irrelevant."

"True. What's relevant is that your *relative* is being completely unreasonable."

She faced the snake and opened her mouth to retort when an explosion erupted behind her. Something struck the side of her head and flung her into him. Her last conscious thought was that the universe was playing some sick joke on her if it had in mind for her to die in this snake's arms.

Chapter One

Paige Hart awoke to discover her brain was exploding.

Or imploding.

Or something else scientific that accounted for the persistent hammer blows behind her eyelids, at her temples, and at the base of her skull.

She knew right away that visual stimulation would be too much to bear at the moment, so she kept her eyes squeezed shut. But slowly she allowed other details to seep in.

She was in a bed. That was good. Better than a coffin, for sure. Well, maybe not, considering there was major drilling going on in her gray matter.

Paige let her hand slide beneath the body-warmed cotton sheet. She encountered more cotton covering her torso, which told her that she wasn't home waking up from a horrible nightmare that had pounded through her head like a wrecking ball. At home she always slept in the nude.

So someone had dressed her in a cotton nightgown and placed her in a foreign bed. Yes, this certainly wasn't her own bed. It was too hard and the pillow too flat and she never used cotton sheets anyway. Flannel in winter, satin in summer.

"Okay, woman," she murmured, "get a grip. Who are you, where are you, and why are you wherever you are?"

Her olfactory senses kicked in. Disinfectant and something else—a sickly sweet scent. "Okay, the where is obvious. You're in a hospital."

That thought alarmed her enough to send her fingers groping over her body, taking inventory. At the same time she wiggled her toes and lifted her legs. The actions managed to make her head pound all the harder, but at least she was assured that all her limbs seemed to be intact.

She wasn't hooked to any life-sustaining equipment that she could hear or feel. No beeping, no sense of anything poked under her derma.

She took a deep breath, her eyes still shut against what she knew would be agonizing light. "Your name is Paige Hart. You're thirty-two years old. Single, thank God. Your parents are William and Lila Hart, currently of Macon. You have six brothers, two sisters, and way too many aunts, uncles and cousins."

At the thought of her huge extended family, she groaned. Because that reminded her of more things about herself. Like the fact that she was an attorney, and from the moment she'd passed the Georgia Bar Exam eight years ago, one after another of those relatives had paraded through her office with a variety of legal problems they wanted Paige to handle.

It didn't matter that she was a tax attorney. That didn't prevent Aunt Lulu from marching Paige's cousin Duane into her office after he was picked up for vandalizing a bridge by spray painting "Jump here" on the side of it. Nor did it matter to her second cousin Bonnie that Paige wasn't trained to handle sexual harassment suits. And it didn't stop the majority of her next-of—and not-so-next-of—kin from naming her the executor of their various wills.

The most bizarre case had been when Jerry, her first cousin once removed, wanted to hire Paige to help him contest the will of his mother, her great aunt Twila. Luckily, Paige had had to decline, as she'd been named executor of Aunt Twila's will, and was able to claim a conflict of interest. So Aunt Twila's estate—all of it—ended up in the hands of an organization called People for a Snake-Free America. Aunt Twila had possessed a real aversion to snakes.

Speaking of snakes, the name Ross Bennett

popped into her throbbing head. Why, she didn't have a clue. She was fairly certain she didn't have a relative by that name, but with her family she couldn't rule it out. No doubt, though, the name certainly left a bad taste in her mouth.

"Think, Paige," she murmured. "What was the last thing you remember doing?"

She gasped as memory tumbled back into her head like an avalanche of bowling balls. Of course! She'd been walking down the hallway of the Fulton County Courthouse, arguing the details of her cousin Jasmine's divorce from Jasmine's husband, Carl Peyton. Arguing those details with Carl Peyton's attorney—the snake, Ross Bennett.

She vaguely remembered being thrown against Ross, something exploding at the side of her head, and brilliant stars bursting behind her eyes before the world went black.

Okay, so that's why she was here. She'd gotten knocked for a loop. But other than a certain tenderness on her right thigh—probably a bruise— she didn't think she'd suffered more than a slight blow to the head.

Well, maybe not all that slight.

Dizzily she wondered what had happened to Ross. The man was a snake, to be sure, but that didn't mean she wished him harm. Maybe she wouldn't mind him having his jaw broken and wired shut, but nothing more serious than that.

And she wouldn't want his wired jaw disfigured

permanently. Because it sure was a nice jaw. It sat squarely below some very sexy lips, a great nose, and a pair of hazel eyes that could probably melt glaciers. Yes indeed, Ross Bennett was one extremely handsome snake.

Of course, good looks couldn't make up for the fact that he made his living from the deaths of marriages. Divorce attorneys were only one very tiny step above ambulance chasers in Paige's estimation. Especially divorce attorneys who were hell-bent on not giving Paige's relative even a fraction of what she deserved. And most especially divorce attorneys like the one she'd had to deal with in college, who'd done everything in her power to ruin Paige's life.

Divorce attorneys sucked. Ross Bennett was a divorce attorney. Ergo, he was a snake, albeit a handsome one. And, unfortunately, a smart one.

Paige prided herself on her zippy retorts, her ability to cut any opponent to the quick. The truly irritating thing about Bennett was his equal ability to snap right back.

He'd caught her off guard that first meeting by matching her cutting remark for cutting remark. And instead of withering before her eyes, like normal people did, he'd seemed to get more and more amused as the slashing continued. Although she'd held her own, by the time she'd left his office, she'd felt a strange concoction of emotions: anger, grudging admiration, and something that felt oddly like a tingling exhilaration, but which she'd decided to interpret as an allergic reaction.

Paige shook off thoughts of Ross Bennett, and turned her attention to opening her eyes, surveying her surroundings, and getting released from this place as soon as humanly possible. She was not a great lover of hospitals.

She cracked one eye open. Just enough to see that there were no visitors in her room, nor any hospital personnel. That was odd. When any member of the extended Hart clan was admitted to a hospital for whatever reason, the rest rushed to their sides and smothered them until the patient had to either recover or croak.

Maybe they hadn't been notified of the explosion yet.

A loud groan to her left had her swinging her head, which she immediately regretted. Pain lanced through her temples and for a moment the room wobbled drunkenly.

She pressed fingers to her temples, trying to keep her brains from spilling out. When the room stopped swimming, she noticed a beige curtain bisecting one side of the room and, obviously, hiding a second occupant.

Another moan came from behind the curtain. Paige wasn't quite sure, but she thought the hospital personnel ought to have been a little more watchful of the two of them. Then again, maybe it was a good sign they didn't need constant monitoring. But she could certainly use some aspirin.

Turning her head gingerly, she surveyed the

room. It looked large enough to hold four beds, but the other side of the room was devoid of anything save two bedside tables. There was a door on the far left and two armoires on the right. The door to the hallway was centered to her left, on the other occupant's side of the room.

Beside it was a large window with its sickly yellow blinds raised. Oddly enough, the hallway on the other side of the glass was so dimly lit she couldn't really make out anything beyond. It gave her a funny feeling of total isolation, but the sound of rustling sheets from the other occupant guaranteed she wasn't totally alone.

Then her eyes lit on a large trash type bin directly to the left of the door to the dark hallway, and the words on it gave her pause: *BIOHAZARD*. And right below that, *Medical Waste* with that strange tarantula-like symbol. Other than the occasional visit to sick relatives, she didn't have much experience with hospitals. But she never remembered a hazmat bin the size of a small truck in any hospital room she'd ever been in.

Directly above it was a steel box anchored to the wall. What its purpose was, she didn't have a clue.

Glancing to her right, she noticed two more windows, affording her a view of the outdoors. Not much to see from this vantage point though. Just a view of the Atlanta skyline, the Nations Bank building towering like a beacon.

She checked her bedside table, and found a

pitcher of water and a plastic cup beside a telephone. Water sounded wonderful; her throat was scratchy and dry. She sat up slowly and swung her legs over the side of the bed. She was barefoot, she realized, and that reminded her she had to have clothes around here somewhere.

Her hand trembled as she reached for the pitcher and for the first time she realized there was a bandage on it. At some point someone must have stuck a needle of sorts into her. As she went to pick up the pitcher she realized just how weak she was from the blast. She needed both hands to pour.

As she sipped, she thought about calling her brother Nick, the only sibling she had in Atlanta, but decided she ought to hear from a medical professional first so she could reassure him she'd be out of here within an hour.

Of course, the place conspicuously lacked medical professionals at the moment. She glanced at the head of her bed. Sure enough there was a call button there. She jabbed it twice for good measure and was grateful it didn't ring in the room.

The other patient had gone quiet, so she resisted the urge to call, "Yoo hoo!"

Testing her legs, she slid from the bed and got to her feet. A bit of vertigo overtook her and she grasped the bedside table to steady herself. Nausea roiled in her tummy, so she took deep breaths and prayed she wouldn't toss her cookies right there.

Her legs felt as rubbery as banquet chicken, so she just stood for a while before attempting to move. Man, she needed aspirin! Where was a nurse? For that matter where was her purse, her briefcase—her *clothes* for crying out loud?

Considering the cool rush of air on her tush, she didn't have to reach around to know that this was one of those hospital gowns that left little to the imagination. Which meant she wasn't *about* to march down that spooky, dark hallway and demand attention.

She turned back toward the door and armoires on the other side of the room. Maybe one contained her clothes, purse and briefcase. With luck, the door led to a bathroom and she could relieve another pressing problem.

Right now that side of the room looked to be miles away and she wasn't certain whether her shaky legs would carry her the entire way. But what the heck. Her bladder was insisting that if she couldn't walk, she should crawl.

Paige took a few shaky steps, relying on the bed for some support. Actually, with each passing second, she felt strength returning, although her headache wasn't receding in the slightest. Okay. Bathroom, clothes-change, medical personnel . . .

Medical personnel. She'd buzzed twice and still no one had arrived. What kind of health-care facility was this? Now that she thought about it, *which* health-care facility was this? The closest one to the courthouse was Saint Catherine's, so most likely that's where she was. Either that, or the one just on the other side of the Twilight Zone, she thought, glancing at the almost black void beyond the window to the hallway.

Desperation to relieve her bladder drove her forward. She was shuffling more than striding, but she was making progress. Mentally patting herself on the back while simultaneously berating the hospital staff, she was halfway to the door on the right when a horrible, awful, despicably familiar snake voice stopped her in her tracks.

"Nice ass, Hart."

Talk about waking up from your average nightmare to a better-than-average fantasy.

Ross hadn't been exaggerating. Paige Hart had one terrific ass. It wasn't a real surprise considering she filled out a business suit better than any lawyer he knew. The first time he'd set eyes on her—the day she'd marched into his office like an angry, avenging angel—his jaw had nearly dropped to his desk. He'd had to consciously stop himself from whistling appreciatively.

Her honey-blond hair had been pulled back in a tight bun and her green cat eyes had been narrowed and shooting flames his way. But even with the evidence of her determined stride and angry countenance, he'd taken a moment to appreciate her female curves, her female chest.

But the moment she'd opened her mouth he'd temporarily forgotten about her pretty face and killer body. "Mr. Bennett, prepare to be taken to the cleaners."

And he'd had to try to ignore that face and body ever since, because within ten minutes of meeting with her—if you could call that sparring session a meeting—he'd learned another important thing about her: She had one of the sharpest legal minds he'd ever encountered. Besides his own, of course.

Which made her dangerous.

Ross didn't like losing. But obviously neither did Paige Hart. And she'd been haggling his client out of more and more assets with each subsequent meeting. If Ross didn't watch it, Carl Peyton would find himself merely a multimillionaire by the time the divorce was settled.

"You!" Paige breathed, and her tone and horrified expression told him right off that she wasn't real happy to see him.

Well, he wasn't exactly thrilled to see her either. If he understood this situation correctly, they were hospital roommates. How that was possible he didn't have a clue. He remembered a blast—apparently Boom Boom Carbone had been at it again—being forced into an ambulance, and then being conked on the head after a deafening crash of sorts. But nothing else until waking and getting a real good look at Paige Hart's fine bottom.

His forehead hurt. He lifted a hand to it, to find

gauze taped over his left eyebrow. Apparently that conk on the head had drawn blood.

"Fancy meeting you here," he said with a grin he didn't mean. The thought of being forced to stay in a room with this fast-talking, faster-thinking shrew gave him a headache of mammoth proportions.

Paige was clutching the back of her hospital gown, even though she was facing him. He wasn't about to complain. The action tightened the fabric across her slender waist and hips, giving him an eyeful. A very pleasant eyeful.

Man, she had great breasts. Nice legs, too. Too bad she had the ferocity of a shark.

Not that he didn't appreciate shark tendencies. After all, he was a lawyer, too.

"Looks like we're roomies," he said, his mouth suddenly dry as sawdust.

"This must be a mistake. How did we get here?"

"I couldn't begin to tell you, darlin'. I don't even know where *here* is."

She eyed him balefully, but as her gaze wandered up to the top of his head, her expression slid from contemptuous to somewhat concerned. Nodding at it she said, "I hope I didn't cause that."

Ross shrugged noncommittally. He knew she wasn't responsible for the blow to his head. That had happened in the crash. How ironic. If not for the zealousness of the EMT, he wouldn't be injured at all. If he were the contentious sort, he'd be writing up a lawsuit the moment he was released from the hospital.

Still, he was nothing if not an opportunist. He could milk this. "Last I remember, you were throwing yourself at me. Really, Paige, all you had to do was ask."

She scowled. "Do you know what happened?"

"No, but somehow I have the feeling Boom Boom or one of his goons had something to do with it."

She rubbed her temple with one hand while clutching at the back of her gown with the other. She glanced over her shoulder while shuffling backwards toward a door at the other side of the room.

"Have any nurses or doctors been in here?" she asked, reaching for the knob.

"Your guess is as good as mine, darlin'. I woke up two minutes ago."

She glared. "I am not your darlin', Bennett."

An idiotic desire to ask her if she was anyone's darlin' had his mouth forming the question, but he squelched it. That was none of his business and besides he didn't like the sour feeling he got at the thought of a positive response.

He'd checked on her enough to know she wasn't married. Routine investigation, naturally. He always learned as much as he could about the adversarial attorneys with which he dealt. That was just common sense.

So he also knew Paige Hart was not a divorce

attorney. When he'd learned that he'd practically rubbed his hands together. Piece of cake—or so he'd thought.

And then he'd met her. He practically shuddered as he recalled that first encounter. He'd vowed there and then never to underestimate another attorney again as long as he practiced law.

Realization suddenly struck him. He was hospitalized. For a blow to the head? That seemed a little extreme. Taking stock, he felt battered and bruised all over, but not severely enough to warrant admission to a hospital. He had a slight ringing in his ears, which was annoying, but not painful. He hoped it was from the noise of the blast, and that it was temporary.

"Dammit, what are we doing here?" Paige complained.

Ross raised a brow. If he wasn't mistaken, that was the first swear word he'd ever heard out of her mouth. Her luscious, pink mouth.

"And why aren't they answering?" she continued, pointing at her bed. "I rang for a nurse."

"Well—"

"Try yours," she demanded in an annoying, imperious tone he'd begun to associate with her. She was one pushy broad. Just on principle—and to annoy her in return—he didn't comply.

"Has it occurred to you," he asked, "that the hospital might be overrun with casualties? My guess is you and I weren't the only ones hurt in the blast. In fact, we might be a couple of the lucky ones."

She shot him a withering look. "Lucky? To be holed up with you? Somehow it doesn't feel quite the same as winning the lottery."

Good thing Ross didn't wither easily. In fact, now that he thought about it, the woman was kind of cute when she bristled. Not all that interested in dying anytime soon, he decided not to voice that observation.

Her eyes lost a bit of their fire. "You might be right," she said grudgingly. "About the number of injured, that is."

Two seconds earlier he'd have bet a million bucks that those words wouldn't pass her lips in this lifetime. At least not directed at him.

She ruined his small flame of triumph by adding, "Going to take up personal injury now, too? Maybe walk down the hall and pass out business cards?"

Her sexy pink mouth suddenly lost a whole lot of appeal. He hid a growl behind a feral grin. "I couldn't possibly compete with you in getting people more compensation than they deserve."

The fire came back to life in her sparkling green eyes, which for some unknown reason made him want to smile. She bared her teeth. "I can't help it if you're a hack."

Before he could retort, she broke eye contact, then continued blindly to grope for the door-knob. She kept her front to him, denying him another view of her very sexy rump. Too bad. His favorite view of her had always been from the rear. Because that meant she was leaving. But he didn't think he'd ever again watch her back end walking away from him without remembering exactly how it appeared in all its naked glory.

He bit back another smile at her fruitless attempts to get the door open. She was way off, and, considering he needed to use the facility as well, he decided to help her out. "A little higher and about six inches that way," he said, hiking his thumb to the right.

She followed through and connected, twisting the knob and shoving the door open. Then she reached in, flipped the switch, and glanced over her shoulder. With a sigh of relief that carried to his ears, she shuffled backward into the bathroom, then slammed the door shut.

As soon as she disappeared Ross lifted his bedsheet and saw he was wearing a gown similar to Paige's. Tossing back the sheets, he gingerly swung his legs over the side of the bed, wincing a bit when the movement managed to make him a little dizzy. Okay, maybe the hospital was just being cautious.

Paige, on the other hand, didn't outwardly appear injured at all, except the way she squinted occasionally and massaged her temple. But if she'd suffered a head injury, shouldn't she remain in bed? She spoke lucidly enough—snappily enough—that he supposed it could simply be a concussion. But even if all she had was a concussion, he didn't think she should be up and about. If she suddenly fainted or something, he wouldn't be much good at carrying her to bed, considering he felt somewhat weak right now.

Curiously, the mental image of hauling her into bed affected him. Sexually. Good God, he knew it had been awhile since he'd had a girlfriend, but he wasn't that hard up, was he? Getting turned on by a shark lawyer who was trying to bleed his client dry? Impossible. Except the tightness in his groin was calling him a liar.

Ignoring that particular part of his anatomy, Ross pushed to his feet, automatically checking his left wrist for the time. But it seemed their clothing wasn't all that the staff had confiscated. He glanced around, but there was no clock in the room. He was due back in court at three o'clock—if there was any courthouse left.

He estimated that the blast happened between twelve and twelve-fifteen, since Paige had waylaid him the moment he'd emerged from the courtroom at the lunch recess. Of course, that didn't mean anything because he didn't have any idea how long he'd been out of it.

If he couldn't make his court date, he'd better get his assistant to request a continuance. Then again, he supposed that if he didn't appear they could easily presume he'd been hurt in the bombing.

Still, he wanted to be certain. With that in

mind, he rang the call button. He needed to blow this pop stand fast if for no other reason than to get away from a half-naked Paige Hart and the strange feelings she caused in his lower belly.

She emerged from the bathroom looking slightly less pucker-faced, but still her green eyes held a wealth of disdain. Ross was about to make another butt remark. But then lights outside their room blazed to life.

By the sound of Paige's squealed gasp, he knew she saw the same huge, stenciled word as he did. It was emblazoned on the window separating their room from the one outside their door.

ENITNARAUQ

Chapter Two

"Does there have to be so much *dirt* everywhere?"

Nick Hart resisted the overwhelming urge to throttle his client's wife. He kept his tone polite. "An unfortunate by-product of construction, Mrs. Jones. You tend to have to dig holes."

Her painted, red lips puffed out in a pout as she surveyed the lot in Buckhead, where she and her husband were building a brand new, three-million-dollar home Nick had originally designed. Of course, his design had been mutilated over and over, every time the twenty-six-year-old bride of sixty-eight-year-old Freeman Jones—media mogul—opened a new issue of *Architectural Digest*. The original three million would probably come in closer to nine. Not that Freeman Jones couldn't afford it.

Just the week before, immediately after the tile had been laid for their outdoor swimming pool, Pamela Jones had whipped open a copy of the April issue and pointed to a photo. "I changed my mind. I want our pool to look like Kathie Lee's."

Nick had had troublesome clients before, and he would have them again. But Pamela Jones was one for the books. He could just imagine his frugal, no-nonsense father's reaction to so much wasted time and money. Master Sergeant Hart would probably recommend tossing Pamela Jones into the brig.

"About the marble in the foyer," Mrs. Jones said, leafing through a copy of *Country Living,* "I'm not quite happy with the—"

"Nick!" a voice shouted behind him.

He whipped around, pathetically grateful for the interruption from the construction foreman— who also happened to be Nick's uncle. "Yeah, Jimmy?"

The portly man puffed as he hurried up to Nick, a frown of worry lining his ruddy forehead. "Just heard over the radio . . . some kind of large blast at the Fulton County Courthouse."

"Blast?" Nick said stupidly.

"Kaboom!" Jimmy elaborated, gesturing big with his hands.

"How horrid!" Pamela Jones commented.

By her expression Nick figured she was picturing the dirt the blast probably conjured. "As in a bombing?" he said, his mind honing in on his sister Paige. Not that he was *too* worried. She spent very little time at the courthouse. Usually she was only there when one of their relatives landed in trouble, and he didn't think any had been arrested lately. But seeing as her office was just two blocks away, the blast might have affected her.

"They don't know yet. Place is in chaos."

"I better get over there," Nick said. The odds were slim, but his mother would have his hide if he didn't make certain Paige was all right.

"But the marble in the foyer!" Pamela Jones protested.

Nick did a quick ten-count. "I'm sorry, Mrs. Jones, but my sister's an attorney and her offices are located close to the courthouse."

"An attorney?" she said, wrinkling her nose in distaste.

Considering Freeman Jones had met Pamela at his sixty-fifth birthday party when she popped out of his cake and danced and stripped for his entertainment, Nick figured she didn't have much room to judge. Then again, could be lawyers conjured nasty images of prenup agreements for young Mrs. Jones. He kept the polite smile on his face by sheer force of will. "Yes. You'll have to excuse me."

"When can we talk marble?"

Jimmy was gaping at the woman as if she were

a lunatic. Jimmy always had been a great judge of character.

"I'll get back to you," Nick told her between clenched teeth. He knocked Jimmy on the shoulder. "I'm sure Paige is fine, but I'll let you know."

"Right away, you hear?" Jimmy said, then backed away from Pamela Jones slowly, eyeing her like a man staring down a rabid dog.

Nick hid a grin while striding for his car. He might have no reason to drive toward the courthouse, but he was going to head in that direction regardless, in hopes of avoiding the foyer marble discussion. Because Lord knew if he gave her another day, she'd likely change her mind yet again. As soon as he turned over the engine and peeled away from the construction site from hell, he pulled out his cell phone and punched in Paige's office number. Her receptionist, Betty Niles, answered before the first ring ended. "Law Offices."

Betty was a fifty-year-old socialite who'd hired Paige to settle some tax issues after her husband had gone to that great bank vault in the sky. One day Betty had stopped by the office to pick up some papers, and encountered chaos. The receptionist had called in sick, and Paige and her other staff were running around like manic chickens while the phone jangled and clients fretted.

Calmly Betty had sat down at the reception desk—muttering something about always wanting to see how the other half lived—and began answering phones. That had been four years ago, and she'd been running the office with an iron fist ever since.

"Betty, it's Nick. Please tell me Paige is sitting in her office frowning over stupid new tax clauses."

"Oh, darling, I wish I could. I haven't heard from Paige in hours. She's missed two appointments."

"She was at the courthouse?" For the first time dread coated his stomach.

"I'm not sure. She stormed out just before noon, growling something about shooting a snake."

He could hear the occasional wail of sirens through the phone. "How big was the blast, do you know?"

"No one can get near the place to find out. Initial reports are hundreds injured, but no deaths reported."

Yet. She didn't say the word, but it hung in the air between them. "Did you feel the blast there?" he asked.

"It rattled the windows a little. And we certainly heard it." Betty took an audible breath. "We've been trying to get through to the hospitals, but it's a zoo at every single one of them, and they're not releasing information on anyone." She let out a haughty little sniff. "I reminded St. Catherine's that I not only sit on the board, but that there is an entire wing of their hospital named after my father." She sniffed again. "They hung up on me."

Nick might have taken a moment to appreciate that in the not-too-distant-future heads would roll at St. Catherine's if he weren't immediately concerned for his sister. "You have no idea which hospital they transported which patients to?"

She rattled off the three largest hospitals closest to the courthouse. Nick knew the locations of the first two, and figured if he struck out at them, he'd get directions for the third.

"I'll find her," he said, trying to assure himself as much as her. After all, his mother would never forgive him if he didn't. One never abandoned a Hart to the vagaries of fate. Not when there were hundreds of other Harts more than willing to step in and punch fate in the nose.

Paige stared at the woman standing on the other side of the large window. Whether a nurse or doctor, Paige couldn't be sure. The woman was dressed in a long, white gown, and she had goggles resting on top of her head and a mask draped over her chest. A stethoscope wound around the back of her neck.

The woman appeared to be in her mid-thirties, with classic, lovely cheekbones and large, gray eyes. Paige couldn't tell what color her hair was because of the cap covering it.

Paige jabbed a finger toward the Quarantine sign then lifted her hands in a "What the hell?" gesture. The woman smiled, nodded, then flipped a switch. Her voice suddenly filled the room, coming from speakers Paige hadn't noticed before. "Don't panic. I'll be there in a moment to explain everything."

Vaguely aware that Ross had joined her to watch the strange ritual the woman began performing, Paige was struck speechless. This had to be a joke. If it wasn't a joke, it was definitely a nightmare.

They stood in silence as the woman covered her shoes and the lower hem of her scrub pants with plastic bootee-type things, tied the mask over her mouth, and donned the goggles.

She moved to the door and opened it. Paige was at least grateful that it didn't look like she'd needed a key, so they weren't exactly locked in here. The woman kept the door held open with her hip while she reached up to that metal box Paige had noticed earlier. From it she extracted two latex gloves, which she snapped on her hands and over the long sleeves of her gown. Effectively, the woman was completely covered, head-to-toe.

"I'm starting to get a complex," Paige murmured.

"No kidding," Ross answered. "You'd think we had cooties or something."

The woman let the door slip closed with a quiet *whoosh*, then faced them. By the way her mask moved, she was probably smiling, but her eyes held more than humor. They held concern. "Not cooties, exactly."

"Who are you?" Ross demanded, and Paige

glanced over to see him scanning the room as if searching for a weapon.

"Please, please, don't be concerned," the woman said. She had a throaty voice Paige guessed men would find sexy. "This isn't as scary as it looks. It's all mostly for your protection as well as the hospital's."

"It looks pretty damn scary," Ross said, and Paige vigorously nodded her agreement. She took a moment to resent the fact that she agreed with the snake on *anything*. She took a second moment to resent the fact that Ross Bennett looked fairly delectable in a hospital gown.

"I'm Dr. Turner," the woman said. "Dr. Rachel Turner."

"Why are you dressed like that?" Ross asked, and Paige nodded again. She was at least grateful to the snake for reading her mind and forming her questions, because she couldn't seem to utter a peep. "And how did we land in a room labeled Quarantine?"

"Please, won't the two of you sit down?" Dr. Turner said. "I'll explain."

Paige's legs were still wobbly, but she managed to make it back to her bed. Ross swept the privacy curtain between them back to the wall so that they could all see one another, then he half-sat, half-stood, his one hip hitched on the edge of his bed.

He had great legs, Paige decided, then shook her head. The blow to her skull was having a very bizarre effect. The last thing she should be noticing right now was her nemesis's anatomy.

The doctor stepped farther into the room and faced them. "I'm not certain how much you remember, but there was a . . . an accident at the courthouse."

"An accident?" Ross snorted. "I'd bet my Beemer that blast was no accident."

"You *would* drive a Beemer," Paige commented.

"Oh, and what do *you* tool around in? A Hyundai?"

"As a matter of fact—"

"Excuse me," the doctor interrupted.

They turned their attention back to her.

"Your guess is as good as mine. All we know is that there was an explosion, and many, many injuries. We probably won't know how many until tomorrow, when all the hospitals coordinate statistics."

"No one was killed, were they?" Paige asked.

"We just don't know yet. None that were brought here," the doctor said. "But there were plenty injured. Too many, as a matter of fact. Our emergency room was and continues to be swamped."

"Is that why you forced me into a room with this . . . this—"

"This what?" Ross asked, his eyes narrowing.

"He's a divorce lawyer," Paige informed the doctor, and by the scrunch of her nose, he guessed she assumed that was all the explanation she needed.

"Is that right?" the doctor responded politely.

"Yes," Paige said. "So you can imagine why I want out of this place."

"So do I," Ross agreed, ignoring the insult. "I have to be in court this afternoon."

The doctor's fully covered head shook. "I'm afraid that's not possible."

"Why are you dressed like that?" Paige asked, her expression full of dread.

"Before I get into that, let me just check you two out."

Paige and Ross both sputtered protests, but the doctor ignored them as she took pulses, checked pupils, listened to hearts. After each test she scribbled notes in the charts that hung from the ends of their beds.

Apparently satisfied, she nodded and placed the instruments she'd used in a cabinet beside the bathroom.

"Ms. Hart, you've suffered a mild concussion. Nothing that a little time and Tylenol won't cure."

"I can do that at home," Paige said quickly.

"I'm sure you could," the doctor replied, then turned her attention to Ross. "Mr. Bennett, you have five stitches in your forehead. But otherwise you didn't sustain any injuries. In fact, the two of you actually saved each other from worse, from what the paramedics told me. Ms. Hart shielded you from the blast, and you broke her fall."

"Did I do that?" Paige asked, pointing at Ross's head.

"Actually, he sustained the laceration in the accident."

"Accident?" Paige said.

"The one on the way to the hospital."

Paige scowled at Ross. Apparently he wasn't going to get any more guilt mileage out of her. Too bad. "Okay, diagnosis is, we'll live," he said quickly, avoiding Paige's glare. "When can we leave?"

"I'm getting to that," Dr. Turner said.

Paige was getting scared. She wasn't an expert, but things looked a little too ominous at the moment. She crossed her arms, tapping her fingers against her skin. It was more an act of nervousness than impatience. She had the feeling they were in for some not-so-good news.

"As I said," the doctor went on in that husky voice, "there were many, many injuries. Too many for emergency services to handle. We had to call in every resource available to us."

Ross grunted his impatience.

The doctor must have heard it, because she arched him a cool look that Paige bet quelled most men. "We were strapped and some ambulance workers who were in the area on another mission stopped to help. They thought they were doing you a favor, when, in fact, it was a mistake, considering what they were carrying."

"What they were carrying?" her patients chimed in unison.

"They were transporting some . . . materials to the CDC."

CDC? The Centers for Disease Control? Suddenly the woman's weird attire wasn't so puzzling. She was protecting herself from infection of some sort. Protecting herself from *them*.

Ross must have reached the same conclusion because he surged to his feet. "What are you trying to say?"

The doctor wasn't cowed. "There's a slight chance that the two of you came into contact with infectious materials when you were transported in that ambulance."

"What kind of infectious materials?" Paige asked sharply.

"We're still getting details faxed to us from the CDC. But the fact is they were transporting some viral cultures and blood specimens, which were jostled and broken in the accident. They didn't realize it until they unloaded you."

"A virus?" Paige squealed. The word AIDS screamed through her aching—and suddenly spinning—head.

"What virus?" Ross demanded.

"The CDC believes it's a new strain of Tibetan Concupiscence Virus. Or TCV."

"Oh, my God," Paige said. She didn't have a clue what that was, but it sure sounded awful, and visions of their skin suddenly breaking out in horrible sores filled her mind.

"Concupiscence?" Ross repeated. Paige could

almost see his mind chugging along. Understanding had his eyes widening. "Horny Monk Disease?" he said dryly, not nearly as panicked as Paige felt he ought to be.

"Oh, you've heard of it?" the doctor said.

"Horny Monk Disease?" Paige whispered.

"They actually call it that?" Ross said, gaping a bit himself. "I was *kidding!*"

The doctor laughed. "No, I don't believe they call it that. At least not in official literature. But you're getting the idea. The symptoms appear to be . . . somewhat unusual."

"Is it dangerous?" Paige asked, not sure she wanted to know what the unusual symptoms might be.

Dr. Turner shook her head. "It doesn't appear to be dangerous to young, healthy adults such as yourself. But it could pose a danger to the elderly, especially if they're already ill. And of course, we wouldn't want children exposed to it."

Ross quirked an eyebrow. "What are these . . . unusual symptoms? And how long do we have to stay quarantined?"

The woman cleared her throat. "Well, some symptoms are elevated heart rate, a warmth radiating under the skin, possible dizzy spells, heightened sexual awareness, and a few other very minor irritations."

"Oh . . . my . . . God," Paige said faintly.

Ross crossed his arms. "I've never actually considered heightened sexual awareness an irritation."

"That's it!" Paige said, pointing at Ross accusingly.

"That's what?" he and the doctor asked at the same time.

"The reason I was ... was ... Never mind," Paige said, feeling her cheeks heat up. Like she'd ever admit she'd been making silent, nonlawyerly observations about the snake the last few minutes. Hospital gowns weren't supposed to look that good. Or skimpy.

Ross grinned, revealing dimples she'd never really noticed before. And a smile that could entice a nun.

Paige shook her head and dragged her gaze from his. "We need two rooms."

"Afraid you won't be able to resist me?"

"Get a life," she said, after a rather unladylike snort. "We need two rooms," she repeated to the doctor.

"I'm afraid that won't be possible. At least not for the foreseeable future."

"Why not?" Paige nearly shrieked. "I cannot share a room with this ... *him*."

"I understand," the doctor said soothingly, although not effectively. Paige felt anything but soothed. In fact, she felt downright near hysteria. "But I'm afraid that until we start releasing some of the other blast victims, we are in dire straits for space. And frankly, the space to handle isolation cases such as this is already at a minimum."

"There has to be some other way," Paige implored, ignoring the smirk on Ross's handsome, disgusting face.

"I'm afraid not," the doctor said. "Not immediately. But I promise we'll try and get you into private rooms as soon as we can."

"Oh, Lord," Paige said, rubbing her throbbing temples. "Nightmare just doesn't begin to describe this situation."

"How long is the quarantine period?" Ross asked.

"Ten to fourteen days, I'm afraid."

"Two weeks?" Ross said. "I can't stay away from my practice that long."

"Well," said the good—or rapidly becoming the not-so-good—doctor, "We'll want to monitor Ms. Hart's condition for the next twenty-four hours, but as long as you're not showing signs of illness, you can have any equipment you may need delivered."

"I'll need a fax machine, my pending files, a set of law boo—"

"Just remember that most of what's brought in has to be sterilized before it can be taken out. And if it can't be sterilized, it leaves here in a hazmat container and is destroyed."

"But I can fax things to my office, right?"

"I don't see why not."

"I need aspirin," Paige whimpered.

The doctor's gray eyes darkened in sympathy.

"I'll have a nurse bring you some Tylenol right away. I'll also bring in a couple of pads of paper so you can make lists of whatever you'd like your families or coworkers to bring you."

"Can we get real clothes?"

"Absolutely. Your comfort is key. But I wouldn't recommend any silk blouses. They stand a good chance of being destroyed in the sterilization process. Try to stick with one hundred percent cotton."

"We want the TV activated," Ross added, grinning at Paige. When she frowned at him, he shrugged and said, "All work and no play and all that."

Paige practically groaned at the thought of "playing" with Ross the snake for days on end. She dragged her gaze from his dimpled grin. "Can we request a brick wall?"

The doctor's throaty laughter filled the silence. "Are you two a little concerned about the symptoms?"

"Not a chance," Paige said hotly. But then she put a hand to her head. "But are you sure there's not an antidote or something?"

"Not one we're aware of at the moment. Like I said, this is all new to us. But I promise the CDC is working feverishly on it." Her eyes twinkled. "No pun intended." The woman laid a gloved hand on Paige's arm. "And we'll be monitoring you closely. We'll do everything we can to keep any discomfort to a minimum."

"How soon will these . . . symptoms begin to appear?" Paige asked, pretty sure she was already a little afflicted, considering Ross Bennett kept getting better looking every time she glanced at him. The toad.

Before the doctor could answer her, the outer door leading into the anteroom opened and a nurse entered. She moved to the intercom.

"Oh, good," the doctor said. "Ms. Hart, Mr. Bennett, this is Nurse Martinez. Maria, Paige Hart and Ross Bennett."

"Hello," the striking Latino woman said, her gaze honing in directly on Ross. Her smile widened considerably.

"Nurse Martinez is one of our finest," the doctor said. "She'll take very good care of you."

"Oh, yes, I certainly will."

Paige wasn't exactly thrilled at the idea that Nurse Martinez looked more than willing to take superb care of the snake. Visions of sponge baths danced through her head. "Aspirin," she reminded the doctor, a little more curtly than she'd have liked.

"Oh, yes." The woman moved to Paige's bed and pulled her chart again. The doctor flipped it open and began making notes. "Maria, let's get Ms. Hart some Tylenol—a thousand milligrams to start—and then more later as needed."

Maria blinked, then glanced at Paige as though suddenly realizing she wasn't a piece of furniture. Finally she nodded.

Dr. Turner turned to Ross. "Would you care for a pain reliever?"

He touched the bandage on his forehead. "It doesn't hurt that bad."

Oh, great, now he was trying to be macho. Probably for the nurse who was looking at him like she was an Ethiopian orphan and he was a seven-course feast.

"Do you happen to know the last time you had a tetanus shot?"

Ross squinted. "Hmmm, actually, no."

"In the last ten years?"

"Definitely not."

"Okay, we'll have to give you a booster."

"Is that going to hurt?"

Paige rolled her eyes. "Men are *such* babies."

"Hey, it's *healthy* to want to avoid pain."

"Your arm will be sore for a few days, yes," the doctor informed him.

"Is it . . . umm . . . absolutely necessary?"

"Sheesh!"

"Unfortunately, yes," the doctor answered. She turned back to the nurse. "Booster shot for Mr. Bennett."

"Got it."

"That's it, then, Maria. For now."

"Not quite," Maria said. "Ms. Hart's brother is here."

And the Hart cavalry begins riding to the rescue. "Oh, thank God," Paige said. "That's Nick. *Please* let me talk to him. He'll know what to do."

The doctor's eyes went wide as baseballs. Her mask flared right about where her nostrils would be. She sucked in an audible breath. "Your brother's name is Nick Hart?"

Uh-oh. "Yes. Why? Do you know him?"

"Please tell me he's not an architect."

"No can do. He's an architect."

"Damn," the doctor muttered, suddenly glancing around wildly as if looking for a quick rock to hide under.

"I take it you know him," Paige surmised dryly. Oh, great. This woman had Paige's life and continued good health in her hands, and Paige's guess was that she had been one in the long trail of broken hearts Nick had scattered from Macon to Atlanta.

Just then Nick barreled his way into the anteroom, displaying his famous lack of patience.

Paige would have been wildly relieved to see him if out of the corner of her eye she didn't notice the doctor go stiff as a steel rod.

"Paige, are you all right?" he asked, his deep voice filling the deadly quiet room and his blue eyes brimming with concern.

His gaze flickered over the doctor but not a spark of recognition lit them. Which wasn't surprising, considering her getup. Then he spotted Ross, and Nick, too, went stiff. "What the hell's going on here? Paige? What are you doing in a room with a *man?*"

Paige sighed. Nick, by virtue of the fact that he

was two entire years older than Paige, believed he was her keeper. He'd been the sole reason Paige had made it through high school with her virginity intact. Of course, he still blamed himself for the disaster her freshman year in college, which was utterly ridiculous.

Paige suppressed a shudder at the memory. "How about if I let the doctor tell you?" she said. "Nick, this is Dr. Turner. Dr. *Rachel* Turner."

"How do you do," he said gruffly, and again there was not an ounce of recognition. "Now tell me what you're doing to my sister."

Paige almost groaned again. If there hadn't been a glass partition separating them, Paige would gladly smack her oaf of a brother right upside his head. Now was *not* the time for him to forget an old girlfriend.

Chapter Three

He doesn't even recognize my name.

It was a very fortunate thing for Nick Hart that Rachel Turner wasn't into violence as a rule. Otherwise he'd have been in danger of severe bodily harm at that moment.

Well, she couldn't actually blame him for not recognizing her in this outfit. Especially since she wasn't the same plump, shy nerd she'd been back then. But he could at least have the decency to remember the name of the woman who had helped him try to pass college biology.

All of the hurt she'd felt that spring and summer came crashing back as though it had been yesterday. Pacing with anxiety during the hour of his exam, each anxious step a pleasantly painful reminder of what she'd given him so freely the night before. And it hadn't all been answers to biology questions.

After the exam, waiting breathlessly by the phone, wanting, *needing* to hear him tell her he'd aced his test, all because of her. Wanting, *needing* for him to show up, take her in his arms and thank her the old-fashioned way.

When she'd heard nothing for hours, she bit the bullet and called *him*. No answer. She waited an hour longer, figuring maybe he was out cele-brating with his fraternity brothers. But then she'd gotten just irritated enough to march over to his dorm room, only to find the door wide open and all of his personal possessions gone. It was as though he'd disappeared into thin air.

Or had never existed to begin with.

Still, Rachel had clung to a thread of hope for nearly another month. Every time the phone rang she'd feel a zap to her heart. And every time it wasn't Nick on the other end of the line she'd be swamped with despair.

And finally one day, when the phone rang and she'd received the worst news of her life, she'd given up all hope, all thoughts, all dreams of Nick Hart.

Until now.

The jerk.

How dare he come waltzing into *her* hospital after all these years, looking even better than he had in college? She would never have believed it possible. But there he stood, his sandy blond hair just a little too long, his blue eyes made even more seductive by fine lines fanning out from them as if he'd spent the last fifteen years squinting into the sun.

His complexion supported that suspicion. He was deeply tanned, and his body was just as broad and hard as it had been in his old football-playing days. Not that she'd thought about him over the years—well, not much at any rate—but she had to admit she'd have loved to know that Nick had gone soft and paunchy. And bald.

No such luck.

He was still the gorgeous man he'd been back then. Too good for a shy, plain coed like her. But miraculously—or so she'd thought at the time—he'd seemed to genuinely like her. And on that final night of cramming, seemed to genuinely desire her.

The man had been the ultimate actor.

"Doctor . . . err . . . Turner, is it?" the idiot said.

Rachel blinked, realizing she'd been so lost in the past, the here and now had slipped out of her grasp.

"I don't know how you know Nick," Paige said in an undertone. "But please don't hold him against me."

Rachel wasn't about to admit that in some distant past she'd definitely held Nick against herself. "Don't worry," she assured the beautiful woman who Rachel now realized looked so much like her brother it almost hurt. "I'm not into secondhand retribution."

"Good," Paige said, looking half-relieved, half-curious.

"I'll have Maria bring in your pain reliever. Start making lists of the belongings you want brought to you. I'll go speak with your brother."

"What are you going to tell him?" Paige asked, suddenly wary.

"Just the facts."

"Please don't tell him ... the ... err ... symptoms."

Rachel glanced over to find Ross Bennett grinning. *Oh, boy.* She had a feeling these two had a history as well. What kind, she didn't know. But this situation was suddenly a little more volatile. She made a mental note to try to expedite the separation of the two if at all possible.

Rachel returned her attention to Paige's brother. She could feel the scowl form on her face. Good thing he couldn't see it. She took a step toward the door. "Mr. Hart, I'll be right out to explain the circumstances. But I want you to step to your left. Whatever you do, I don't want you touching me." Boy, now there was an understatement. "Got it?"

His frown was disgustingly sexy. She remembered it from college. The way those hard lips had turned down slightly whenever he was working through a particularly tough problem. The way his sandy eyebrows arrowed downward; the way his eyes darkened slightly. A kissable frown. Now there was a new concept. And one she didn't have any intention of exploring.

Rachel watched Nick silently move to his left, his eyes fixed on his sister, his expression brimming with concern. Well, what do you know? He *could* care about someone other than himself.

Rachel took a deep breath then marched to the door to the anteroom. She opened it, then propped it on her hip as she pulled off her gloves and dropped them in the hazmat bin inside the room. She backed into the anteroom and let the door *whish* shut on its own.

Before the knob even clicked into place, Nick stepped toward her and began barraging her with questions. "What happened to my sister? Why is she quarantined? What the *hell* is she doing in there with a man?"

"Stay back!" Rachel said, and was horrified her voice came out sounding panicky. Contamination wasn't the only thing she feared, although she hated admitting it to herself. His proximity after all this time was making her heart do nasty things. Because she couldn't help but remember the last time they'd been this close. Even closer. He'd kissed her good-bye, thanked her for *everything*, then waltzed out of her life.

"Nick!" Paige's voice sounded through the intercom. "Quit badgering Dr. Turner! This isn't *her* fault!"

The man obediently stepped back again, then

said in a low voice he probably hoped wouldn't carry to the other room. "She's going to be all right, isn't she?"

"She's going to be fine. Let me get out of this gown and scrub down, then we can go out in the hall and talk."

For some reason she was loath to reveal her face. She realized that at this point she didn't want Nick Hart to recognize her. She didn't want to experience the hot humiliation of seeing him get all uncomfortable when he realized she was at least one of the women he'd used and dumped in his youth.

So she dawdled a bit as she put away the stethoscope, removed the plastic booties and dumped them in the red plastic-lined, corrugated hazmat box and removed the gown and dropped it in the "sterilize" bin.

She did all this without looking at him, but out of the corner of her eye she noticed that he seemed surprised by what she wore underneath. She didn't know what he'd expected her to be wearing, but apparently scrubs weren't it.

The moment of truth arrived. Self-consciously, and still avoiding his gaze, she untied her mask, pulled off the goggles, then removed the cap and shook out her hair.

Sucking in a deep breath, she turned to face him. His perusal was agonizingly slow and thorough, as it appeared he was cataloguing every feature she possessed.

His smile, too, was slow in developing, but it was filled with all the wrong messages. Instead of recognition, it conveyed new interest. The jerk. She hadn't changed *that* much. So her hair was much shorter than in college, but it was still dark brown and unruly. So she wore contacts now instead of glasses, but her eyes were just as gray as they'd been back then. So her face had thinned down when she'd dropped twenty pounds, but it was *still* her face, the one he'd gazed down on with what she'd thought was so much passion and heat.

She wanted to kick him. She wanted to scream and beat her fists on his chest. She wanted to ask him how he'd done on that damn biology exam.

Because she wasn't about to do any of those things, she moved to the sink and began scrubbing her hands and arms with disinfectant soap.

"That getup isn't much of a fashion statement, is it?" he asked, that dry undertone of humor so achingly familiar, it caused a lump to form in her throat.

She swallowed. "It's not meant to be."

"Two minutes ago I wouldn't have guessed there was a woman under there, much less a gorgeous one." He thrust out a hand. "Nick Hart."

Oh, yes, she'd shoot him if she had the chance. Straight through his heartless chest. As she finished drying off with paper towels she looked pointedly at his hand, then up to his face. *Nice to meet you* would be a lie on two levels. First it *wasn't* nice, and second, they'd already met. So she stuck with, "How do you do?"

She almost winced. Even to her own ears she sounded like a humorless prig. Well, what did she care? She certainly never planned on sharing laughter with the man again in this lifetime.

His hand dropped slowly and his smile faded. But instead of showing consternation at her chilly response, he just seemed to show curiosity. He looked deeply into her eyes and for a moment Rachel held her breath, mesmerized.

His head tilted as he kept his eyes locked on hers, and he frowned slightly. "Have we met?"

Rachel's heart stopped for a painful moment. "What makes you think that?"

"I don't know. You just . . . look familiar somehow."

"Trust me, Mr. Hart. Had we met before, I'd have remembered."

He grinned. "Is that a compliment?"

"No."

"Wow," Ross said after the doctor sailed out of the anteroom with Paige's brother hot on her heels.

"Wow, what?" Paige asked him, still staring at the outer door, now shut.

"Did you see those sparks flying?"

"Sparks?" she said. "More like daggers."

"What do you think that was all about?"

"With Nick, I make it a policy not to try and guess."

"I'm thinking history there," Ross said, proud at his keen observations of human nature. Of course, his recent observations weren't exactly bending toward the inner workings of people, but on nature of a totally different sort. Like the kind that sent up a prayer of thanks to God for doing such a fine job in creating women. One woman in particular at the moment. The one stuck with him in a hospital room.

He didn't think that the virus they were supposedly exposed to had anything to do with it just now. He'd always conceded that Paige Hart was one sexy broad. So the fact that he found her really appealing right now was just a reasonable response from any normal, healthy male.

"What are you looking at, Bennett?"

Ross blinked, realizing he had, indeed, been checking her out in a somewhat lascivious manner. Who wouldn't? "You."

"Well, cut it out."

"Kind of hard when you're the only other person in the room, and there's not a book or newspaper in sight."

"Start counting tiles or something," she snapped.

Ross pressed his lips together to keep from chuckling. Up until recently, he'd considered her prickly manner a real pain in the ass. But for some reason he was beginning to enjoy it. In fact, he decided, shifting on the bed, he was beginning to respond to it. Which was absurd, but there you had it.

She wrapped her arms around her waist and hugged herself, looking around. "Could things get any worse?"

Ross shrugged. He wasn't exactly happy with the situation either, but he was slowly discovering a few benefits. "We're still breathing. The alternative wouldn't be much fun."

She nodded thoughtfully. "There are so many things I'm going to need."

She'd agreed with him. That wasn't all that fun. "Same here. But if it's as she says and we can't take everything back out that's brought in, it's going to be an expensive proposition."

"*We* didn't cause this situation, why should we have to pay for it?"

"Oh, I fully plan to recover the expense, but the initial outlay will probably have to come straight out of our pockets." He stood up and propped his hip against his bed. "Although I have an idea how we could minimize it some."

"How's that?" she asked, shooting him a leery look.

"We could share."

Paige's cat eyes narrowed even further. "Oh, yeah, you'd love that, wouldn't you? Raiding my files when I'm not looking."

He stood up straight at that. "Hey, I could get offended."

She snorted. "You're a divorce attorney. You

vermin don't know how to be offended. Just offensive."

Okay, that had crossed the line from sparring to just plain insulting. Insulting wasn't nearly as cute as sparring. And he wasn't about to justify his choice of professions to her. His reasoning for specializing in divorce litigation was his alone, and way too personal to reveal to anyone. "Have it your way. It just seems ridiculous to waste the money on two computers, two faxes, the whole works, when we might have to leave them behind."

She digested that for a moment with a prudish pressing of her lips. Ross had the feeling she hated to agree with him on anything, no matter how reasonable.

Other than being opposing attorneys in a divorce case, he couldn't quite figure out the origin of her dislike of him. After all, there were two sides to any divorce, and though he fought some bloody battles for his clients, when the war was over he and the other attorney in the case would shake hands and buy each other drinks. It was simply what people in their line of work did.

It sort of irritated him that he cared what she thought at all. What did it matter? Just because she was an intelligent, beautiful woman shouldn't make a difference. He'd dated his share of successful women in his thirty-three years, and they had all seemed to like him well enough. He'd even learned the fine art of breaking off the relationships with barely any hard feelings. Most of his former girlfriends were still good friends.

That thought reminded him of Tina, his neighbor, whom he'd dated for several weeks over a year ago. He needed to get hold of her as soon as possible and ask her to take care of his Persian cat, Sammy, while he was locked in this hole. He hoped she wasn't off on some exotic modeling assignment.

"Okay," Paige finally said, interrupting his budding mental "to do" list. "I suppose we can share a fax. But not a computer."

"Man, you are one suspicious female," he complained. "This could possibly turn out to be pure hell."

"Ha! Consider who I'm dealing with here."

He stalked over to her, his gaze boring into hers. "You know, I'm getting just a little tired of your derogatory remarks. Other than the fact that I'm an attorney, you don't know a thing about me."

She opened her mouth, a retort just begging to fly from her lips. But nothing came out. After a moment, she shut it again with a click of her teeth. "True," she said, in about the most begrudging tone Ross had ever heard. He had to stifle a smile at the reluctant admission.

"I mean," he added, deciding to drive home the point, "I don't kick puppies, I don't steal candy from babies—"

"I get your point," she interrupted. "I had no right to judge. I'm sorry."

Wow, another first from the woman. An apology. He considered asking her to repeat that into his miniature tape player once it arrived, just to have it on record for posterity, but Ross decided she might not take kindly to the request. As it was, she didn't look very happy about having to concede that he was right. But she'd done it. Which actually managed to hike up his admiration for her a half-notch or so.

Maybe the next two weeks wouldn't be so agonizing after all.

"You just like to fleece poor defenseless women."

Then again, maybe they would.

Ross just rolled his eyes. He wasn't going to get into a debate about his questionable ethics. He lived just fine with his ethics, thank you very much. He slept like a baby at night. Well, most nights. "Your cousin Jasmine's about as defenseless as a tiger."

Paige pressed her lips together again, but she couldn't quite manage to stifle the humor that glinted in her eyes. And what that brief sparkle did to her face and his groin was just plain indecent—in a really pleasurable way.

Ross shook his head. He was a perfectly healthy male who had perfectly healthy needs and desires. But he couldn't remember the last time a woman's almost-smile had produced a sharp spike of lust in him like that. Especially immediately after that same woman had been doing everything in her power to let him know her very, very low opinion of him.

"Must be the virus."

Paige went still. "What?"

Ross blinked. Had he said that out loud? He must have, considering the look of near-panic that now graced her delicate features. He waved. "Nothing."

"What must be the virus?" she persisted.

Sheesh. Now how did he answer that? "I don't know. I just sort of got this strange feeling."

"What kind of strange feeling?"

He racked his brain trying to remember some of the more benign symptoms the doctor had mentioned. He finally remembered one. "I just sort of got dizzy there for a moment."

Relief blazed from her eyes and she smiled. "Oh. Yes, well, that could be the aftermath from the blast, too."

"True," he said, deciding not to elaborate on what other symptoms seemed to be popping up whenever the woman's lush lips tipped upward. "Have you been experiencing any . . . odd feelings?"

Her smile vanished. He could see warring emotions tugging at her. Apparently she couldn't decide whether to tell the truth. Finally, she sighed. "Maybe some that are unusual. Yes. But so far nothing that can't be completely ignored."

He almost laughed at that. So it took some effort to nod solemnly. "Of course. Easy to ignore."

Just then the doctor and Paige's brother returned to the anteroom, her brother looking thunderstruck. Paige practically leapt toward the intercom button. "Doctor? Are you certain there's no known antidote? We've been talking, and it appears we're already starting to get . . . sick."

The doctor stared at her for a moment, then did her very best to appear to ponder the situation. "Unfortunately, none that we're aware of."

"Then you need to get one of us out of here as soon as possible," Paige said, her voice practically croaky with desperation.

"We're working on it."

"So am I, Paige," her brother chimed in.

"But . . . err . . . Ms. Hart?" the doctor said.

"What?"

"The two of you were exposed less than four hours ago."

"So?"

"There's just almost no chance that you'd begin to experience any symptoms already. At least none caused by the virus itself."

Paige's hand dropped from the intercom switch as she slowly turned to face Ross. And she wore about the most horrified expression he'd ever seen.

Chapter Four

It had taken nearly four hours, and it had been an incredibly painstaking process, but finally Ross and Paige's hospital room had been transformed into an odd cross between a studio apartment, an office, and, unfortunately, a room for contaminated people.

Paige had been completely bemused by the process. First, the doctor had brought in notepads and pens so Paige and Ross could draw up their lists of necessities. Then, because those pads couldn't leave the room except in a hazmat container, they'd had to hold up their lists while Nick, on the other side of the glass, copied them to his Palm Pilot.

Nick had copied Paige's list first. Then when he

began working on Ross's, she'd slipped away to take a shower. Because boy, she'd begun to feel itchy. Not necessarily all on the outside, either.

If the virus hadn't had time to kick in, how could she explain her sudden awareness of the snake, whom she was fairly certain she'd loathed when she'd awakened that morning?

Well, she hadn't actually *loathed* him. Paige made it a personal rule to try and hate no one. Everyone in the world had some redeeming quality; some just hid them better than others. And Ross Bennett was *really* good at hiding his.

Not that she wanted to probe to discover any good qualities he might possess. It was bad enough that she suddenly found the turkey attractive on the outside. Learning about any good parts of his internal makeup could prove disastrous. Especially if these subtle feelings of lust she'd been experiencing were about to increase in intensity. As long as she disliked the man, she could resist physical temptation.

She hoped.

She glanced up from her new laptop, which she'd been loading with various programs for the last thirty minutes, to study the man. He, on the other hand, was busy setting up their new shared fax. He, too, had showered, the moment their clothes had arrived. So his teak hair was still damp at the temples. In profile he was as good-looking as he was face-to-face. Right now he was bent over and frowning in concentration.

She'd had to suppress a squawk of irritation when she'd seen that his choice of clothing consisted mainly of running shorts and T-shirts. Plain old rubber flip-flops on his feet completed his look.

He could have done her the favor of covering up his legs. She didn't need the distraction of his leg muscles flexing with every move he made. And when he needed to bend over, he could at least be polite enough not to do it with his back turned toward her. A position that displayed the contours of his butt in mouth-watering detail.

Paige shut down her computer and closed the lid. "I think we need rules."

Ross swiveled his head in her direction, a concentrated frown still on his face. "Huh?"

"Rules. As long as we're stuck here together, I think we need rules."

His eyes narrowed. "What kind of rules?"

She waved. "Rules for coexisting."

He straightened and turned to face her head-on, crossing his arms over his chest. "Such as?"

"Such as . . ." She glanced around wildly, trying to come up with concrete ways of saying, *Don't be sexy in front of me.* Not exactly easy when his bare legs were screaming for her touch. "Well, for example . . . when my curtain is drawn, you don't cross that line."

"I'd consider that common courtesy."

"Okay, Rule Number Two—"

"Wait. We have to have Rule One-A."

"We're making up subrules now?"

He ignored her. "Rule One-A. For every rule you try to impose, I get to make one up, too."

Paige was immediately unhappy with Rule One-A. Unfortunately, it was only fair. But being fair to a snake with great legs didn't appeal at all. She sighed. "Fine."

"Should we be writing these down?" he asked, eyebrows raised. He lifted his right arm. "Although I'll have to ask you to take that on. My arm hurts from the shot."

Paige set her laptop aside and grabbed a legal pad. "Rule Number Two: No stupid television shows."

"Define stupid."

"You know. *Three Stooges* kind of stupid."

"Rule Two-A: No soap operas."

She wrinkled her nose at him. "I don't watch soap operas."

"Good."

"No cartoons, either," she added for good measure.

"Not even *The Simpsons?*"

"Well, *The Simpsons* is okay, I guess." She absolutely loved *The Simpsons*.

"How about *The Roadrunner?*"

"I bet you just drool at the thought of handling the coyote's product liability claims."

"The thought has crossed my mind."

"No roadrunner."

"Gee, you sure know how to ruin a guy's fun."

"Rule Three: When I'm conducting business on the phone, you don't eavesdrop."

"You know, if you keep up this flattery, I might start to get an ego."

"Agreed?"

"Agreed. Can I eavesdrop on your personal calls?"

"No."

"Shoot."

That tugged a reluctant smile from her. "And I won't eavesdrop on yours."

"My life's an open book, babe."

"Oh, no doubt. A little black book, I'm guessing."

He arched a brow at her again. "Just so we understand each other. Not only am I a snake, but now I'm a womanizing snake at that. Is that right?"

"If the water moccasin fits."

"Cute. Real cute."

Paige took a shallow breath and glanced down at her notes. He was definitely cute. Of course, she never remembered being quite this judgmental about a man before. True, he was an opposing attorney, but that shouldn't give her reason to make all kinds of unflattering assumptions about him. It wasn't like her at all, and she didn't care for herself at the moment. "I'm sorry," she said softly, still avoiding looking into his enigmatic eyes. "I . . . don't know why . . . why you seem to bring out the worst in me."

"It's probably the old Bennett charm."

Paige suppressed an honest-to-goodness snort. Although she was not really thrilled to learn that he *was* sort of charming in an irritating way. "Bottle it and make a buck."

"Not a chance. I'd get sued for false advertising."

She smiled but still didn't look up. It unnerved her that he wasn't being real snakelike at the moment. She'd felt more at home knowing him as a jerk. But they had to room together. Why not get along? "How about we call a truce for the duration?"

"I'm willing if you are," he said, and then reached out and took her chin.

Paige jumped and her startled gaze whipped up to meet his. "What . . . what are you doing?"

He shrugged. "Just got a little tired of talking to the top of your head."

His touch was warm and electrifying.

Her heart thumped hard in her chest and heat unfurled in her belly. She knew she should shove his hand away but it felt so darn good. Too good. Way, way too good.

Reluctantly she lifted her chin, breaking contact. His fingers hovered for a moment before he dropped his arm to his side. For the tiniest moment, confusion blazed in his hazel eyes before he blinked and quirked a smile at her. "Let me guess. 'Rule Number Four: No touching.' "

"Ooh, that's a good one," Paige blurted. She

began scribbling furiously. "No touching. Definitely."

"No matter how much we want to touch?"

Her pulse kicked up another notch. "No matter how much," she agreed. "Because truly, we'd never know if it's the virus. And we don't want to do anything we'd regret when we're better."

"Okay, so how about Rule Four-A: We stay busy with games and work to keep from being tempted?"

She pointed her pen at his nose. His really great nose. "Excellent idea. We'll play games. That'll be good. Nothing dangerous about games."

"And watch TV."

"Sure. Right. That'll be good."

"And maybe read dry legal briefs."

At the word "briefs" Paige's eyes, of their own volition, traveled straight to the man's shorts.

She'd seen him put away the clothes that had been delivered to him earlier. So she was acutely aware that Ross Bennett favored colorful Calvin Klein briefs.

Not that she cared.

She dragged her gaze away from the man's crotch. Unfortunately, not before he'd caught her ogling him. His eyebrows were slightly raised, and his mouth was pressed tight, obviously in an effort not to grin.

"Definitely no touching," Paige croaked.

*   *   *

It was on the second drive home from the hospital when realization struck Nick like a wrecking ball. His car's wheels spit gravel as he pulled off the road and screeched to a halt.

Rachel Turner. Oh, Lord! *Rachel Turner.*

How had it been possible that he hadn't recognized her? True, it had been fifteen years, but how could he forget the best night of his life? Sweet, sweet Rachel, who'd spent countless patient hours trying to teach a dumb young kid basic biology concepts. Who'd so innocently given herself to him that final night. Who must have wondered why he'd disappeared on her the following day. Who, by the time he'd rushed back to campus at his first opportunity, had vanished.

He'd spent months trying to learn what had happened to Rachel. But it had been as if she'd never existed; as if she'd been a figment of his teenage imagination.

He'd been angry. So angry! He'd known it was his fault for rushing home—leaving before he explained to her what had happened and why he had to go. He'd known that more than likely she'd make the assumption that he'd used her that night. That he hadn't been as wildly hot for her as he had, in fact, been. That although he hadn't been a virgin that night, as she'd been, he'd almost felt like one, so in awe was he by the way she'd entrusted her body into his care.

"Damn," he muttered as he yanked up the parking brake.

No wonder she'd been as chilly as a snow cone today. Not that he considered himself unforgettable, but he seriously doubted that Rachel had forgotten the man who'd taken her virginity. Stolen it, he'd bet she believed now.

As he thumped his head on the steering wheel, Nick tried to decide how to handle Rachel now. Boy, how he'd like to handle Rachel now.

She'd been adorable in college. She was sexy as red-hot sin now. The moment he'd laid eyes on her this afternoon, he'd known he wanted to ask her out. Of course, she'd been absolutely not interested.

And why would that surprise him? He'd already blown it by not recognizing her right away. Should he approach her again and tell her he'd remembered? Maybe apologize for his sin this morning. And for the one fifteen years ago.

Would she listen? And even if she listened, would she care? Had she been as devastated by his sudden disappearance as he'd been when he'd returned to find her gone?

Had she been hurt? For how long? Even though it was ancient history, Nick felt a cold fist squeeze his gut at the thought. He'd *never* meant to hurt Rachel. He'd truly cared about her, loved the way he could be himself around her. He'd enjoyed her quick and easy wit that turned into shy mumbling whenever anyone else was around. It had made him feel special that for some reason she trusted him enough to open up to him when she was obviously not so free and easy with anyone else. Especially other guys.

When they'd been alone together, she'd been so much fun. The stories she'd concocted on the spot to help him remember biology terms had had Nick rolling on the floor half the time. And it had worked. To this day he knew what a lysosome was. Since its nickname was the "suicide sac," she'd told him to remember it by thinking of it as cheating on your wife. When you *lie-so-some*body won't find out, you make your own suicide sac and sleep in it.

He'd known that his friends considered Rachel frumpy. Geeky. Not dating material in the least. So over the months that Rachel had so selflessly tutored him, he'd kept his growing attraction to her quiet. Not that he was ashamed of her, just that he didn't want to hear the derogatory remarks some of the bigger idiots might toss out about her.

He'd even kept his attraction to her *from her*. Because he'd been so afraid to scare her off, to lose that camaraderie they'd built. But that last night . . .

Nick shook his head. This was ridiculous. Even if she'd cared about his sudden disappearance then, she certainly had gotten over it long ago. Obviously she'd moved on, and quite successfully. *Doctor* Rachel Turner. He smiled at that. She'd achieved her dream. He didn't know where or how, but she'd done it. Good for her.

Then it hit him. Doctor Rachel *Turner*—her maiden name! Did that mean she wasn't married? No, it meant nothing these days. Married women didn't necessarily take on their spouses' surnames any longer. Then again, when he'd been checking her out up and down, left and right, he'd definitely not seen a ring. Which probably meant nothing for a doctor in a hospital.

What he *had* seen was a smart, successful, beautiful woman with a body he'd definitely like to get to know more intimately.

And now she probably hated his guts.

Shit.

Ross stared at the papers Paige had just handed him. He skimmed them a moment, then burst out laughing. "You're kidding, right?"

"Not at all."

He began reading again from the beginning.

AGREEMENT FOR CODE OF CONDUCT

1. PURPOSE.

WHEREAS, the undersigned parties desire a peaceful and harmonious existence in the course of their daily affairs, and

WHEREAS the parties find themselves inextricably coexisting in a constrained environment for reasons not of their design or desire, and

WHEREAS the parties have consented to govern their behavior by a mutually agreed upon code of behavior negotiated by them during their period of hospitalization,

THEREFORE it is resolved that the following rules shall govern their behavior:

2. TERM OF AGREEMENT. The term of this agreement shall be for the remaining time that the undersigned parties are in quarantine.

3. PROVISIONS. By mutual consent of both parties, the following rules shall be observed by both parties.

Rule 1. Concerns of individual parties.

a. Physical privacy. When the privacy curtain has been drawn closed, neither party shall effect entry, ingress, invasion, or intrusion through that barrier, nor shall either party attempt to bypass, circumvent, or otherwise circumnavigate said barrier.

b. Equity. For every rule or provision of this agreement made by either party, a matching rule or provision may be made by the other party.

Rule 2. Television programming.

a. Stupid programming. During the term of this agreement, neither party shall indulge in, nor subject the other party to, stupid television programming. Under this agreement, stupid television programming includes, but is not limited to:

    i) *The Three Stooges,* and

    ii) cartoons other than *The Simpsons.*

b. Soap operas. Neither party shall indulge in, nor subject the other party to any programming of daytime dramas, i.e. soap operas.

Rule 3. Telephone privacy.

a. Neither party shall eavesdrop upon or otherwise listen to the business or personal telephone conversations of the other.

Rule 4. Susceptibility to symptoms arising from illness.

a. Touching. Neither party shall touch, paw, palpate or otherwise handle the other.

b. Diversion of attention. Both parties agree to occupy their attention with diversionary activities to alleviate prurient, licentious, libidinous, or salacious inclinations. Such diversionary activities include, but are not limited to,

i) professional work, and

ii) the playing of games of an uninflammatory and temperate nature.

Rule 5. Conduct with medical personnel.

a. Neither party shall eavesdrop upon or otherwise listen to the medical consultations or conversations with any physician or medical professional.

b. Both parties shall refrain from making wisecracks or disparaging remarks about the other to any doctor, nurse, or medical professional. This includes, but is not limited to, lawyer jokes.

4. ACTIONS NOT PROHIBITED. Nothing in this agreement shall be construed as a prohibition against either party for taking actions necessary for the mutual or individual welfare of any party in exceptional circumstances. "Exceptional circumstances" include, but are not limited to,

1. Acts of medical aid or assistance which might be deemed appropriate by a reasonable person in ensuring the well-being or safety of either party.

2. Acts of an incidental nature which may be deemed appropriate by a reasonable person for the performance of their professional duties or obligations.

5. NO PARTNERSHIP. This agreement shall not be construed as any statement of partnership between the parties to this agreement. No partnership exists between the parties of this agreement.

Ross glanced up from the papers. "You expect me to sign this?"

"Of course."

"But my arm is still sore."

"Tough it out, cowboy."

"And we don't have anyone to witness it."

"We'll work on the honor system."

"Who says I have honor?"

"Not me."

Ross wasn't thrilled about signing the document. Even if it really didn't have any "teeth," he didn't like violating anything he'd signed in good faith. And he didn't have much good faith about not touching this woman.

He grabbed his pen and began scribbling.

"What are you doing?"

"Adding a final clause or two."

"We don't need any final clauses."

"Yes, we do."

He continued writing, pausing every once in a while to make certain he had the wording exactly as he wanted it. Finally, he passed the "document" back to her.

6. AMENDMENT. This agreement may be modified in part or in whole at any time with the mutual consent of both parties. Such amendment to this agreement need not be in writing for the amended agreement to be in force, but both parties agree to make such amendments in written form by attachment to this agreement in such time as is reasonably practicable.

7. INDEMNIFICATION. Both parties agree to indemnify and hold harmless the other party for any liability which arises from this agreement. Parties agree to defend and indemnify each other against any claims made against them by a third party which arise as a result of their entering into this agreement.

8. SEVERABILITY. If any part of this agreement is determined by any competent authority to be in violation of law or incompatible with medical protocol, or if any part of this agreement is proclaimed to be invalid, such part shall be deemed severable from this agreement and the remaining provisions of this agreement shall remain in force.

She looked up, eyes squinty with suspicion. "Cute."

Ross shrugged. "Standard stuff. Take it or leave it."

She stared at him for a hard moment, then took up her pen. "You really are a snake."

He grinned. "I know."

"Scrabble? I guess that's okay."

Ross didn't smile, although he really wanted to. Paige Hart might be a suspicious, judgmental shrew, but she was a pretty one. Really pretty. Gorgeous, actually. And she was all his . . . for a while. "Your bed or mine?" he asked, gazing at her with the most innocent expression he had in his repertoire.

She peered at him through narrowed eyes. "How about on the floor?"

He shrugged. "Not as comfortable, but okay." He unwrapped the plastic from the brand new game board. "How about you making us cocktails, while I set us up?"

Paige grinned and bounced off her bed. She strolled to the cooler her brother had brought them and opened it. "Root beer, cola or seltzer?"

Ross didn't answer for a moment. He was way too busy appreciating how Paige Hart filled out a pair of jeans. It didn't help that he'd gotten an eyeful of exactly what her tush looked like in all its naked glory.

Still bent over, Paige twisted to face him. "Ross?"

He dragged his gaze from her back end to stare into bottomless green eyes. And every hormone he possessed began humming. His heart accelerated alarmingly. His blood pumped so hard, he could hear it roaring in his ears and feel it pooling in his groin. And in that moment he wanted Paige Hart more than he'd ever wanted any woman in his life.

Paige didn't have a whole lot of experience in the sexual tension department, but she was pretty sure that stunned and smoldering look in Ross's eyes was a bad sign. Worse, her body was responding to it. Her skin was suddenly tingling and her pulse kicked into overdrive. She took a couple of deep, calming breaths, which obviously weren't deep enough, because she wasn't calming down.

He really was a handsome beast, the clod. And he was looking at her like she was candy and he was a sugar-deprived child.

Only he wasn't a child. He was a grown man. With a full set of working body parts. And all she could picture right now was seeing and feeling those parts in action.

Paige shook her head and turned back to the cooler. "Preference?"

"You. Naked."

Paige snapped straight, but couldn't turn to look at him. "Do you think the bug is kicking in?"

"Something sure has."

"Well, we've got to ignore it."

"Are you saying you're feeling it, too?"

"I . . . I'm not sure." She put a hand to her head. "I don't feel so good."

She heard him drop the game and surge to his feet, and still she didn't turn to him. He laid a hand on her arm and her flesh burned where he touched her. "Want me to call a nurse?"

"No. No, I don't feel sick." She glanced down at his hand, so big and warm. "You're touching me."

His hand dropped and she felt the loss acutely. "Sorry."

"Let's . . . just play."

"Fine by me." Ross reached around her and pulled a can of root beer from the cooler, and Paige inhaled deeply. His scent was a sexy mixture of soap and man. Before Paige did something really dumb, like throw herself into his arms, she grabbed a root beer, too, popped it open, and breathed in again, replacing his scent with the soda's.

She decided that going for a light, carefree attitude was the better part of survival. "I have to warn you, I'm pretty good at Scrabble."

"I'm shaking in my vowels."

Paige grinned reluctantly. "You should be."

They sat down, both cross-legged, and Paige watched him surreptitiously while Ross set up the game. This would work. An innocuous game was just what they needed to take their minds off one another.

They chose tiles and Paige won the right to go first. She studied her letters for a moment before starting off by laying down the word E-A-S-T.

Ross marked down her score, then studied his own tiles for a moment. She watched as he added a B and an R to her word.

Looking as innocent as a newborn, he calculated his own score, then glanced up. "Your turn."

She wasn't going to react. Even if unbidden, her own breasts tightened just seeing that word. She studied her tiles and came up with the word A-F-T.

Ross didn't even hesitate as he added S-H to that one.

Paige's jaw dropped, and of course her gaze drove straight to his crotch. He didn't notice, seeing as he was whistling tunelessly as he added up his score and picked new tiles.

Suddenly this game wasn't quite so innocent. And two could play at it, too. With the S from his SHAFT, she spelled the word S-N-A-K-E. She shot him a triumphant smile, but he didn't notice that, either.

"Good one," he murmured, "Twenty points." And without hesitation he spelled the word B-E-D.

Paige growled, then formed the word T-U-R-K-E-Y.

Ross sipped his soda while he studied his letters. Then he added T-H-R-O-B to the top of BED.

Oh. My. God. She stared blankly at her letters as a throbbing sensation began in her nipples and rippled downward. It took several seconds and a few deep breaths to get it under control. She pressed her lips together and formed the word R-U-S-T.

Ross used a T and a blank to embellish it and make it THRUST.

"Cut that out!" she demanded, around a small gasp.

He glanced up, eyebrows raised. "Cut what out?"

"As if you didn't know."

"I'm just playing the hand dealt me, so to speak," he said blandly.

"We're supposed to be playing this game to take our minds *off* sex."

The gleam in his gray-green eyes was so hot and erotic her heart lurched to a halt. "Is your mind on sex?" he asked, his voice low.

"It wouldn't be if you didn't keep tossing out words like that!"

His mouth didn't tip up in a smile, but his eyes twinkled as he raised the soda can to his lips. Paige watched in fascination as he drank, her eyes fastened on his Adam's apple, which undulated lazily with each swallow. Until this moment she would never have guessed that a man's throat could be sexy. And she really, really resented that his was. How was she supposed to resist temptation if he kept doing things like walking and swallowing?

A hysterical burst of laughter bubbled up, but she pressed her lips together to keep it from breaking free. There wasn't a doubt in her mind that this virus had taken hold. She'd dated enough men over the years to know that throats weren't sexy. It had to be this horrid disease's fault.

She had to start thinking unsexy thoughts before smoke began pouring out of her ears. She searched her brain, trying to come up with something, *anything*, that couldn't be misconstrued.

"Your turn," he said.

"Soooo . . . how do you think the Falcons will do this year?" she asked as she perused her letters.

In her peripheral vision she saw him grin, his dimples digging into his cheeks. "Big football fan, are you?"

She didn't know a football from a Frisbee. "Oh, yes. Great sport."

His grin grew wider and he surged to his feet. Dropping his empty soda can in the trash, he bent to grab another one from the cooler. "Well, I think if the QB learns some patience and can manage to stay in the pocket, and if he gets some help from his tight ends, they should at least be contenders."

Speaking of tight ends, Paige's gaze fastened on his. The man had a world class butt.

"They've got to move the chains this year, too."

Move the chains? They used chains in football? Paige wanted to ask what kind of chains those would be, but she didn't dare. All her mind could conjure was shackles that would make a person helpless and at the mercy of a sex partner. Now she *knew* this awful virus had taken over her brain, because even though she'd never been into bondage, it was a totally erotic image. What would it feel like to be at the mercy of Ross Bennett's sexual advances? To lie there while he gently—or not so gently—ravished her?

She didn't have a clue how or when she'd come to the conclusion that Ross would be a gentle, giving lover. Up until hours ago, she'd have bet her entire savings that he'd be utterly selfish in bed—a real oaf. Not that she'd thought of him in that light before a few hours ago.

And she shouldn't be thinking about him that way, now.

"To do that," Ross went on, oblivious to her lascivious thoughts, "they're going to have to find holes and penetrate them."

Okay, so football was officially a dangerous topic. "So, how about those Braves?" she squeaked.

Chapter Five

"You have to get me out of here," Paige whispered into the phone. She kept a keen eye on the bathroom door, waiting for Ross to emerge.

"I'm doing the best I can," Nick said around a sigh. "But Dr. Turner wasn't kidding, Paige. Between the bombing and the flu epidemic, the hospital is splitting at the seams. All of them in the greater Atlanta area are overflowing."

Paige scowled at the Scrabble board, almost completely filled now with words like DESIRE and LUST. How Ross had managed to get letters that spelled out so many suggestive words, she had no idea. Near the end she'd used two of her last three tiles to create the word PEN. Ross had innocently said, "Oh, and the only two letters I have left are I and S." That's when she'd quit. No more Scrabble for them.

"The Macon contingent will be there tomorrow, Sis."

Paige cringed. "How many of them?"

"I told Mom just the immediate family."

"That many?"

"Probably."

There was one good thing about that news that she could see. If they had an endless parade of visitors, they wouldn't have time to think about sex. Well, maybe they'd still think about it, but they wouldn't be able to do anything about it.

"I hope you told her I'm fine."

"I *tried*."

Paige rolled her eyes as Ross emerged from the bathroom. He shot her a questioning look, but she just turned away. "If you could keep working on that little problem," she said.

"Speaking of little problems," Nick responded, "I have one of my own."

He sounded so glum, Paige felt a jolt of alarm. "What is it?"

"You know your Dr. Turner?"

"Yes."

"So do I."

"Tell me something I don't know."

"You knew? How?"

"I saw her reaction to you when you arrived the first time. So, what'd you do to her? Your usual wham-bam, I'm outta here, ma'am?"

"Paige!" He sucked in an audible breath, then blew it out. "What makes you think I did anything to her?"

"Call it an educated guess."

"Well, I . . . uhm . . . uh . . . knew her in college."

Uh-oh. The old *uhm-uh* routine. This was worse than she'd thought. "Say no more. I can pretty much guess the rest."

"It's not *exactly* what you're thinking."

Yeah, right. The man seemed to forget she'd known him her entire life. "It's not?"

"Well, a little."

Paige rolled her eyes again. She had to be saddled with a brother who attracted women like honey attracted bears, but who had no intention of ever committing to any one of them. "Thanks a bunch. Now I probably have an attending physician who hates me by osmosis."

"Has she been treating you badly?"

"No, she's been really nice, actually. Especially considering I'm related to someone who at one point *'uhm-uh'* broke her heart."

"I didn't mean to!"

"You never do," Paige responded quietly. And she meant it. Nick might be a babe magnet, but he'd never mistreat the women he dated. He was too kind-hearted for that.

"I'm trying to figure out a way to approach her and . . . uhm . . . uh make things right. Got any suggestions?"

"Wear armor."

"I figured as much," he said glumly. "Why do you women have to be so damn testy?"

"Oh, please."

He muttered something under his breath that Paige was pretty sure she was better off not hearing. "Well, do you have everything you need for now?"

"Yes. More than enough," she said, scowling at the Scrabble game again.

"And they're treating you right? Betty said she put in a call to make sure they would."

Paige smiled at that. She could imagine that phone call. Her socialite secretary was one tough cookie. "Yes, except for the fact that they're in here every two hours poking and prodding. Just how often does one need one's vitals checked?"

"Just do everything they say, kiddo."

"Do I have any choice?"

"No." He paused for a second. "I don't suppose you'd consider dropping hints to your doctor about your really cool older brother?"

"Wow. I didn't even know I *had* a really cool older brother."

"Very funny. And unwise, considering I'm your lifeline between quarantine and civilization."

Paige grinned. "Look, pal, I'm not really in the mood to be on the receiving end of an enema or something. Fight your own battles, bro."

* * *

"Mr. Bennett, please pick up the privacy telephone below the window," Dr. Turner requested from the anteroom.

It was the following morning, and a nurse had just left the room carrying two vials of their blood as if they were filled with poison.

Ross glanced over at Paige, then shrugged, walked to the window, and snatched up the receiver.

He wasn't about to inform the doctor that he'd barely slept last night because he'd been fighting a hard-on that could have drilled through brick.

Just listening to Paige's soft, steady breathing as she'd slept had kept him tossing in agony. In slumber she'd been completely oblivious to the danger just ten feet—and one flimsy curtain barrier—from her.

This just wasn't like him. He prided himself on a healthy libido, but usually it kicked in only when he was certain the lady doing the kicking wanted him just as badly. Obviously Paige found the thought of intimacy with him about as appealing as defending a first-degree murder case in Texas.

And yet everything about her had him mentally salivating. The way she rubbed her earlobe when she was concentrating on something. The way her breasts rose and fell underneath her shirt with every breath she took. The way she smelled of all things female. Sunshine. Flowers. Rain. *Sex.*

She definitely exuded sex. In every single way.

Paige Hart suddenly equaled sex, and he needed her. Bad.

Desire clawed through him like a hungry kitten, and it made him really testy. The way he saw it, it was all Paige's fault. Well, maybe the virus had something to do with it, but really, she was mostly to blame. After all, the doctor standing out in the anteroom was definitely a desirable woman. But the virus wasn't making him lust after *her*. His mind, his body, his soul were yearning for only one woman. And that one didn't want him touching her.

"Mr. Bennett?"

Ross glanced back at the doctor and put the phone to his ear. "Hmmm?"

"Before we begin, I need to ask you, would you be more comfortable with a male doctor?"

"Why would I be?"

"We'll need to ask you some sensitive and personal questions, so if you'd feel more comfortable answering them with a male doctor, I'll be happy to refer your case to one. Dr. Grant is a highly qualified—"

"You're the one in contact with the CDC, right?"

"At this point, yes. But several of us are in consultation."

Ross looked into the doctor's intelligent gray eyes and shook his head. "I'll take my chances with you, doc."

"You're sure?"

"Yes."

"Okay, but if at any time you change your mind, just let me know."

"Will do."

"Are you experiencing any of the symptoms we discussed?" she asked, her pen poised over a clip-board.

Yes, dammit, an erection that won't quit. "Nothing unusual, I don't think."

"Have you ever been diagnosed with high blood pressure?"

Ross shook his head. "My blood pressure's fine. I get a physical every year, and it's never been a problem."

"I see. Well then, we'll want to keep an eye on it for the next couple of days. It seems to be slightly elevated. Not dangerously, but still on the high end of normal."

Testosterone overload. "Stress."

"Stress?" she asked, tawny eyebrows raised. She really was pretty. Not his type, but pretty.

That thought brought him up short, considering that not twenty-four hours ago she'd have been *exactly* his type.

"You'd be stressed, too, if you were locked up in here," he griped.

"Your temperature is a bit high, too, but that could be normal for you."

After three frigid showers, I should be suffering from hypothermia. "I don't feel sick."

He heard Paige rooting around in the cooler,

and then the *schtick* of a soda can opening.

"Are you experiencing any satyriasis?"

"Satyriasis?"

Sploosh.

Ross turned in time to watch Paige sputtering. The root beer she'd been sipping now graced the front of her shirt and the floor at her feet. She stared at the mess, then him. With eyes wide as saucers she stammered, "I . . . I think I'll just wait in the bathroom and . . . and clean up."

She made a beeline for the bathroom, slamming the door behind her.

He turned back to the doctor. "She's one up on me, I guess. I don't have a clue what satyriasis is."

"Unusually frequent, prolonged, and sometimes painful erections. Excessive sexual craving," she said matter-of-factly.

"Oh." Ross felt his ears heat up, but he went for a casual shrug. "Not much more than usual, I guess. I mean, it's normal in the morning. Right?"

"Well, yes. But was it unusually . . . intense?"

He moved closer to the window and lowered his voice. "Yes, it was a killer," he admitted. This was embarrassing, but he figured lying about it wouldn't help their cause much. They needed to be cured, as fast as possible. Otherwise he was going to suffer agony the next few days until they could split him and Paige up.

That thought, for some dumb reason, didn't appeal to him. Even if she caused him immense pain, if he had to be stuck in a hospital room, he'd rather have her be there with him. Why should he suffer alone?

The doctor didn't react except to nod and make notes on the chart. She was one cool customer, this Dr. Turner.

He lowered his voice even further. "Don't you people have some kind of anti-Viagra drug or something?"

"Unfortunately, at this point we don't want to give you anything that could mask any symptoms you might experience. We need to know what we're dealing with here."

"Terrific."

She lifted big gray eyes to meet his. Though she wasn't smiling, there was a definite gleam there. "I'm sorry," she said, with all the sincerity of a used car salesman. "But you know, we've come a long way with medical science. For example, did you know that it's been proven beyond a shadow of a doubt that *it* doesn't cause blindness?"

Ross didn't immediately catch her drift. While he mulled that over, he watched her cheeks blush lightly. When it finally dawned on him, he grinned painfully. He couldn't believe he was having this conversation with a stranger, doctor or not. He cleared his throat. "Thanks, doc, I'll keep that in mind."

"Is there anything else you need to tell me? Any other unusual symptoms."

He shook his head. "Other than that one problem, I feel great. Although I could stand some real food."

"You're welcome to have a friend bring in anything you'd like. Your diet's not restricted in the least."

"Really? That's great."

"Go for it." She laid down his chart and picked up another one. "Can you ask Ms. Hart to come out?"

Gladly. Can't wait to hear this. Ross swiveled on his heel and strolled to the bathroom door. "Oh, Paige," he said, rapping lightly. "The doctor would like to see you."

She swung the door open, glaring at him. "You. In here."

"Aww, that's no fun."

"Tough."

She marched by him to the window, then turned to glower at him until he shrugged and stepped into the bathroom, *almost* closing the door the entire way.

The rule about eavesdropping on conversations with the medical staff aside, he couldn't help it if she spoke loud enough to carry to his ears. Therefore, he felt no compunction about listening intently.

Although it *did* remind him of days long past, when he'd stand at his bedroom door and listen to his parents' shouting matches, cringing, swallowing hard, silently begging for the yelling to stop.

He shook off the feeling. This was completely different.

Then again, Paige wasn't making it easy. She pitched her already throaty voice low as she and the doctor spoke. Since he couldn't hear the doctor's questions, he had to figure they'd be pretty much the same ones she'd asked him. Except for the erection part.

Did women get satyriasis? He didn't have a clue. But if Paige was experiencing anything like it, he wanted to know about it.

"Antsy. I really want out of here," Paige said.

Ross frowned, not sure why that bugged him, seeing as he wanted out, too.

There was a pause, then, "I . . . don't know what you mean. . . . Well, I wouldn't if that snake Bennett wouldn't keep . . . doing things."

Another pause. "Well, you know, he swaggers around here strutting like a bull in heat."

Did bulls go into heat? he wondered idly.

"And, you know, he won't wear anything but shorts."

Ross stared down at his shorts. Nothing wrong with them that he could see.

"And he plays dirty Scrabble . . . No, not cheating exactly. I mean, well, never mind."

Ross grinned.

"Yes! Well, I mean no. I don't *hurt* anywhere, if that's what you mean. Although it feels awfully hot in here."

Ross nodded his agreement, although all the heat he felt was on the inside.

Several heartbeats later, she said, "I . . . suppose not." Then, "Yes. I want this virus to go away . . . Oh, we're infected, all right. That's the only explanation I can think of . . . Explanation for why I . . . I"—she lowered her voice to a whisper, but Ross still caught it—"find that slug attractive."

Ross grinned again, ignoring the slug part and honing right in on the attractive part. So she was definitely in as much pain as he was. Good.

The doctor and Paige talked for a couple more minutes, and then Paige said the weirdest thing. "My brother should be coming back again today."

"Especially Nick," she added after some comment from the doctor. "He's the greatest brother in the world. And a fantastic architect."

Ah, she was talking her brother up. But Ross could imagine how the doctor was reacting to that news, considering her reaction to the man when he first arrived.

A moment later he heard her cradle the phone. He quickly pulled the door closed and strode over to the sink and leaned against it, whistling casually. She knocked and said, "You can come out now."

He took his time walking to the door and opening it. Paige stood there, two bright red spots staining her cheeks. She gave him a pucker-faced look that would make anyone else unattractive.

On her it looked good. "You better not have been listening."

"Why would I do that?"

"Rule Five: No eavesdropping on conversations with the doctor."

"Rule Five-B," he retorted. "No more wisecracks to the nurses."

She blinked innocently. "Why, whatever do you mean?"

"Oh, I don't know," he said, stalking her so she had to start backing up, "like this morning when the nurse asked me where I got my incredible eyes."

"I didn't—"

"Oh, but you did. 'He probably cashed in on a living will,' I believe were your exact words."

Her eyes widened. "You have good hearing."

"Yes, I do."

She glanced over to the glass, then back at him, her eyes narrowing suspiciously. "I'll keep that in mind."

"I have a lot of good qualities," he said, backing her up right to the foot of his bed. "Want to see one or two?"

"Dr. Turner?"

Rachel's heart lurched at the sound of Nick's voice. The chart in her hand clattered shut. She sucked in a deep breath and let it out slowly, before turning to him. "Yes, Mr. . . . . Hart, isn't it?"

Something flickered in his blue eyes and it took

a couple of heartbeats before he answered. "Yes, that's right. Nick Hart. Paige's brother."

"What can I do for you, Mr. Hart?"

"Just Nick."

"What can I do for you, Just Nick?"

His lips twitched. "Well, for starters you can tell me how my sister's doing."

"One moment, please," she said, then took her good old time finishing making notations on the chart in her hand, then sliding it back into the rack. She stuck her pen behind her ear, then crossed her arms over her breasts. As ridiculous as it seemed, her body was responding just at the sight of the man. This did not make Rachel a happy camper.

Leaning back against the nurse's station, she said, "Your sister is doing just fine."

"Have you learned anything new?"

"Not so far. We just sent the second set of blood samples to the CDC. It'll be a while before we hear results."

"Is she in any pain?"

Rachel almost laughed at that. Although she'd named the virus to Nick yesterday, she hadn't gone into details about the symptoms. Apparently concupiscence wasn't one of the biology terms she'd taught him those many years ago.

"No, no pain per se. Although she's understandably itchy to get out of there."

"When will another room open up so she can have her privacy?"

"Not in the foreseeable future, I'm afraid. But the two of them seem to be getting along as well as expected."

That wasn't quite true, but there really was nothing she could do about their situation at this point. And she remembered enough about Nick Hart to know he was a bear when it came to family.

"If you'll excuse me," Rachel said and began to walk by him.

"Wait!" Nick grabbed her arm and pulled her back.

"Let go of me, Mr. Hart," Rachel said, in as strong a voice as she could muster. Which, unfortunately, wasn't all that strong, considering just the feel of his hand on any part of her body robbed her breath.

He did let her go, but he still managed to block her path. His gaze traveled over her features like a whisper. Finally he said, "You know, I knew a Rachel Turner in college."

An explosion erupted in the vicinity of her heart. He knew. Or he thought he knew. "It's not an uncommon name."

"She was beautiful, like you," Nick said, his voice pitched low and gravelly.

"You don't say," Rachel replied, trying to get around him. Her insides were shaking like a rattle.

"And she wanted to be a doctor."

"Hope she made it. Would you please excuse me? I've got patients to see."

"And then she disappeared on me."

"*I* disappeared on *you!*"

"So it is you." His mouth set grimly. "I returned to school. Why didn't you?"

"None of your damn business." They were attracting attention, so Rachel lowered her voice. "Leave me alone, Nick."

"Have dinner with me."

"Not a chance in hell."

"Lunch."

"No."

"Coffee."

"No!"

"We've finally found each other again after all these years. I think we owe it to ourselves to get reacquainted."

"You know, strangely enough, I don't give a damn what you think."

He reached out a hand but Rachel flinched, and he dropped it. "Give me a chance to explain."

His blue eyes were pleading and Rachel had to steel herself against their lure, their mesmerizing appeal. "Nick, it's ancient history. There's nothing to talk about, nothing to explain."

He shook his head and opened his mouth, but from behind him some woman yelled, "Nicky!"

He rolled his eyes and glanced over his shoulder, then turned back to her. "This isn't finished, Rachel."

"Yes, it is, Nick."

She skirted around him and started down the hall.

"We'll talk about it later," was Nick's parting shot.

Rachel didn't bother to answer, but she shuddered inside. Another thing she remembered about Nick Hart: When he set a goal, he moved heaven and earth to achieve it.

"Not this time, Nick," Rachel muttered under her breath.

Chapter Six

"Have you ever noticed that the Queen of Diamonds is kind of a babe?"

Paige stared at Ross as though he'd lost his mind. Which he very likely had. He was in deep trouble if a playing card was turning him on.

Paige had been doing some work, and Ross had tried as well. But he hadn't been able to concentrate because he'd kept getting distracted by the way she typed.

Her fingers were delicately formed and small, and her nails were really very pretty. And the way they set the laptop to clacking as she typed was too darn sexy.

To get his mind off those fingers and how they'd look skimming over his flesh, he'd grabbed a deck of cards and started playing solitaire. It hadn't helped to relieve the tightness in his groin one bit, and he'd started wondering if any man had ever died of a prolonged erection.

He'd considered taking the doctor's advice, and had even headed to the bathroom at one point, but he'd turned back in disgust. He knew that the relief would be too short-lived. Gone, in fact, the moment he stepped out into the room and caught sight of Paige again.

"The Queen of Diamonds?" she repeated, breaking into his errant and unwelcome fantasies.

"Maybe it's all the jewels," Ross said, attempting not to flush like an idiot.

"Oh, well that makes sense," she said, the sarcasm dripping like a melting ice cream cone. "A divorce attorney getting turned on by jewels."

Ross tossed down the deck of cards. "Okay, that's it." He fairly leaped off the bed. "I've had about enough of your innuendoes concerning me, my career, my motives. Lady, you don't know a damn thing about me, and yet without any of that knowledge, you've appointed yourself prosecutor, judge and jury. And I've pretty much had it."

She had the grace to look ashamed. She punched a couple more keys on her computer, then dropped the lid. "Look, I'm sorry, Ross," she said. But when she glanced up at him, her eyes glittered with something that wasn't even in the ballpark of remorse. "It's just that, well, I . . . know someone who was badly burned by a divorce attorney years ago. The lawyer was ruthless, unethical, and she didn't give a damn who she burned, just so long as her client got the goods. It left a lasting impression."

"Gave us all a bad name, huh?" he asked, wondering if her parents, like his, had gone through a nasty divorce.

Paige snorted none too delicately. "Well, what do you expect when you make your living off of other people's misery?" she asked, and not all that unkindly. She truly looked puzzled.

He would have liked to ask what happened to her, but he had the feeling dredging it all up wouldn't exactly further his cause.

Although why he even had a cause, he didn't have a clue. What did he care what Paige thought of him? Only he did. Dammit.

He shrugged. "I look at it this way. The couples were miserable long before I stepped into the picture. It's my job to make certain my client isn't even more miserable down the road, when she finds herself strapped for money to put food on the table or dress her kids."

She digested that in silence for a moment. Then she nodded. "Okay, I'll accept that you honestly believe that. And I'll try not to take more swipes at you."

"Thank you."

"But I'm not guaranteeing anything."

"Fair enough."

Her brows furrowed as she studied him as if he were a nasty subpoena. "You seem to bring out the worst in me." She paused and her lower lip trembled. "And I know I'm being unfair." Her breath hitched, and Ross sent up a silent prayer that she wasn't going to get all emotional on him. He preferred her sassy over upset, any day of the week.

"I honestly don't know what's wrong with me, Ross," she added, covering her face with her hands. "I'm usually a pretty nice person."

His earlier outrage vanished faster than witnesses at a mob trial. Especially when he couldn't get the sound of his name on her lips out of his head. Or the gleaming honey-blonde hair now covering her hands and face.

He walked over to her bed while his heart did painful cartwheels. Women in distress really bothered him. A lot. After years of hearing nothing but distress in his household, he treasured peace and contentment. No messy and loud relationships.

"Hey, I'm sorry," he said, unable to resist the temptation to touch her hair. "You don't know anything good about me, either, so I suppose it's not a stretch to make some assumptions."

She glanced up, and he was horrified to see those deep green eyes misty as morning moss. "I just don't know why I'm acting this way."

He forced himself to drop the silky strands of her hair. Sitting on the edge of her bed, he said,

"Well, let's see. You've been in a bomb blast, you've been exposed to an unknown virus, and you're holed up like a prisoner with a virtual stranger. I'm thinking you have plenty of reasons to be upset."

She blinked. "Oh, great. Now you're going to be nice about it."

"There *are* some people who think I'm a nice guy, you know."

"But this is a bad thing."

He blinked back at her. "It is?"

"Yes. You're already too good-looking and intelligent. Nice makes it even worse."

"Makes what even worse?" he asked, fighting a grin.

"This . . . this disease."

His eyes fastened on her luscious lips. "I was thinking about that . . ."

"Uh-oh," she said, then sniffled a little. Her lips trembled up into a ghost of a smile. "That sounds ominous."

He grinned back at her. "Well, not really. I was just thinking, if we're feeling this way, why try to fight it?"

Her eyes widened. "What do you mean?"

"I'm thinking we ought to maybe toss out the no-touching rule."

"That would definitely be dangerous."

"But quite possibly fun. What better way to pass the time?"

She stared at him for a moment before shaking

her head. "No, I think it has the potential for disaster."

"How?"

"Well, what happens once we get out of here? We just wave, say 'it's been fun' and go on our merry way?"

"If that's what we want," he responded, although for some odd reason, that scenario held very little appeal.

"What if only one of us wants that? What then?"

He could see her point. But he didn't have to like it. "I guess you're right," he said, standing. "It could spell trouble."

She nodded, but he could swear her eyes held disappointment.

Without thinking, he reached out and touched her cheek. Sure enough, her skin was as soft and silky as it looked. "How about just a kiss?"

She sucked in an audible breath. "That could be dangerous, too."

Disappointment sluiced through him, but he smiled and dropped his hand. "You're right, I suppose."

He turned back to his bed.

"Oh, what the hell," she blurted, and grabbed his wrist and swung him back to her. She practically threw herself in his arms. "One kiss won't hurt."

Ross was stunned for all of a nanosecond. "Rule Four-A," he reminded her.

"So sue me."

He hadn't gotten where he had in the world by passing up opportunities when they jumped in his lap, so to speak. He cupped her head, his fingers plowing through the hair at her temples. Then he lowered his lips to hers.

At the first touch of her sweet mouth, explosions started erupting all over his body. He tipped her head to the side and groaned all at once, then captured her lips again and deepened the kiss, coaxing her mouth open and hot under his. He tipped out his tongue and licked at her lower lip.

She tasted like heaven. Her kiss was soft and yielding, yet demanding, and Ross wasn't certain he'd ever enjoyed a kiss this much. She lit him up, set him on fire. As he plunged into her mouth, his one hand slid down to the small of her back and he pulled her against him, leaving little doubt about how much he wanted her.

She moaned, pressing into him, and the feel of her pearled breasts against his ribs almost undid him. "God, Paige," he whispered against her lips. She felt so small to him. His hand nearly spanned her back.

Her hands climbed up his chest then circled his neck, leaving him free to go on a Lewis and Clark expedition of her soft curves. And he was very happy with that exploration. And excited. Way, way too excited. If she kept kissing him like this, he was going to ravish her whether it was a good idea or not.

Her scent coiled around him, playing havoc

with his senses. She wore no perfume, so it was purely the clean, erotic scent of a woman.

Paige suddenly pulled back, staring at him wide-eyed and breathless. Her lips were kiss-swollen and so lush he wanted to devour them.

"Well," she said, stepping back. "Well, that was quite a . . . a—"

"Treat?" he asked, really sorry it was also over.

"Experience," Paige countered.

"A really good one."

"Probably too good," Paige agreed with a quick nod. "One we'd be dumb to repeat."

"Oh, I don't know about that—" Ross replied, but his argument got interrupted by the light blazing on in the anteroom. Paige jumped away from him faster than a crook jumps bail. She scrubbed a hand over her mouth, then finger-combed her hair.

Ross took a moment to appreciate the rapid rise and fall of her breasts before turning to see who was coming to interrupt them yet again.

His jaw nearly dropped as a motley crew of non-hospital personnel poured into the outer room.

"Oh, jeez," Paige muttered.

"Who are all these people?" Ross asked. There was a middle-aged couple, an older lady, twin girls about sixteen years old, and a young man about twenty, carrying what looked like a calculator in his hand.

"My family. Or about a one-percent contingent of them." She squared her shoulders and moved

114

to the intercom, flipping it on. "Hey, all."

An older version of Paige—but with blonder hair—spoke first. "Paige, honey, how are you do-ing?" Her eyes worriedly roamed over Paige, no doubt checking for signs of injury.

"I'm fine, Mama. Y'all really didn't even need to make the trip."

Okay, that was Mom. Which led Ross to con-clude that the tall and elegant man beside her, with his arm draped protectively around her shoulders, was Paige's father. Obviously no messy divorce there.

The man said, "What's this report I hear that one of my little soldiers has taken a hit?"

Oh, boy. Military. Ross would bet his Rolex on it.

"I'm fine, Daddy. Truly."

The short older woman with cotton-white hair stepped forward. Digging through a huge black purse, she pulled out a roll of candy and held it up. "I brought you some Life Savers, Paige, honey. Wintergreen. Your favorite."

Ross watched Paige cross her arms. "Where'd you get them, Aunt Rose?"

"The gift shop downstairs."

"Did you pay for them?" She turned back to Ross and said in an undertone, "Aunt Rose has a bit of a sticky finger problem."

"Is that any way to thank your aunt?" her ap-parently kleptomaniac relative asked, sniffing.

"I'm sorry. Thank you," Paige said. "You need

115

to leave them out there. A nurse can bring them in later."

Aunt Rose meandered to the cabinets and laid the roll of candy on the counter. Ross watched with no small amusement as she opened and closed drawers. She seemed fascinated by a pair of latex gloves, and began trying to casually drop them into her purse.

"Mama," Paige said, then nodded toward her aunt. Her mother swung around and gently took the gloves from Aunt Rose's hand.

"We're using your apartment as our base of operations, baby," her father said. "We're not bugging out until you're safely back in friendly territory."

"Oh, that's not necessary, Daddy! I'm just fine."

"Have you been eating strawberries, honey?" her mother asked.

"No."

"Then why are your lips swollen?"

Ooops.

Paige rubbed her mouth. "Umm, maybe something hit me in the blast."

"Let me see your teeth."

"Mama, I'm *fine.*"

One of the twin girls stepped forward and tapped on the glass with a purple fingernail. "Hey, Paige, this is, like, way weird. What's wrong with you? How long do you have to be here? Why aren't you in hospital clothes? You don't look sick at all, except a little flushed. I have a date next week with James, and I was hoping you'd come home to do my hair. Will you be out by then?"

Ross knew a strange desire to breathe for the girl, because he hadn't seen her stop to do it for herself yet.

"And who's *he?*" the girl finished, pointing at him. "He's cute."

Paige apparently chose which questions she preferred answering. "I'm afraid I don't think I'll be able to get home in time for your date."

"Nick told us you were holed up in quarters with someone," her father chimed in. "Introduce us to your bunkmate."

Paige glanced over her shoulder. Her expression part exasperation, part apology and part plea. Ross shrugged and moved closer, conjuring a smile.

"Everyone, this is Ross Bennett," she said, waving in his direction. "Ross, these are my parents, William and Lila Hart."

"How do you do?" Ross said.

"A pleasure to meet you," her mother said, while her father checked him over as if putting him through inspection. By the look in his eyes, he didn't appear to be too impressed.

"The woman over there trying to pilfer latex gloves is my Aunt Rose."

Aunt Rose waved, then began inspecting another drawer.

"The chatty one here is my sister, Carmen, and the strong, silent type is my sister Camille."

The one named Camille shot him a tentative smile.

"And the young genius here is my cousin, Nathan."

The young genius in question was busy punching numbers into his calculator, occasionally pausing to shove his glasses higher up on his nose. "How much do you weigh, Paige?" he asked without even looking up.

Paige flushed. "Well, uh, I don't remember," she responded, sliding a look in Ross's direction.

"Nathan," Aunt Rose chastised as she dropped an unknown object into her purse. Apparently Paige didn't catch it, because she didn't react. And Ross wasn't about to squeal on the woman. If Aunt Rose stayed long enough, she'd clean out the entire hospital. "One never asks a lady her weight or her age."

"I was just trying to determine the proper dosage of acetaminophen that should be administered."

"The doctor already figured that out," Paige said quickly.

"Why are you quarantined with a cute guy?" Carmen reiterated. "How come you get all the luck?"

Paige's expression did little to indicate she felt even remotely lucky at the moment. She waved vaguely. "It was a fluke."

"Paige, honey," her mother said in a low tone, as if Ross wouldn't be able to hear her. "Your great aunt Alicia needs your help with her will. When will you be able to work on that?"

"She's changing it *again?*"

Her mother nodded. "Lester's out."

"Who's in?"

"Harmen Steinhope."

"The taxidermist?"

Her mother nodded again. "They make a real cute couple."

"This week," Paige muttered as she swung on her heel and headed for her bed. She picked up a legal pad and pen, then returned to the window, scribbling the entire way. "Okay, I'll get to that as soon as I can."

"Good. Because she's not getting any younger, you know."

Ross glanced at the pad Paige was scribbling on, and his jaw nearly dropped as he saw the to-do list, littered with names of cousins, aunts and uncles. Just how big a family did this woman have?

Just then Nick and their doctor entered, and relief shone on Paige's face. Her aunt beamed a smile at Paige's brother as she lifted a papery cheek for a kiss, while surreptitiously closing her bag.

"What are all of you doing in here?" the doctor said. "They're only supposed to get two visitors at a time."

"If they only got two at a time, they'd be getting visitors twenty-four hours straight," Nick said dryly.

"Oh, no! You mean there are more outside?" Paige asked.

"Filling the waiting room."

The doctor turned to Nick. "You mean, all of those are yours?"

"Just about," Nick said.

Paige's father faced the doctor and held out a hand. "Master Sergeant William Hart, Retired, ma'am. What intelligence do we have on this bug?"

"How do you do, Master Sergeant?" she replied. "Intelligence is sketchy at best. But we've got a full analysis team working on a sit-rep and planning tactical contingencies, sir."

He peered at her. "You bone military like a pro, doctor. Were you ever in the service?"

She held out her hand again. "Captain Rachel Turner, U.S. Air Force Reserve. It's good to have you with us, sergeant."

Ross noticed Nick's jaw dropping at that announcement.

Sergeant Hart beamed. "Ah, air force. Isn't that the life? Out for a quick bit of fluff action in the morning, and snug in a comfy bed after supper."

The doctor smiled. "You obviously have never slept in an air force bunk or you'd know there's nothing comfy about them."

"True enough, captain! Now what can Hart Company do to help out?"

"Sir, I need to secure the area so I can assess my patients."

"Say no more." He smartly clicked and turned back to his family. "Attention to orders," he said, checking his watch. "Let's break from here and rendezvous in the mess at thirteen hundred hours."

"We love you, baby," her mother said softly, laying her hand on the glass. "If you need anything at all, please let us know."

"I love you too, Mama," Paige said, lifting her hand as well. It gave Ross an eerie sense of being in prison, which, to be honest, was fairly close to the truth.

Paige dropped her hand. "And I will."

Ross watched Paige's family march out, and a sort of melancholy stole over him. He'd actually enjoyed the eccentric group.

Family. It had been years since he'd thought about how much he used to crave one.

But ten minutes in the company of Paige's, the craving returned to symbolically knock him upside the head. It wasn't a pleasant feeling.

Chapter Seven

"I'm *so* sorry about that," Paige said five hours, two doctor visits, and about a hundred Hart relatives later. They both collapsed on their respective beds.

He rolled his head to look at her. "Sorry about what?"

Her hand raised and fluttered the air. "About them."

"Your family?"

"Oh, yes."

"Don't be. I enjoyed them. But remind me never to leave my wallet out around Aunt Rose."

She chuckled, but then peered over at him. "Either you're extremely nice, or you are the biggest bullshitter this side of the Mason-Dixon."

"No, I mean it. I didn't have much family. Almost none, in fact. I thought it was great."

"Really?" she asked, and sounded wistful, like she thought no family would be a *good* thing. "How many brothers and sisters?"

"None. Only child."

"Aunts, uncles, cousins?"

"None, none, none. At least none alive. I had an uncle, but he was a confirmed bachelor. Which my dad should have stayed," he muttered under his breath.

She rolled to her side and propped her head in her palm, curiosity lighting up her green eyes. "What do you mean by that?"

He didn't want to talk about it. Well, actually, he realized that wasn't exactly true. He never used to want to talk about it. But with Paige's eyes and face and hair mesmerizing him, he found himself somewhat eager to hold her attention. And to tell her the truth.

Not to mention, the way she was lying displayed her curves in gorgeous detail. The small swell of her hips that tapered to a tiny waist. The breasts that begged for a man's touch. The long and luscious legs. Of course, he would be better off not noticing those things. So he determinedly returned his attention to her face.

He shrugged. "Just that my folks weren't exactly the Cleavers."

Her eyes dimmed with sympathy, which would normally raise his hackles. But she didn't look like she felt pity. Just a certain sadness. "I'm sorry."

"Yeah, well, that's life."

"Did they divorce?"

"Oh, yeah."

"How old were you?"

"Seven."

"I'm sorry."

"I'm not. Well, at least I'm not sorry that they separated. It was preferable to killing each other."

"Who did you live with?"

"My mother. For two years. Then my father, until I went to college."

"Did your mother . . . die?" she asked, swallowing hard.

Ross shook his head. "No. But she received nothing out of the divorce. And she had no real skills, other than housekeeping. So she became a maid. We eeked out a living. My father finally convinced her I'd be better off with him. It broke her heart, but she eventually agreed."

Understanding dawned in her eyes. "Is that why you became a divorce attorney?"

"It played a part, sure. I wanted to make sure no woman was left penniless and powerless again."

"Don't look now, but in our case your client is Carl Peyton, not my cousin Jasmine."

He snorted. "Jasmine is in no danger of being left penniless, Paige."

Irritation sparked in her eyes for a moment, but then it was gone. "That's true, I suppose."

"And the bottom line is, I take on plenty of pro bono work for women who find themselves divorced or divorcing deadbeat dads. I have to take on some big power clients just to pay the bills."

"If your dad was a deadbeat, he wouldn't have wanted you to come live with him."

"He wasn't a deadbeat dad. In fact, he was a darn good one, once my mother and he split. He was a deadbeat husband. The rules were different then. He managed to get the court to agree with him that if he couldn't have custody, which he fought for, then he shouldn't have to pay, either."

"Wow. I'm glad the rules have changed."

"It's still a battle occasionally."

"And . . . what about your mom?"

He smiled. "She's great. The happiest day of my life was the day I showed up at the house where she was working, told her employer she was quitting, and dragged her out of there."

"Where is she now?" she asked softly.

"Florida. Happily retired and married to a really great guy."

"And your dad?"

"Happily a bachelor and still working in California."

She hesitated, then asked, "Is that why you've never married? Because you didn't want to end up like your folks?"

Ross sat up. "What makes you think I've never been married?"

She popped up, too. "You have been?"

"No."

He could swear relief passed over her features.

"And no, that's not why I've never been married. I know there are good and bad marriages out there. I mean, look at your folks. It's obvious they're still devoted to one another and their children. I'm not gun-shy at all. Plain and simple, I've never been in love with anyone enough to want to spend the rest of my life with her. And I won't ever be another statistic. When I marry, it's going to be for good."

She nodded, thoughtful.

"How about you?"

Laughing, she said, "You've seen my family! I haven't had time!"

Somber, Paige was beautiful. Laughing, she was breathtaking, and Ross was annoyed to find himself getting aroused from her laughter alone. He shifted uncomfortably. "What do you mean?"

She forked both hands through her hair, which managed to thrust her breasts against her shirt, and Ross's mouth went dry and his running shorts suddenly began to shrink. Or so it felt. "I'm the first lawyer in the family," he heard vaguely, over the roaring in his ears. "Doesn't matter that I'm a tax attorney. As far as my family's concerned, I'm an attorney for all reasons. Do you know how many times I've had to represent Aunt Rose alone?"

He was pretty certain that was a rhetorical question. At least he hoped so. Because at the moment his brain was devoid of all blood. It had all gushed, headlong, to his groin.

He jumped up and began pacing. Something had to give here. Like Paige.

"What's wrong?" she said, her voice low with worry.

"I think we need to make love," he blurted.

Paige stared at the man. Was he serious? Just like that, *We need to make love?* How was she supposed to respond to that? Well, she knew how she *should* respond—with outrage or disbelief or something like that.

But her body wasn't cooperating. The idea of making love to the man held a lot more appeal than it should. Mostly because she'd been touched by his story about his parents.

The man had entered his profession for almost *noble* reasons. And the moment he'd begun making a good living at it, he'd stormed in to take care of his mother. And despite a shaky home life during his formative years, he didn't carry the baggage around with him. He had no twisted ideas of marriage as some fate worse than death.

Not that she was in the least thinking of him in terms of marriage, but she'd never been attracted to men who couldn't or wouldn't commit for their own paranoid reasons.

Of course, her brother Nick was like that to a certain extent. And he didn't have the excuse of a lousy role model. Ross did, but wasn't relying

Trish Jensen

on it as a reason to keep women at bay.

"Hello?" he said, snapping her out of her musings.

"Wh . . . what?" she said, her voice shaking more than it should.

He held out his arms. "I don't know about you, but I'm wildly uncomfortable at the moment, Ms. Hart."

"You think it's the disease?" she asked, stalling for time. Not that she would agree to this insanity in the end, but because her body was crying for her to do exactly that.

"Who knows?" he replied. "Who cares? I want you. From that kiss earlier, I'd say you aren't exactly disinterested."

"I think," she said, "we ought to mull this over a while, before we jump into something we might regret."

"What's to regret? We're both adults. We're mutually attracted to one another. Why not give each other pleasure?"

Just looking at the man gave her pleasure. Kissing him had been like a dream. She couldn't even begin to imagine how good making love with him would feel. Did she want to find out?

"What are you thinking, Paige?" he asked in a husky whisper.

She didn't know. "What about birth control?" she argued, although her voice had lost authority. And her head was having trouble reasoning properly.

128

The hope in his hazel eyes died a quick death. "I forgot about that."

She latched onto that excuse with every thread of sanity remaining in her. Which wasn't a whole spool, for sure. Nodding, she said, "The last thing we need is to make that kind of mistake."

He rubbed the back of his neck tiredly. "Of course. You're right."

She was ridiculously disappointed he hadn't put up more of a fight. After all, there were definitely ways of making love that didn't include intercourse. Why wasn't he mulling those over?

Get a grip, Paige. But she couldn't seem to, because now images of his hands on her, exploring her, just about stole her breath. "I suppose there are other . . . err . . . things we could do," she heard, then glanced around to see who'd voiced that thought, only to discover to her horror that it had been her own traitorous mouth.

He cocked his head as he looked at her with a twinkle in his eyes. "You mean, like necking?" He strolled closer and touched her cheek, which she'd guess was flame red at the moment. "You mean, like playing baseball? I haven't done that since high school, but if I remember correctly, it was a lot of fun."

She was about to blurt out another ridiculous suggestion when the anteroom light went on again. She and Ross groaned in unison.

He glanced down at his shorts. "I am in no shape to handle visitors."

Paige couldn't help but check his predicament. And was somewhat shocked to see it was a big predicament, so to speak. Just talking about necking could do that to him? She felt a zing low in her belly at the thought of what touching him might accomplish.

"Who is it?" he asked, keeping his back to the window. "More relatives? If so, I'll just close off my bed with the curtain."

She looked over his shoulder. No, it wasn't any member of her family, or even a nurse or their doctor. This time it was a drop-dead gorgeous brunette Paige was certain she'd seen in magazines or on calendars or something. The woman was clad casually in a tan sleeveless vest shirt, and her dark hair was held up in an artless ponytail, high on her head. She was smiling and pointing at Ross.

"It's for you," Paige said, trying to keep the irritation out of her voice. She had the feeling this woman wasn't his relative in any way, shape, or form.

He glanced over his shoulder, and his face split in an all too happy grin. But then he turned back to her and took a few deep breaths, before swiveling and heading for the window and flipping on the intercom.

"Hello, sweet stuff," the woman cooed.

"Howdy, beautiful."

The woman held up a huge picnic basket. "Brought you everything you asked for."

130

"Thank you, thank you. You saved our lives."

"Anything for you, love. The nurse told me to leave it out here."

"That's fine. Perfect."

"I'd love to stay and keep you company, but I've got a shoot over in Buckhead."

"Oh, don't worry about it. I'm just wildly grateful."

"You keep that in mind, ya hear?" the woman purred, before blowing Ross a kiss and sashaying out the door.

All the desire that had been building in Paige for the last several minutes whooshed straight out of her body. To be replaced by something she could only describe as homicidal in nature.

"At what point in that 'I think we should make love' argument were you planning on mentioning you have a girlfriend?" Paige asked fifteen minutes later, once the nurse had hauled in the basket and left.

Ross glanced up from the feast in the basket. "Huh?"

It didn't take a genius to recognize she was a little hacked off. Well, a lot hacked off. Her face was the color of a fire truck and her eyes blazed like a three-alarmer. And when she pointed at the window, her hand shook. "The girlfriend."

He straightened. "Tina?"

She crossed her arms over her chest and tapped her foot. "There's more than one?"

"She's not my girlfriend. At least, not anymore."

"Right."

"No, I'm serious," he said, even while his inner voice was wondering why he felt a not-so-subtle desperation to make her believe him. He didn't make apologies or excuses to anyone. Ever. "We dated a couple of times, but that's it. She's just my neighbor."

"What was all that love and smoochie stuff, then?"

Ross shrugged. "She's a model. I think they're genetically engineered to flirt with every man they meet."

She seemed to mull that over for a moment, giving Ross time to ponder whether he'd just encountered jealousy. Considering her opinion of him was a step below her opinion of things she'd encounter under a rock, that was a pretty far-fetched notion.

Yet, no other explanation made sense. She couldn't possibly be strictly jealous of Tina's looks. Tina was beautiful, but Paige was perfection incarnate.

That thought and the accompanying response from his body, brought him up short. This disease was playing havoc with his gray matter. No doubt about it. He was experiencing all kinds of feelings he'd have never thought possible. His sudden wistful longing for a huge extended family, for example. Not to mention his wholesale attraction to a woman who considered him pond scum.

But he couldn't help but tease her. "Why, Ms. Hart, you're not jealous, are you? After all, you've got me all to yourself right now. And you have my utter permission to have your way with me."

She rolled her eyes and crossed her arms. "Oh, please. If I had my way with you, you'd be catching a one-way flight to Timbuktu."

Ross laughed. He was really beginning to like her prickliness. Although why, he couldn't guess. He'd never been attracted to sassy-mouthed women before as far as he could recall. But he figured he'd also seen her frightened, vulnerable side, and he much preferred her feisty to scared.

Her scowl faded slowly as she sniffed the air. "What's in the basket?" she asked. "Whatever it is, it smells wonderful."

He winked at her. "Pure ambrosia."

"Yeah?" She shuffled her feet. "Are you going to share?"

He pulled the bottle of wine out of the basket. "Hope you like cabernet."

Paige was in heaven. Almost. As they sat on a red-and-white-checked picnic blanket she surveyed the feast before them. Ross's *friend* had loaded the basket with freshly steamed king crab legs, plump, sweet grapes, cheese and crusty French bread. Paige *should* be content. Especially since Ross denied any relationship with that . . . that . . . person. But this pesky, nagging buzzing in her lower belly was giving her fits.

Ross held up his plastic cup. "Here's to freedom."

"Oh, I'll definitely drink to that," she agreed. This forced confinement was driving her batty. And so was Ross Bennett. Especially when he kept forgiving her for making assumptions about him. If he'd just be more of a jerk, he'd be a lot less of a temptation.

"This is wonderful," she added after sipping the wine. "All of it. Thank you."

"My pleasure," he responded, smiling softly.

That smile was definitely *her* pleasure. Or, more likely, her downfall. She dragged her gaze from the danger and got busy cracking another crab leg and digging out the delicate meat. Except her hands were shaking, and she couldn't quite manage it. Ross took the crab leg from her. His warm fingers brushing over hers, and her nerve endings exploded.

She snatched the crab leg back from him and tossed it aside. "Who are we kidding?" She grasped his T-shirt and pulled him to her. He didn't seem as startled this time. The way his lips landed on hers with such ferocity told her he'd been waiting for her to do exactly this.

They kissed as if they had one minute to live, the intensity that of a bubbling volcano. Their mouths moved in a frenzy and desire erupted, hot and flowing. Their hands groped and grasped, which just fueled their hunger.

His hands roamed over her like a crazed blind

man learning Braille. Everywhere he touched her she came to immaculate life. And everywhere he touched her seemed to have a direct line of nerve endings leading straight to her breasts and between her thighs.

Paige had never been so needy in her life. She wanted the man so badly she wanted to scream with it. Ross cupped her bottom and pressed his hard erection against her sensitized center and she gasped into his mouth. He raised his head and looked down at her, his eyes smoky green with desire. "I want you. It's killing me, I want you so much."

Oh, man, she wanted him too. She wanted his hands all over her, his naked flesh brushing against hers, pressing her down as he mindlessly ravished her.

Paige's breath chugged in and out of her lungs like a struggling choo-choo. Her hands glided over his body of their own volition, reveling in the hard, corded strength in muscles bunched and tensed and ready to pounce. Her head swam and her body sang. She vaguely remembered that there were a boatload of reasons why they shouldn't be doing this, but at the moment she couldn't drum up even one. The only thought that had any power in her head at the moment was that she wanted him driving into her so desperately she might die from it.

And as suddenly as the fevered kissing began, it ended.

Ross moaned and stood up. "Lord, Paige, you just don't have a clue what you do to me."

She scrambled to her feet, too, then wobbled a little and blinked to try to clear her head. Ross's hands grabbed her arms to steady her. Or maybe to steady himself. She dragged in a gallon of air and held it for a moment as she searched his handsome face.

At least he looked as unfulfilled as she felt. His lips were pressed tightly together and a muscle ticked in his jaw. His eyes were a smoky mixture of lust and regret.

"What's wrong?" Paige asked when she found her voice. It came out as a croak.

He cleared his throat and swallowed. Twice. "We're due for a vitals check in less than an hour."

"So?"

"Less than an hour," he repeated, as if the phrase was self-explanatory.

She peered at him in exasperation, her body still throbbing in protest. "Your point being?"

He stared at her, wide-eyed for a moment. "My point being there's not enough time."

Her jaw went slack. "Not enough time? An hour?" she squeaked.

"Lady, when we make love for the first time, it's going to last a helluva lot longer than an hour."

It was her turn to stare. In truth, there were several parts of that statement to which she should be reacting. Like he had said *when* rather than *if*, as though their joining was a foregone conclusion and it was only a matter of time.

And speaking of time, was it really possible for people to make love for that long? Thinking back on her few experiences, she couldn't remember it lasting longer than ten or maybe fifteen minutes tops. What in the world could two people do for that long? And how in the world would one survive sustaining these intense feelings without exploding?

She wanted to ask but she was afraid it would make her look naïve. Obviously he was pretty certain it could be done. And as the heat between them cooled a bit with space and time, she decided that all the possibilities running through her brain were merely curiosity. And the tingles pinging through her body were merely a byproduct of that curiosity.

Yeah, right.

She shoved hair back from her face. "It's just as well," she said, going for a casual shrug. "Like you said before, we have no protection."

"For what I have in mind, we won't need protection."

She gaped at him. "For over an hour?"

"A whole lot longer than an hour," he said, then winked.

She was so caught up in her imagination, it took her a few moments to register that her phone was ringing. Actually, it took a smug grin from Ross and one hand waving in front of her face and the other pointing to her bedside table. She shook her head to try to clear it of way too many erotic thoughts, then moved to the phone.

"Paige Hart."

The babbling on the other end of the phone was so incoherent, she didn't immediately recognize the voice of her cousin. "Whoa, Jasmine, slow down. Take a deep breath and say that again. I didn't understand a word you said."

Jasmine did, then started over. As Paige listened, and finally comprehended what Jasmine was telling her, she slowly swiveled toward Ross, her eyes narrowing on the snake. Oh, she should have known. How foolish could she be?

His eyebrows shot up and he held out his hands in an innocent "What?" gesture that she didn't buy for a moment.

When Jasmine finally sputtered to a stop with a wailed, "What are you going to do about it?" Paige considered exactly what she'd like to do about it. Like run a stake through the snake's nonexistent heart.

She turned her back on him and said, "Don't worry about it, honey. I'll look into it. I promise. Just relax and leave everything to me."

She hung up and once again faced the jerk, even as embarrassment at her capitulation to his manipulation burned through her.

"What?" he asked, his "not guilty" look firmly in place.

"You bastard."

Chapter Eight

"What'd I do now?" Ross asked in a weary voice.

"As if you didn't know."

"I don't have the slightest idea."

She pointed a shaking hand at the phone. "That was my cousin, Jasmine."

"I gathered that much."

"Carl dognapped Doodle."

"He did *what?*"

"You heard me. He stole her dog."

"Wow. No way."

"Don't act like you didn't know he was going to."

"I had no idea."

"Oh, really?" Man, she couldn't believe she'd practically thrown herself at this slug. "Then where do you suppose he got the notion to leave Jasmine a note stating that possession is nine-tenths of the law?"

Ross visibly gulped. "Well, I might have mentioned that, but in no way was it in relation to Doodle."

"Carl is going to pay through the nose for this stunt."

"Hold on," Ross said, lifting his hand. "Let me talk to him. See where his head's at."

"In a guillotine if he doesn't return Doodle posthaste."

Ross moved to his phone. "All but done. Sort of. Let me see."

She stood there glaring, fists on hips. It was *so* unfair to be attracted to a gorgeous creep who was working for the man making her cousin's life hell.

The gorgeous creep pulled an address book from his bedside table and flipped through it, then picked up the phone and began to punch in numbers. After three he stopped and turned back to her. "No offense, but a little privacy here?"

Paige shot him one final fulminating look, then swung around and began marching to the bathroom.

"Paige?"

She stopped, but didn't turn to look at him. She figured her punishment for being such an idiot could be refusing to let herself drink in his disgustingly handsome face. "What?"

"My chances of getting to fool around with you tonight have diminished dramatically, haven't they?"

"They've downright vanished, mister," she said, ignoring the annoying disappointment lumping in the pit of her tummy.

"Even if I straighten this out?"

It almost strangled her to choke out, "Even if you straighten this out."

"Damn," he said softly.

Paige forced herself to continue toward the bathroom, even as her mind echoed his sentiment. *Damn.*

Rachel was exhausted. Bone-deep exhausted. As she headed to her car in the underground physicians' garage she entertained fantasies of the bubble bath and the whodunit mystery awaiting her at her condo.

The last two days had been a nightmare. She'd never seen the hospital so overrun with injuries. No deaths from the bombing, thank God, but everything from contusions to concussions to broken limbs to . . . viral infection.

She grimaced just thinking about that. What sin had she committed that led fate to drop Nick Hart back into her life? It had to have been a doozy. After fifteen years, you'd think he no longer had the power to affect her in any way. But just seeing him again had nearly sent her into cardiac arrest.

Rachel unlocked the door to her Lexus and yanked it open. She squared her shoulders before climbing inside, determined to purge all feeling. Determined to wipe all thoughts of that sorry excuse for a man from her mind. Determined not to engage in a pitiful round of what-ifs.

Nick had made his choice a lifetime ago, and she wasn't about to allow him to try to make amends now. If his conscience was nagging him, too bad. In fact, good. He deserved to feel a world of guilt.

Nodding to herself, she fired up the engine and cruised up the ramp of the garage, focusing on that bubble bath and book.

Busy purging her mind, she almost didn't spot the lone figure that appeared from the shadows and strode into the middle of the drive, effectively blocking her path. Was the person insane?

She blinked. The person was Nick. And he had a determined look on his face that bode trouble.

Rachel's heart zoomed into overdrive. She glared at the man as she lowered her window. Leaning her head out, she yelled, "Move it or lose it, Hart."

"I'm not moving until you agree to talk to me," he said, and the pitch of his voice did amazingly insane things to her belly.

"I'll mow you down like a blade of grass."

"Fine. Then you can tend my wounds."

"Like hell."

He tsked. "Are you forgetting your Hippocratic Oath, Dr. Turner?"

"The only hypocrite here—"

"If you'd give me ten minutes, I could explain."

She considered revving her engine, but the fear that the car would shoot forward and hit him kept her from doing it. Not that he didn't deserve it. But it would be a real shame to mar the stark male beauty of that man's body.

He was dressed in thigh-hugging jeans and a camel chambray shirt, open at the throat, sleeves rolled to below the elbow. He'd filled out in all the right ways, Rachel thought begrudgingly. He'd always been big and hard, but his shoulders had expanded even more, if that were possible, making his hips appear slimmer in contrast.

"Get out of my way, Nick," she said, and was horrified to hear the catch in her voice.

"No." His eyes glittered and his jaw spasmed. Rachel recognized the stubborn stance. Nick Hart never backed away from a challenge, nor gave up against staggering odds.

She remembered that his stubbornness was the reason he'd sought her services as a biology tutor in the first place. In front of an entire class, his biology prof had snidely suggested he take some other class to fulfill his science requirement, likening his brain to one of those footballs Nick threw up and down the field. That was all the challenge Nick had needed to make certain he passed that course. With single-minded fanaticism, he'd grilled other students until he got the name of someone who'd be willing to "coach" him. And then he'd called her.

Rachel had known who he was. After all, he was their football team's great hope for a run at the national championship. She'd been so intimidated that a gorgeous star athlete had come asking for her services, she'd initially refused. In fact, she'd refused about ten times. But the man wouldn't give up until she'd agreed.

And look where that got her.

Rachel shook her head. She knew darn well that Nick would stand there all night if he had to. The stubborn son of a—

"Please, Rachel. Just have one drink with me. That's all I'm asking."

Even her bones ached, she was so tired. Yet the look on his face was somehow compelling. Exhilarating. Like she was mainlining adrenaline.

She sighed. "I'm not getting rid of you, am I?"

"Not until you hear me out."

"Get in."

He went still as a statue. "Really?"

"You have five seconds to get in this car, or I'm running you over."

It took him less than two. He pulled open the passenger door and flung himself inside. "Now that's the open-minded Rachel I remember," he declared, buckling himself in.

"You just caught me at a vulnerable moment," she retorted. "I'm too tired to argue." She glowered at him for good measure. "Where to?"

"Your place?"

"Not a chance."

"My place?"

"Even less of a chance."

"The Fox and Hound?"

"You're buying."

"I wouldn't have it any other way."

Ross was bored. Well, not bored exactly, but restless as hell. He needed a distraction from the woman who sat not twelve feet from him, emanating hostility, indifference, and sex.

The shorts she wore left her long, bare legs up for open perusal, and no matter which way she situated them, they looked mouth-wateringly good. Her attitude should have turned him off completely, but somehow it didn't. Not when he recognized that her prickly disposition had everything to do with protecting her family.

He couldn't relate. But he'd love to. He'd love to know what it felt like to have family members that you'd protect at all costs. Well, he'd ridden in to save his mother, but within two months she'd been happily married to a guy who'd made it abundantly clear that Ross wasn't needed.

That was it. He didn't feel needed by *anyone*. Save maybe Sam, who sure seemed to love him. Especially when he popped open those cans of Fancy Feast.

But although he loved his kitty, Sam wasn't exactly familial. She was more like an owner or land-lord. And she really didn't need anything from him but food, litter, and his chest.

He'd love to care about someone enough to go to bat for her, no matter how in the wrong that person was. Which Jasmine was. Carl Peyton was a nice guy at heart. And he really had no problem with making certain that Jasmine continued to live in the style to which she'd become accustomed. Of course, the man could afford to be generous.

But Ross didn't believe for a moment that Jasmine was fighting for custody of Doodle the poo-dle for any reason other than spite. Carl had described Jasmine's reaction to the gift of the dog, and she'd made it perfectly clear that if the dog wasn't adorned in rock-sized diamonds, the dog was a worthless gift.

But if Jasmine wanted the dog, Paige was going to fight tooth and nail to make certain Jasmine got the dog. Jasmine was family, and Paige fought for her family. Ross hadn't known Paige that long, but he'd already gleaned that about her. It was an admirable trait in a pain-in-the-ass sort of way.

"Jasmine's still not happy with the arrange-ment, you know," Paige said, as if she could read his mind.

Ross sighed. "He's agreed to turn the dog over at our next meeting. What more does she want?"

"She's convinced that he's going to feed Doodle steaks and generally spoil him rotten so he won't want to come home with her."

"Jasmine's the suspicious type, isn't she?"

Paige opened her mouth to argue, but then she grinned. "A little. I think it runs in our family."

Ross stared at that smile, and hormones bolted awake with a suddenness that was almost scary. He was in trouble if just a look from her gained him an instant hard-on. If she continued with the no fooling around rule, he was in for an agonizing few days.

He dragged his gaze from her and looked around desperately for a distraction. His eyes landed on the television. "Mind if I turn on some TV?"

She closed the folder holding briefs she'd been perusing and set it aside. "Good idea. I could use the distraction."

Ross went still. "From what?"

"Huh?"

"Distraction from what?"

She waved a hand in the air, but refused to look at him. "From . . . umm, work?"

She was *asking* him? "Are you sure you don't need distraction from thinking about getting down and dirty with me?"

"Oh, *please.*"

His grin widened. "Please what?"

"Please check your ego at the door."

"Hey, I'm not egotistical!" he protested.

She snorted.

"Well, not much."

She snorted louder.

"Admitting that I know you have the hots for me is *not* egotistical. I'm just being honest."

"I don't—" She cut herself off, then shook her head. "Okay, maybe I do a little. That doesn't mean I plan on doing anything about it. You're a snake and you are representing my cousin's soon-to-be-ex-husband. Therefore, any intimate contact with you would be foolish. So turn on the dang TV."

Ross turned on the dang TV. "What are you in the mood for?"

"Something funny?"

He flipped through channels until he hit a *Seinfeld* rerun. "How's this?"

"Good," she said, then fluffed her pillows and sat back.

Except it was the "Master of Your Domain" episode, which Ross thought was pretty darn ironic, considering the circumstances. He pretended great interest in the TV, although out of the corner of his eye he could see Paige squirming a little more and more as sex—or lack thereof—was the central issue of the episode.

"Can we watch something else?" she asked a few moments later, desperation roughing up her plea.

"Why?" he asked, eyebrows raised innocently.

"Just change the channel."

He shrugged and did as she asked, holding back a grin. He flipped until they hit an episode of *Friends*. One where Monica and Chandler couldn't keep their hands off each other. Ross figured the universe was on his side tonight.

Paige lasted through about five minutes of that before she choked out, "Something else?"

Frasier was in heaven because he was sleeping with a supermodel. "Change," she ordered.

Melrose Place. Need he say more?

"That show's been off the air for years!" she complained.

"Ah, yes, the wonders of cable."

"Isn't there some kind of sporting event on or something?" she asked. He flipped some more, and she practically screamed, "That one!" when a cooking show appeared. Except the Galloping Gourmet was describing chicken breast picatta in purely lustful terms.

She didn't even have to ask this time. Ross was getting hot around the collar, too. TV was proving to be no distraction whatsoever.

"Where are the Three Stooges when you need them?" Paige mumbled.

Ross's eyebrows shot up. "I thought you hated the Three Stooges?"

"I do."

"Ah," is all he could think of to say. He had to admit that it did his heart good to know she was suffering right along with him. The more she suffered, the more she'd forget her reasons for not wanting to mess around with him. If the television kept cooperating, she'd be flinging herself at him in no time. And being the gentleman he was, he could hardly refuse her.

Unfortunately, she caught him grinning at the thought. "What seems to be so funny?" she growled.

"Er . . . I was just remembering one of my favorite Three Stooges episodes."

Her eyes narrowed as she studied his mouth. "That was not a *nyuck, nyuck, nyuck* grin."

"It wasn't?"

"No."

"What kind of grin was it?" he asked out of curiosity.

"That was a cat circling the canary grin."

"Oh."

She folded her arms under her awesome breasts. "Why do I have the feeling I'm the canary?"

He shook his head. "No, no, no. If I were circling you, which technically I'm not actually doing, it sure wouldn't be to hurt you."

"What would it be to do?" she asked, and although still frowning, a flair of heat lit up her green eyes, which Ross considered a major victory.

"To make you moan with pleasure."

She moaned, but it wasn't exactly a pleasurable sound. "You're driving me crazy. Turn on ESPN."

The universe was still on his side. ESPN was airing a Braves game. "Baseball," he said with a grin.

Paige sighed her relief. "Good. That should be boring enough."

"So tell me, Legal Eagle, when was the first time you got to second base?"

Chapter Nine

"Thanks for agreeing to talk to me," Nick said, after their drinks had been delivered. He looked Rachel over, soaking in her features like a cactus after rain. She wore a moss green cotton polo shirt that did amazing things to her large gray eyes. He'd seen her eyes sans glasses that last night they'd been together, of course, but he'd forgotten just how beautiful they were.

"Like I said," Rachel retorted, breaking into his thoughts. "I was too tired to argue." She squeezed the lime into her vodka tonic.

He looked closer, and did feel a twinge of guilt when he saw the dark smudges under her eyes. "I won't keep you long. At least not tonight."

She choked on her drink. Blinking rapidly, she

said, "Tonight's the last night you're keeping me at all."

Not a chance, Nick thought, but decided not to voice it. Fate had dropped her back into his life, and he wasn't going to pass up the opportunity to get to know her all over again.

He'd been young and cocky when he'd known her before. Yet he'd really cared about her. And in his youthful arrogance, he'd been utterly shocked when he'd returned to school the next fall, only to learn she'd dropped out of not only college, but out of sight.

He'd been so busy playing ball that he hadn't had time to scour the earth for her, but he'd never forgotten her. Though she hadn't been the sexiest woman he'd ever met, their lovemaking had been unlike any he'd experienced before, and he'd fully planned on returning to school for more of her sweet, sweet love.

But she'd vanished.

Boy, had she grown up. In all the right ways. He'd been crazy attracted to her as a young girl. He was even more so, now. Not because she'd slimmed down, or because she was a successful doctor, but because she'd matured into a confident, competent, drop-dead gorgeous female. If she was still as sweet and kind as she'd been then, it was a potentially lethal combination.

"Are you really in the military?" he asked.

"The reserves, now. But yes, air force for four years."

"Why?"

"Why not?" she countered.

"You were doing really well in college. Why would you quit to join the air force?"

She shrugged, but didn't answer him.

"Please tell me I didn't drive you away."

Rachel set down her drink and smiled, but it wasn't a charming smile by a long shot. "Don't *we* have an overblown sense of importance?"

"Rachel—"

She leaned forward. "My leaving had absolutely *nothing* to do with you."

He didn't know whether to be happy or insulted by that. "Well . . . good."

"Although it might have been nice to have gotten at least a thank-you after your exam."

"I'm so sorry about that. I really am. You'll be happy to know I aced the biology exam."

"Oh, I'm ecstatic," she responded, deadpan.

Well, okay, he couldn't blame her for not feeling triumphant after all this time. She'd been so determined to help him make a good showing back then. But considering the circumstances, that was probably the wrong thing to mention.

"Was I supposed to assume that the . . . night before was your way of showing gratitude?" she asked, her voice going even lower and huskier. "Pitiful, plain Rachel Turner should have been pathetically grateful that the big man on campus actually deigned to introduce her to sex."

"No! Rachel, it wasn't like that at all."

She ignored his denial, and her face was slowly turning red. "How you must have laughed with your buddies in the locker room. 'Look what I had to do to get tutored.' "

"Dammit, I'm telling you it wasn't like that!"

"What was it like then, Nick? What possible excuse have you come up with?"

"I had a . . ." He hesitated, because he didn't feel comfortable airing Paige's misfortune, "family emergency."

She laughed. A full, throaty sound that would be sexy if it weren't so filled with disbelief. "Oh, that's rich."

"On my grandmother's grave," he said, holding up a hand. "It's the truth."

"A family emergency that just *happened* to come up right after finals." It wasn't a question, but a patent, flat statement.

"Actually, the emergency had come up a few days earlier, but my folks didn't want me distracted from finals, so they didn't tell me until I called that day. As soon as I heard, I packed up and left. I know it was brutally unfair not to take the time to call, but all I was thinking about was my sister, Paige."

Rachel went still. "It involved your sister, Paige?"

"Yes," he said, and hoped she didn't ask for details. It had been a horrible time in Paige's life, and he knew she'd smack him for divulging what had happened to her.

"Do you see the irony here?" she asked, after another dainty sip of her drink. Her tongue popped out to lick moisture off her lower lip, and Nick reacted a little too strongly to the gesture. *Way* too strongly to the gesture.

He sucked in a breath. "Irony?" he gritted out.

"You're saying Paige is the reason you took off. And Paige is the reason you're back."

"True," he said, and smiled his best smile. "Remind me to hug her for that later."

She almost slammed down her glass. "No need. Because this is where it ends." She stood up.

"You haven't finished your drink," he said desperately.

"I've had enough. Of it and you." With that she flung her purse strap over her shoulder and began to march out.

Nick jumped to his feet, not having taken even a single pull on his draft. He tossed a tip on the table, then followed her. He caught up with her at the door. Holding it open for her, he asked, "Have you really become this unforgiving?"

"Yes."

He grabbed her arm. "Why, Rachel?" he asked softly. "What has happened to you? The kid I knew in college was the most forgiving, sweetest girl I'd ever met."

"I grew up."

"We had something then. Maybe we could get it back."

She glanced down at his hand, locked on her

upper arm, then looked back up at him. "What makes you think I want to get it back?"

"You wouldn't be so angry now if I hadn't hurt you badly then."

She went still, and then to Nick's horror, her eyes filled with moisture. Blinking, she said, "It's old news, Nick."

He pulled her to him and hugged her. She went poker stiff, but didn't jerk away. "Please, please, please let me make it up to you," he whispered in her hair. "I'll do anything you ask. I'll take you anywhere you want to go. Just don't let this opportunity for us to be part of each other's lives go."

"You're not going to give up, are you?" she asked, pulling back to look up at him with watery eyes.

"You know me," he retorted, smiling.

"Unfortunately," she muttered.

"Please, Rachel."

Her breath hitched. She was silent for a good twenty seconds. Finally, she said, "I am *such* a sucker."

Nick couldn't believe how strong the sting of hope was that zapped through his chest. "Let me make it up to you," he repeated, even softer this time.

More silence. Then she whispered, "How?"

"Go out with me," he said, stroking a knuckle down her soft cheek. "Please."

She took another noisy breath. "That's a really terrible idea."

"No, it's not. I promise, if nothing else, you get a free meal out of it and possibly a fun evening. What have you got to lose?"

"Plenty."

"One night out of your life."

She rolled her eyes. "All right."

"Really?"

"One date."

"That's all I'm asking." *For now.*

"And then you'll leave me alone."

No way in hell. "If that's what you want."

"Friday night?"

He would have chosen tomorrow, but three days wasn't *too* long to wait. "Perfect."

By the next morning, Paige was ready to chew nails. Baseball the night before hadn't proved distracting in the least. Not when Ross kept trying to get her to engage in a conversation about running bases. And he wasn't talking at a baseball stadium. When she'd refused to answer him, he'd given her detailed reports on who and where he'd managed to run them himself.

She'd opened a book and pretended to ignore him, but images of him groping Sally Jean Rippen in the backseat of a Chevy—while *Star Wars* played at the drive-in—wouldn't go away. With her brothers always watching her like hawks, she hadn't had much chance to do any teenage exploring herself. But she had a sneaking suspicion that if she'd known Ross Bennett in high school, she'd have moved heaven and earth to find out what it felt like to be groped by him.

And she was much more impressed than she ought to be that Ross had been a lot more interested in Sally Jean's assets than Princess Leia's. After all, wasn't *Star Wars* the ultimate guy movie?

If she'd slept ten minutes last night, she'd be surprised. But after taunting her relentlessly with talk of sex, Ross had finally given up, wished her good night, and promptly fallen asleep. The turkey.

After more poking and prodding by nurses this morning, and after a pretty lousy breakfast, Paige was attempting to keep herself busy putting out family fires. But she was doing a fairly rotten job of it, because awareness of the man was practically driving her insane.

He was wearing running shorts again. This time red. His Oxford shirt was white, and not only opened at the collar, but opened all the way down. She wanted to scream at him to button up, but was afraid he'd take that as a sign that his bare chest was enticing. Which it wasn't. Well, yes it was, but she'd eat worms before she'd say so.

Just to get him back, she'd donned a pair of ratty cut-off shorts—short being the operative word—and a tank top that wasn't skin tight, but close. He'd nearly swallowed his tongue when she'd emerged from the bathroom. Which had been tremendously satisfying, even if she pretended not to notice his reaction.

He'd been on the phone most of the morning himself. But every time he glanced her way, he winked, smiled or did something else to make her nuts. So Paige decided to give as good as she got. She grabbed nail polish out of her suitcase and began painting her toes. Pure joy flooded through her when Ross stopped speaking in mid-sentence, and it took him some time to remember he was on a phone call. When he did, his terse "I need to call you back," made her even happier.

He stared at her feet. "Lady, you are playing with fire."

Paige raised innocent brows. "Excuse me?"

"If you refuse to let me ravish you, you had better stop that right now. I won't be responsible for my actions."

She stretched out her leg to admire one completed foot. "You have a toe fetish, do you?"

"Not before today. But the idea suddenly has a lot of appeal." He took a noisy breath. "What color is that polish?"

"Flamingo."

"Flamingo," he repeated, still staring. "I bet it glows in the dark, doesn't it?"

"Yes."

"Do you wear it on your fingernails, too?"

"Sometimes."

"Boy, could we have fun with that."

She stifled an extremely delighted smile. "*Please.* Show some restraint."

"You like using restraints, do you? I think I could come up with something."

Her internal smile up and vanished. And, unfortunately, not out of revulsion at the thought. Not that she'd ever had bondage issues, but really, she should be a lot more outraged than she felt.

Not only that, but once again he'd managed to turn the tables on her. He was a wily snake, for sure. Here she'd been delighting in making him all hot and bothered, and instead *she* was the one who suddenly felt on fire. Even the toenails she was painting suddenly seemed to tingle. She quickly finished off her other foot, then capped the polish and shoved it back in her bag.

Waving her hands a little too frantically over her toes to dry them, she refused to look at Ross again. She just knew he'd be sporting that too-intimate smile, the one that said, "I'm picturing you naked."

Relief flooded through her when the light in the anteroom flashed on, and she glanced up to see Dr. Turner smiling in on them. Although she was getting mighty sick of her vitals being taken constantly, it was, for once, a welcome distraction.

The doctor flipped on the intercom. "Good morning to you both."

"Good morning," they responded in unison.

The doctor began donning all that quarantine equipment, which Paige found she was getting used to. And actually, was grateful for. Because she sure as heck didn't want to be responsible for spreading this absolutely horrid affliction. No one should have to suffer through being hot for someone they didn't like.

But even as she thought it, she knew in part she was lying to herself. There were bits and pieces of Ross Bennett that were utterly likeable. Which didn't make her happy.

The doctor finished dressing, then opened the door and reached in for gloves. After slapping them on, she picked something up from the counter, then entered their room. Paige noticed it was a file folder, which the doctor handed to Ross. "Your secretary asked me to give this to you."

Ross glanced at it and nodded. "Thanks," he said, then dropped it on his bed. "What's new, doc?"

"The report on your latest bloodwork from the *CDC* is in. You'll be relieved to know you're both still showing no signs of infection."

The doctor didn't know it, but that news gave Paige no relief whatsoever. And besides, she just didn't believe it. Not with the way her body had been acting lately.

She chanced a peek at Ross, expecting to find a matching look of disbelief. Instead the turkey was smiling widely at her. "Isn't *that* good news?"

Paige snorted, but then remembered herself. "Oh, definitely. But not surprising, seeing as I'm experiencing no symptoms *whatsoever*."

He broke out laughing. "Your nose is growing, counselor. Good thing you're not under oath." After he sobered, he turned back to the doctor. "Doc, is there something you can do about those middle-of-the-night vitals checks. Really, it's worse on our health to get continually woken up."

His expression was the epitome of innocence, but Paige wasn't fooled. This man had a penchant to harbor some kind of ulterior motive for just about everything. "Doesn't bother me," she said, crossing her arms over her chest.

"That's not what you were saying last night."

"I'll have the orders changed immediately to two checks a day," the doctor said. "Once in the morning and once at bedtime."

"You're the best, doc."

Paige rolled her eyes.

The doctor glanced back and forth between them, but luckily she seemed too professional to react to the outrageous idiot. "Who first?"

"Ladies first," Ross said, and managed to actually sound magnanimous about it. Which of course was a sham.

But Paige didn't care. She offered Ross her best fake smile and sailed to her side of the room. The doctor followed her and slid home the privacy sheet.

By this time Paige knew the drill. She sat sideways on her bed, legs dangling, and held out her arm for the blood pressure machine.

"Seriously, how are you feeling?" the doctor asked in a low voice.

"Fine," Paige prevaricated somewhat. After all, she didn't have a sore throat or cold or flu or anything. Just a horrible case of raging hormones.

The doctor nodded as she began to pump. "Your brother will be relieved to hear it."

Paige rolled her eyes. "He hasn't been hassling you, has he? I know he can be a pain."

"Maybe a little more diligently than your average overprotective brother. But he's not too bad."

"Good."

The doctor noted her blood pressure on her chart. "Still a little elevated."

"Yours would be too if you had to hole up with a totally aggravating man."

Dr. Turner laughed. "I know all about aggravating men."

"My brother being one of them?"

The doctor looked up, her gray eyes narrowed. "What has he told you?"

"Just that there's a history there somewhere."

The doctor sighed. "We went to college together for a while."

"Really? You went to Georgia Tech?"

"For a while."

"Same here. But I transferred after my freshman year," Paige said, hoping the bitterness didn't display itself in her voice.

"That would be after Nick's junior year?" the doctor asked.

"Yes."

"That's when he and I lost touch. He vanished right after his finals, and by the time he returned, I'd left, too."

Paige went still, even as the doctor stuck a thermometer in her ear. "Uh-oh. He disappeared?"

"Yes."

"Right after finals?"

"That's right." The doctor finished her routine exam, completed her notes, then said, "All done."

She began to turn away, but Paige stopped her with a hand to her arm. "Has he ever told you *why* he vanished abruptly?" she asked, even though she was pretty sure she would dread the answer.

"He made some vague excuses, sure."

That answer wasn't as bad as she'd dreaded. Obviously, Nick hadn't told this woman the entire truth. Which, considering, she really should have expected. Nick was a lot of things, but disloyal had never been one of them. Yet it was pretty clear that the woman wasn't all that satisfied with his answer, and Paige wasn't about to be the cause. "He disappeared that spring because of me," she said quietly.

The doctor peered at her, apparently gauging the truth of those words. Finally, after a moment, she shook her head. "Well what do you know?" she mumbled. "The guy actually told the truth . . . for once."

Chapter Ten

"So . . . we're not infected. So far, at any rate," Ross said, the moment the doctor took her leave.

"The hell we're not," Paige retorted. "It might not be showing up in our blood yet, but we *have* to be infected."

"Why can't you just admit you're attracted to me the good old-fashioned way?"

"Impossible."

He crossed his arms over his chest. "Why is that?"

Paige waved vaguely, and avoided looking at him. "You're not my type."

"Really? What's your type?"

She glanced over at him, checking out every inch.

Probably to find a few glaring faults. "You're too big."

"You're into midgets?"

"I mean too broad."

"You go for scrawny?"

"And I like intellectual men."

"Don't look now, but I can read."

"And I most definitely do not date divorce attorneys."

"We all have to make a living somehow. What have you got against divorce attorneys?"

Her eyes darted around the room. "Isn't it obvious?"

"No."

She shrugged one shoulder. "As I believe I've mentioned, I've had a bad experience with one."

His mouth dropped open. "You? Personally? I thought you said you've never been married."

"I haven't."

He stepped in front of her and stuck a knuckle under her chin, forcing her gaze to his. "Tell me," he said softly. "Tell me what the bad experience was."

She stared at him for several seconds, then shook her head. "You'd just think I was an idiot."

"Lady, I've seen you in action, with Jasmine's case, and a whole slew of others you've been working on since we've been here. The last word I'd use to describe you would be idiot."

Her skin was so damn soft, and her lips would tempt a monk. And those moss green eyes just about begged a man to ravish her. Except right now they seemed stormy and slightly tormented. He braced himself for her to tell him it was none of his damn business. So when she began blurting out her story, his hand dropped from her chin in shock.

"When I was in college, I started dating a man. He was actually a professor. Not one of mine, mind you," she added hastily.

"Of course not," he agreed. "Was he your first?"

"My first love? Well, no. I was pretty head-over-heels for Tommy Dushevski in second grade."

"Lucky Tommy."

She pushed lightly at his chest and he took the hint and stepped back, giving her space. Jumping from the bed, she began pacing.

Ross didn't know why she was actually honoring his request to tell him what happened to her, but he realized he was much more interested in her story than seemed warranted. And that he was bracing himself for some news that would really tick him off.

Which was surprising, in and of itself. Not that he didn't hate hearing about *any* woman being screwed over, but that it was *this* woman, who was a formidable adversary. But a damn beautiful one.

She'd been leaving her hair down, and it was much longer than he'd have guessed from the prissy little buns she wore when working. And it had lovely waves to it, too, which he'd bet would turn even wavier in the Atlanta humidity. He'd bet it took on the "just had wild sex" appearance if left untended.

He dragged his thoughts from taking that road any further for now, seeing as she'd begun speaking again, and he wanted to concentrate on her story.

". . . I thought Professor Drew Stengal was the one. I really did."

Ross would bet his law practice this had been the man to whom Paige had given her virginity. Women were real sentimental that way.

"What happened?" he prodded when she went silent for a moment.

She whirled to face him, her nostrils flaring slightly, and her eyes stoked. "Mrs. Drew Stengal happened."

"Oh, boy."

"No kidding, the jerk."

"I take it you didn't know there *was* a Mrs. Jerk Stengal."

"Of course I didn't know!" she practically shrieked. "What do you take me for?"

Ross held up his hands. "Whoa, sorry. It was something of a rhetorical question."

Squeezing the bridge of her nose, she said, "No, I'm sorry." Her hand dropped. "I was *so* stupid."

"Naïve," he amended.

"No. Stupid. It never occurred to me why he wouldn't want me to have his phone number. I thought it was just his policy because it was unlisted. I never questioned why his apartment was so shabby and practically empty—except for a luxurious bed, of course."

Well, that answered that. They'd definitely been lovers.

"It never crossed my mind to question why, whenever we went out, it was always to some out-of-the-way place at least sixty miles from Atlanta. I thought he was being romantic." She snorted. "Like I said. Stupid."

"Paige, you were young and trusting. And the man was a sleaze. My guess is, you probably weren't his first. He had the slick lines and the easy lies down pat. Trust me, I've encountered hundreds like him in my career. They're scum."

"And you've probably represented a bunch of them," she said, although the usual disdain and fire wasn't evident in her voice. In fact, she said it in a way that gave him hope he was making headway with her opinion of him. "Not a chance, darlin'. The first thing I ask any potential client is whether cheating on his or her part was at the core of the divorce. If it is, I kick the bums out of my office. I don't represent adulterers."

She went still, staring at him. "Honestly?"

"Scout's honor."

Her honey-blond hair fell forward as she lowered her head and shook it. "I wish you'd quit doing that."

"What's that?"

"Saying things that make me dislike you a little less."

He considered this a major concession on her part, but decided it wouldn't be prudent to say so. "Sorry about that. So what happened?" he asked, although he could pretty well imagine. Her name and reputation were dragged through the mud.

"What else? My name and reputation were dragged through the mud. I was the 'paramour.' Can you believe that? Paramour. What kind of dumb legal term is that? And of course no one but my family would believe I was so clueless."

He was batting a thousand so far, but wasn't real happy about it. "I'm so sorry," he said, and meant it. If that jerk college professor were standing in front of him at this moment, the man would have a broken nose faster than you could say "assault."

"His wife was out for utter revenge. I was subpoenaed. Forced to tell all the gory details of our relationship. Of how much money he spent on me during our relationship, so his wife—and her divorce attorney, I'm guessing—could file a judgment against him to recover those mutual assets."

Ross winced. He knew what that meant. She'd been forced to recount how many hotels they'd visited, vacations they'd taken, dinners he'd bought her, jewelry, clothing, the works. She'd been compelled by a zealous divorce attorney to reveal all. "Dissipation is the legal term for that," he murmured.

She nodded, her eyes a little too bright for his comfort.

Well, that explained that. Why she was so willing to think the worst of him. In a way, he couldn't blame her. She'd been badly burned by a member of his profession.

He was at somewhat of a loss as to how to comfort her. After all, why would she want or accept comfort from someone who represented everything she loathed? But he'd be damned if he wouldn't try.

Moving to her slowly, lest she decide to use him as the symbol of all she despised, he touched her arm. "I really am sorry you were put through something like that."

"You know what really stinks?" she asked, her voice a little watery.

"What?"

"I believe you."

Why that just about busted his heart wide open, he couldn't say. "I'm glad. It's true."

"You know what's worse?"

"What could that possibly be?"

"I want you."

Ross was prevented from exploring Paige's declaration—from exploring Paige, for that matter—for the rest of the day. Between nurses and a few thousand of Paige's closest relatives, they hadn't been alone for more than five minutes.

In one way it was just as well, because he got some much-needed work done. Still, he kept one ear tuned to Paige's conversations with her family.

And grew increasingly amazed at how she shouldered the weight for so many of her relatives. And even though he envied the love and camaraderie among all of them, he understood her occasional frustration. How she managed it all, he couldn't fathom.

But his admiration for her was growing in leaps and bounds. Especially now that he understood her original animosity. He couldn't really blame her for having a soured view of divorce attorneys. But his dilemma, as he saw it, was to make her see that *some* members of his profession really did perform a service for their clients.

Then again, why it mattered to him, he couldn't say. Or more appropriately, he didn't want to ponder too closely. Of course he'd want the woman he was going to make love with to have at least a modicum of respect for him. That was a given.

At least now. He couldn't say it had always been a given.

The last of Paige's relatives left and she shuffled back to her bed, rifling through pages and pages of written notes on a legal pad. She plopped down wearily, grumbling under her breath.

"What?" Ross snapped closed his own briefcase.

"Thank your lucky stars you don't have any family," she said, around a sigh.

"You mean to tell me out of all of those people, there isn't a single lawyer among them?"

"My cousin Luther is a prothonotary. And Jillian's a notary. But that's about as close as they get."

Poor thing. Ross lifted his can of soda. "Here's hoping you have at least one pharmacist in the crowd, then."

Paige's lips tugged up in a reluctant grin. "My uncle Hugo."

"Bet he's a busy man."

This time she actually laughed, and Ross couldn't believe what the sound did to him. Or the sight of her dazzling smile, and glowing green eyes. The woman was breathtaking when she wasn't scowling at him. *Literally* breathtaking, he realized, when his lungs began burning.

He sucked in air. "Would you like a glass of wine?"

"Oh, that sounds marvelous," she said. "Just the thing to help me unwind."

Ross jumped from his bed, grateful for the bagginess of his shorts. It was embarrassing how greatly she'd affected him with merely a smile. But he vowed there and then that he'd do whatever it took to keep a smile on her face as much as possible. And all the ways he could accomplish that crashed through his head and down his torso.

He uncorked the bottle of wine and poured what remained from the night before into two plastic cups. Strolling over to her side of the room, he handed her the glass.

"Bless you," she said, and it sounded heartfelt.

She took a small sip and moaned her appreciation. Then she rolled her shoulders, and stretched her neck from side to side. "What a day!"

"How about you turn around and I'll get rid of the kinks."

"Really? You mean it?"

"This is going to come as quite a shock, so brace yourself. But you are looking at possibly the only divorce attorney in the history of the world that doesn't lie."

She snorted, but did it with a grin, which he considered a major step forward. He felt like he'd just been promoted from pond scum to fertilizer or something.

Paige scrambled to turn her back to him. In the guise of just getting it out of the way, Ross lifted her hair into his hands. He rubbed the silky blond strands between his fingers before laying it over her shoulder. He almost groaned aloud, her hair felt so soft. He could just imagine it stroking his skin as she straddled his naked body and leaned down to kiss him.

With more strength of will than he'd known he possessed, he set aside his prurient thoughts and concentrated on the massage. He began with her shoulder blades, which were tight, but delicate in a female kind of way. Man, he loved the way women were built. Especially this woman.

"Ohhhhhh," she moaned. "That's wonderful. Where'd you learn to do this?"

He shrugged, even though she couldn't see it. "I took on a case for a massage therapist once. She couldn't afford to pay in cash."

"Oh, please."

"No, really. It was totally legit."

"Uh-huh."

Behind her, Ross smiled, and moved to the outer portion of her shoulders, digging his thumbs into tense muscles. "Have I mentioned I really admire the way you take care of your family?"

Her laughter was part chuckle, part euphoric groan. "Do I have a choice?"

"That's the cool part. Of course you have a choice. And you choose to help any way you can."

She craned her head to look at him. "Do you really believe that?"

"I'm the nonprevaricating type, remember?"

"Sometimes it feels a little overwhelming."

"I'll bet. Tell you what. As long as we're stuck here, why not divvy up your list? Give me some of the relatives and let me handle them."

"I couldn't ask you to do that."

"You didn't ask. I'm offering."

She moaned again as he started working her upper back. "Now, no offense, but I don't think my relatives could afford your fees."

That stopped him in his finger-wandering tracks. "Are you telling me," he waved at her legal pad, "you do *all* that legal work pro bono?"

"Please don't stop," she pleaded, so he resumed

the massage. "No, I couldn't possibly do it all for free. I'd be bankrupt in a week. But I charge a 'family' rate."

"Well, whatever you charge, I'll charge the same."

She turned her head again. "Why? Why are you offering?"

" 'Cause I'm a nice guy?"

She stared at him a moment. "Okay. How are you at wills?"

"I can certainly make them legal."

She grabbed up her legal pad and rifled through the pages. "Aunt Alicia needs some revisions made to her will."

"Oh, right. Lester's out, the taxidermist is in."

She stared at him again. "Is it possible? A man who actually pays attention?"

He decided not to take offense. "Your family is interesting, to say the least."

Paige laughed, which made him feel ridiculously gushy inside. "That's a nice way of putting it." She tore a page from her pad. "Aunt Alicia is no exception."

Ross glanced at the list of changes. In addition to Harmen the taxidermist, Aunt Alicia had added several other benefactors. "Mel Gibson?" he asked, raising a brow.

Paige turned to face him, apparently figuring her massage was over. "She saw *The Patriot* last week and thought he was cute."

"What did Harrison Ford do to earn her disfavor?"

"Nothing, just the luck of the draw. Aunt Alicia believes in loving only one movie star at a time. She's loyal that way."

"Oh."

Paige leafed through the pad some more. "Maybe you can advise Uncle Troy on his little problem."

"What little problem would that be?"

"He got caught trying to buy illegal grenades."

"Uncle Troy's a terrorist, is he?"

"Only against gophers."

"Excuse me?"

"Gophers. Uncle Troy's a farmer, and the gophers are wreaking havoc on his crops."

"So he wants to blow them away?"

"Nothing else has worked."

"I see."

"And how about my first cousin once removed, Stephanie?"

"Is your entire family in legal trouble?"

"Oh, this is a drop in the bucket," she said, waving.

"What's going on with Stephanie?"

"Well, she's a beautician."

"Uh-oh. I hear a bad perm day coming on."

Paige nodded. "*And* dye job."

"Maybe she should find another line of work?"

"Oh, no! She's very good! Usually. She was just a little angry that morning."

Ross checked Paige's notes. "So this Shirley Nusbaum is suing her for pain and suffering?"

"Yes. Which is pretty much a joke, seeing as Stephanie had just learned the night before that Shirley was having an affair with Stephanie's boyfriend."

"Now that was pretty dumb on Shirley's part. *Never* tick off your hairdresser."

"So true." She must have noticed his lips twitching, because she grinned. "Go ahead and laugh. It's all right. I understand completely."

Problem was, her smile didn't make him want to laugh. It made him want to kiss. Deeply. Hotly.

Her smile faded slowly, so he had a feeling she was doing a good job of reading his mind. He touched her cheek. "Did I hear you right earlier? You want me?" he asked softly.

"Unfortunately, yes."

"Why unfortunately?"

Her eyes slid shut. "I have the feeling it's going to turn out to be a mistake."

"Why?"

"One of us might get burned. And no offense, but I don't want it to be me."

"I'm not into rejection as a rule, either."

"Ha!" she said, popping open her eyes. "My guess is you've never been rejected in your life."

"Not true," he replied, dropping his hand. "Funnily enough, there are plenty of women who find me highly resistible."

"You don't say."

He nodded. "It came as a real shock to me, too."

Her laughter bubbled. "Poor thing."

"Well, if you feel bad for me, you might want to give me a break here."

"Pity sex?" she asked, one brow raised.

"If that works for you. However, I can practically guarantee you won't be feeling sorry for me by the time I'm through with you."

She sucked in an audible breath. "What if one of us is infected, and the other isn't, and we end up passing the virus to the other person?"

"We've been sharing the same air for a few days now. I can pretty much guarantee if that were the case, we've already passed the virus along."

"You know, I bet you are hell on wheels in court."

"I've won my share of arguments."

"What if it's bad for us to . . . err . . ."

"Derive the ultimate pleasure?" he suggested.

"Exactly," she said, smiling her relief.

"I can guarantee you that isn't the case."

"How do you know?"

"If you'd heard the suggestion the good doctor made when I complained of . . . discomfort, you'd have no doubt."

She looked confused for a moment. "Surely she wouldn't suggest we fool around."

"Not with each other, no."

Her brows furrowed for a thoughtful moment. "Oh!" Understanding dawned, and she blushed.

"So you see," he said gently, helping her to understand that this was inevitable, "There's just no reason not to."

She glanced at the clock. "Well, we have a vitals check later."

"True. We'll wait until after that so we'll have all night."

"All night?" she squeaked. "I thought you said an hour?"

"I said, *much* longer than an hour."

"But all night?"

"All night," he promised.

Chapter Eleven

That night Rachel let herself into her condo, exhaustion dragging her down like a lead weight. She kicked off her shoes and wandered into the kitchen, hoping a miracle had occurred and some faery had snuck in while she was at work and stocked her refrigerator.

No miracle. There was a box of baking soda, ketchup that was likely five years old, and several bottles of spring water. It would take a better chef than she to make something edible out of that.

Chinese or pizza? Considering her current exhaustion, that was a monumental decision. In fact, if she stayed awake long enough to accept the delivery it would practically be a miracle. But she was hungry, and if she didn't eat something she'd wake up with an agonizing headache in the morning.

The good news at the moment was that both the Chinese and pizza delivery places were on her speed dial.

Just as she reached for the phone, her doorbell rang. She spun and glared at the door. Unless some food delivery person had anticipated her order, she was in no mood for company.

Walking to the door she glanced through the peephole. Some young kid stood there with a gaily wrapped present in his hands. She opened up and conjured a smile.

"Delivery for you, ma'am."

"Really? How nice."

She couldn't imagine what the occasion was, couldn't imagine who would send her something for no good reason, but Rachel liked surprise gifts as well as the next person. She grabbed her purse and pulled out a five for a tip, which seemed to please the delivery boy very much. He grinned and rushed off, and Rachel closed the door, taking the gift into her living room. She sat on the couch and tore the small envelope from the wrapping.

Rachel,
Saw this in a gift shop and remembered how much you loved collecting these. I'm looking forward to Friday night.

N

Nick. She had a fleeting thought about returning the gift unopened, but curiosity got the better of her. Had he really remembered her old hobby? She tore the paper from the box and opened it. And her heart practically exploded. He *had* remembered her passion for antique music boxes. This one was beautiful, the wood surface gleaming and in pristine condition. A bouquet of roses was carved into the top.

She opened the lid and the notes from the tune "Then You'll Remember Me" from the opera *The Bohemian Girl* drifted to her ears.

"Oh, Nick," she whispered.

Tears popped into her eyes and she blinked, trying to fight them. After all these years he'd still remembered. He had no way of knowing that she'd had to sell her collection shortly after leaving Tech. It had nearly killed her to do it, but at the time money was so tight, and she couldn't justify the frivolous hobby. Over the years she'd thought about starting a new collection, but just hadn't gotten around to it.

In college he'd teased her about the boxes. He'd called it a sissy hobby, but he'd always done it with a charming smile, so she'd just punch him in the arm and sniff indignantly.

This music box was absolutely beautiful, and must have cost him a fortune. Should she accept the gift? And if she did, what did that say? That she'd forgiven him for the past?

She was utterly torn. As much as she'd instantly

fallen in love with the box, she really couldn't see keeping it. It broke her heart, but she just couldn't.

With a reluctant sigh she closed the lid and set the box down. Reaching for the phone she dialed the hospital and asked for Paige Hart's room. When Paige answered, she sounded strangely out of breath.

"Paige, it's Rachel Turner. Are you all right?"

"Oh! Yes, yes, I'm fine."

"You're sure?"

"Yes. Positive. I was . . . working out."

"Oh. Well I'm sorry for interrupting."

"No problem. What can I do for you? Is this a phone consultation or something?"

"No, actually, I need a favor, if you don't mind."

"Name it."

"Would it be possible for you to give me your brother's phone number? I . . . need to talk to him about something."

"I don't see why not." Paige rattled off the number, and Rachel took special note of the area code. "Is that . . . uh . . . the number to his hotel room?"

"No, that's his home number."

Oh, boy. For some reason she'd assumed he was here merely to watch over his sister during her enforced stay in the hospital. It never occurred to her that they shared the same city. This made matters much, much worse.

At least, that's how she interpreted her heart's raging reaction.

"Well, umm, thanks so much."

"May I ask why you need to talk to him? It's not about me, is it?"

"No, no. He just . . . had something delivered here, and I need to return it to him."

"Ahhh, trying to woo you, huh?"

"Is this standard operating procedure for him?" Rachel asked, not real happy that she might just be one in a long string.

Paige's voice pitched low. "I know he must have hurt you in the past, Dr. Turner. But I promise that he's a really nice guy underneath it all."

Rachel's eyes landed on Nick's gift. "Well," she conceded, "the gift *was* pretty thoughtful. But I just can't accept it."

"What was it, if you don't mind my asking?"

"A music box. A *beautiful* music box."

There was a long pause. A really long pause. "A music box?" Paige finally said in a near whisper.

"Yes. Why?"

"Does it have carved roses on the lid?"

"Uh . . . yes. How did you know that?"

"Does it play 'Then You'll Remember Me?' "

Rachel sucked in a hard breath. "Yes. Why?"

"Do you collect music boxes?"

"I used to."

"Dr. Turner, my brother bought that music box years ago. He delivered more pizzas, mowed more lawns and flipped more burgers than you can imagine to be able to pay for it."

Rachel's stomach flipped. Over and over. "Please don't tell me," she whispered, "this was between his junior and senior year of college."

"Okay, I won't."

"It was, wasn't it?" she demanded, almost sick.

"It was."

Rachel was too stunned to even say goodbye. She just dropped the receiver into its cradle. How dare he?

The son of a bitch was wonderful.

"What was that all about?" Ross asked, lifting his head from Paige's knee, which he'd been exploring in minute detail.

She dragged breath into her lungs. The man was just too damn sexy. And relentless. The fact that she'd been on a phone hadn't even made him pause. He'd just continued to nibble his way up her leg toward her shorts. It had taken monumental effort to concentrate on what the doctor was saying.

She and Ross were both wearing shorts and T-shirts. And Ross wouldn't even be wearing the shirt at all, except in deference to the night nurse who'd come to make the final check of the evening.

They were alone. Finally. For the entire night.

"Hmm?" she said, having completely forgotten his question.

"I don't remember," he murmured, then slid up her body to cover her mouth with his.

His kiss was earth-shattering. Warm and strong lips molded her mouth, but touched every nerve in her. His tongue stroked hers, and yet it felt like it was also stroking her skin, her breasts, everywhere.

He raised his head and stared into her eyes. "You. Naked. Now."

"Likewise," she said, her voice throatier than she'd ever heard before. She grabbed the hem of his T-shirt and began yanking upward.

Ross raised his arms and let her strip him at her leisure, which wasn't all that leisurely. She was frantic to see this man's chest again. But this time she would also touch it, taste it, *use* it for her pleasure.

And with luck, his.

That thought conked her just as she pulled the shirt over his head, and she froze. The situation struck her. She had no experience whatsoever with what they were about to do. Her experience was pretty much limited to allowing one scumbag of a professor access to her body, and that man had been content to use it the old-fashioned way. She had no experience with *this*. What if she screwed it up, so to speak? What if she totally humiliated herself? What if he laughed at—

"Uh, Paige?" Ross said, his voice coming out a bit muffled from underneath his shirt.

"Yes?"

"Customarily you take it all the way off."

Still, she didn't move. Fear of failure seized her and wouldn't let go. "Ross?"

"Uh-huh?" he grunted.

"I have a confession to make."

"Now?"

"I think it's necessary." She tugged his shirt back down, even though she'd have rather confessed to the cotton, and not his handsome face.

"What is it?"

"Can you . . . can you sit up for a second?"

"Only if you want to sit on my lap."

"Be good for just a second. This is hard enough as it is."

He frowned, but sat up, saying, "Honey, I planned on being as good as I can be. And hard doesn't even begin to describe this situation."

"I don't . . . umm . . . understand the rules here."

"What?" His eyebrows screwed downward. "What's so hard to get, gorgeous? We want each other. Period. What?"

"Don't laugh, all right?"

He ran his hand through his hair. "Trust me, I'm not laughing."

"I don't know how to do this, okay?" she said, getting a little irritated.

He stared for a moment. "You've never had sex?"

She sighed. "I've never had *non* sex."

"We're not having *non* sex. We're having un-usual sex."

"Fine. I've never had *unusual* sex."

He sat unblinking, but his jaw dropped a little. "You mean, your refusal to talk about playing baseball as a kid was because you actually never played?"

"I had lots of older brothers." She waved, avoiding his eyes.

"Are you saying you don't know what to do?"

She nodded. "I'm pretty pitiful."

"That's not pitiful. It's kind of endearing."

She wrinkled her nose at him. "Don't patronize me, counselor."

"That's the last thing I'd do, Paige. I mean it. And I'd really, really like to be the one to show you."

"How? I don't even know where to begin."

He sat in pensive silence for a moment, scratching his jaw. Then he finally looked up with a wicked gleam in his eyes that spelled mischief. "I'll tell you what. How about if I teach you how to play baseball?"

"That's so . . . so juvenile, don't you think?"

"Oh, no. It's as age-old as the game itself. It was just a way for young people to articulate what they wanted." He stroked her cheek. "It'll be fun, you'll see."

"Well, okay."

"We need to do a little prep work first, okay?"

"Like what?"

"Can you pull out some of that flamingo nail polish?"

"Why?"

"I want to paint your fingernails."

It took a lot longer than Ross liked for Paige's nail polish to dry. His body, his mind, his hormones were impatient. But as he helped her blow on the polish, his brain started racing with what he'd learned. How was it possible that a beautiful woman in her early thirties had never experienced the thrill of foreplay? The only explanation could be that the creep of a college professor who introduced her to sex had introduced her to the joys of male egocentric sex. Instant gratification for him. Nothing but frustration for her.

But if the jerk had been her first—and it certainly sounded that way—then she'd have no frame of reference for comparison. Which meant she had no frame of reference for what they were about to do together. That made Ross excited and scared shitless at one and the same time.

"Dry," she whispered.

"Huh?"

"My fingernails. They're dry."

Ross's apprehension vanished as the anticipation took over. He snapped off the light on her bedside table, both to ward off a bout of shyness on her part, and to test the power of flamingo nail polish. Oh, definitely, her nails were glowing in the dark of the room. This was going to be fun. And sexy as hell, if all went well.

"What . . . what now?" Paige asked, her voice endearingly wobbly.

"Lie down on the bed."

"Shouldn't we get . . . err . . . naked first or something?"

"The rules of baseball are that we begin fully dressed."

"Fully dressed?" she said, laughing. "We're both wearing shorts and T-shirts."

"That's plenty."

"Okay."

"Lie down, Paige."

She swung her legs onto the bed, then lay down on it, smack dab in the middle. It was dark enough in the room that he could merely see the outline of her body, but that polish made it easy for him to notice that her hands trembled slightly. He was reminded of a sacrificial lamb.

He reached out to stroke her silky hair. "Another rule of baseball. If at any time one of us is uncomfortable, we can call time out on the game right then. Got it?"

"Yes," she breathed.

"Now, scoot over a little, love."

She hesitated with what looked like a frown of confusion pulling at the corners of her mouth. But then she scooted. Closer to his side of the bed.

He stifled a laugh. "The other side, honey."

"Oh!" She slipped over to the far side of the bed.

Ross climbed onto the bed, lying on his side, facing her. He draped his left arm across her waist. "Remember. We can stop anytime."

"I know."

If she stopped him, he'd probably die right there in her bed. His body was dealing with a fever he'd never quite experienced before. "Okay, I'm tossing out the first pitch. You hit and get to run to first base, *if you want to*."

"I'm pretty sure I know, but just to be sure, what's first base?"

"Kissing. Just kissing. Do you want to make it to first base?"

"Oh, yes!"

Her enthusiasm was adorable. And sexy. He lowered his head slowly and settled his mouth over hers. At first he kept the kisses short and nibbly, taking the time to enjoy the taste of her, the scent of her skin.

She moaned a little, which was all the encouragement he needed to deepen the kiss. But first he lifted his head and whispered, "Next is advanced first base. Do you want that?"

"Please."

This time when he kissed her, he coaxed her lips apart. Slanting his head, he experimented with the perfect fit, then touched his tongue to hers. She whispered, "Oh!" into his mouth and a firestorm raged to life. Instead of lying docilely, accepting his attentions, she began lending her full participation. In the kissing, the touching, the twisting restlessly, pressing her body closer to his. Her arms locked around the back of his neck in silent demand for more.

And Ross eagerly gave it to her, beginning a wild dance of tongues and lips. It took all he had not to explore all the parts of her calling to him. The kisses could have lasted minutes or hours, he lost all track of time as he reveled in her sweet mouth, the soft skin of her face, the silky strands of her hair. Sensation took over and his blood thickened in his veins while his heart threatened to explode against hers, raging just as fast against his chest.

Ross had always enjoyed kissing. But never like this. This was a mating, not just a prelude to something more. So as much as he did want to get on with the game, he could bide his time, because this felt so damn good all on its own.

Finally, with a groan, she turned slightly, breaking the kiss. Still, he didn't stop, just began worshiping her face and neck.

"Ross," she breathed.

"Mmm?" He worked his way up to her petal soft earlobe.

"Second . . . second base," she gasped. "What . . . is it?"

"Touching your breasts," he breathed almost soundlessly in her ear. "Do you want to go there?"

"Can I . . . touch yours too?"

He was going to burn up. No doubt about it. "If you want to."

"I do."

He took her mouth again, then felt for the hem of her T-shirt. Slipping his hand beneath the cotton, he slid his fingers up her waist and ribs, hesitating a moment before touching her, trying to regain control of his own sparking senses.

"Hurry," she demanded.

"Slow and steady, baby."

"No." She grabbed his hand through the cotton of her shirt and pushed it upward, until he was cupping the underside of her right breast.

"Oh," they said in unison. Even flat on her back, her breast was full and heavy and fit perfectly in his hand. He ran his thumb over her hardened nipple and she gasped again.

"Feel good?"

"Oh, yes." Her arms unlocked from around his neck and she ran them down his shoulders. "My turn."

"Oh, no you don't. I'm not done exploring this base."

His fingertips glided across the valley between her breasts, and he cupped her left one, paying it equal attention.

And Paige really began to squirm in earnest. Her hands frantically tugged at his shirt, and she finally successfully gained entrance, warmth meeting heat. "Oh, so good," she murmured. "So smooth."

Ross sucked in a breath as her fingertips whispered over his nipples. Had he known before that his chest could be such an erogenous zone? He didn't know, and he was sinking so fast into mindless lust, he didn't care. Just felt.

"Third base," she choked out.

He kissed her deeply, before lifting his head and staring into her face. His eyes had adjusted to the darkness enough to see that hers sparkled with almost a wild intensity. "Advanced second, first," he informed her in a gritty voice he barely recognized.

"Show me."

She was quickly transforming into a rampant little hussy. He loved that about her. He raised her up to a sitting position and pulled her shirt over her head. Before he could lay her back down, she tugged at his, too, and he let her.

He gently pushed her down on the pillow again, then threw a leg over her hips and straddled her. And got his first perfect view of her breasts. "God, you're beautiful."

"You, too," she said, going straight for his nipples again.

He could take about another five seconds of that before he felt the pressure build in his groin to catastrophic levels. He grasped her tiny wrists and spread her arms wide, then lowered his chest to hers, taking her mouth again and swallowing her groan and his, as hard flesh met soft and yielding.

Then he slid down her body, ignoring her murmur of protest, and took a breast in his mouth.

"Ross!" she cried out, and her back arched involuntarily.

"That's it, baby, enjoy," he whispered. He tongued first one breast, then the other, moistening and soothing the hardened areolas. Well, maybe not soothing, seeing as she was practically writhing under him. Like a little tiger she growled and yanked her wrists from his grasp. Her fingers threaded through the hair on the back of his head and pressed his mouth more forcefully against her flesh.

"Third base?" he asked after long, lingering moments worshipping her chest. He had the feeling she was more than ready to do advanced exploring, and frankly, he was too close to the edge of oblivion to hold back much longer.

She surprised him with her strength, pushing at his shoulders. "No. Not until I get advanced base two."

"You're really into this equal opportunity stuff, aren't you?" he said between gritted teeth. He wasn't sure he'd survive advanced base two at her hands. Or, more appropriately, lips.

But if she wanted to give as good as she got, he could hardly deny her. Even if it killed him.

He rolled onto his back and braced himself. But nothing could prepare him for her tentative, but excited exploration. She rose to her knees and stared down at his chest, her eyes gleaming, but her hands a little twitchy, as if she didn't know how to proceed from there.

"Touch me with your mouth," he suggested.

And damn, she took directions well. She kissed his throat first, lingering over the frantically beating artery at its base. Her fingers fluttered over his temples and cheeks, then down to his shoulders. And then her lips traced a fiery trail of kisses down lower and lower, until they latched on one nipple.

"Oh, God," he said, bucking up in response.

Her head jerked up and she looked at him, worrying her lower lip. "Did that . . . hurt?"

"Hell, yes. In the best possible way."

Her smile was delighted, and she returned to her task, obviously emboldened. Ross closed his eyes against the too erotic sight of her head bent to his body. But he couldn't block the sensation of her hair tickling his burning flesh. Or her tongue laving across his nipples in longer and more heated strokes.

Feeling the eruption imminent, he grasped her shoulders and pushed her up and over, onto her back. "Third base," he tried to say, but didn't know if it came out sounding anything vaguely like that.

"I . . . I think I know where this is headed," she whispered.

"You always were a bright woman."

He bent to her breast again while his hand slipped down to unzip her shorts. Without pulling them off, he slipped his fingers under her panties and between her legs. She exploded immediately, crying out and convulsing under his touch, which just about made him come with her. He continued stroking her until he was certain he'd wrung every bit of euphoric sensation out of her. Finally she clamped her hand over his, gasping and giggling at once. "Stop! It's starting to tickle."

Ross grinned. Now that was interesting. After orgasm she got ticklish. Armed with knowledge like that, Ross was dangerous. Cool.

"Oh, Ross, what did you just do to me?" she whispered, smiling.

"Line drive to center field," he said, grinning down at her. "Knocked in the winning run."

"Oh, no, you don't. This game isn't over yet. I get my inning at bat."

He groaned, but he wasn't exactly unhappy about that, seeing as his erection had become more than painful. He had the feeling she wouldn't have to take too many pitches to get what she wanted.

He allowed her to push him back, then gritted his teeth while her soft, warm hands stretched the waistband of his running shorts and she shoved them down his legs. "Holy cow," she said under her breath, before wrapping her fingers around him.

Ross just about spontaneously combusted. He shut his eyes on a low moan, then opened them again to watch her mouth begin lowering to him. "Oh, God, what are you doing?"

"What else?" she asked, her voice husky and low. "Advanced third base."

"Oh, God."

Chapter Twelve

Rachel was much more nervous than she felt was necessary, considering the situation. After all, she'd been on dates before. Not many, but enough to know that she'd never felt this roiling in the pit of her stomach—merely at the prospect of going out with someone. Nick would be ringing her doorbell in less than ten minutes—if he was on time. Better yet, maybe he'd chicken out and not show at all.

That thought, for some unfathomable reason, wasn't as appealing as she would like.

As she gave herself a final once-over in the mirror, she thought about just how she was going to thank Nick for the beautiful music box, and then clunk him over the head with it. How dare he have worked hard to purchase it for her so many years ago? How dare he keep it all this time? She'd been much better off believing he was a user and a bastard. Finding out he was at least a little sentimental had ruined her self-righteous peace of mind.

Still, just to show him she was no longer interested—and possibly convince herself as well— she'd selected this outfit carefully. It was an ankle-length, black, cotton, sleeveless dress, with a white cotton short-sleeved shirt underneath. It completely disguised her figure, so he couldn't accuse her of trying to entice him. At the same time it wasn't so informal that she'd feel out of place if he took her to an upscale restaurant.

The doorbell rang at the same moment her clock chimed the hour. Talk about being on time. Although it shouldn't surprise her, seeing that even as a cocky college student, he'd always been punctual.

As she dragged her feet to the door, she placed a hand over her racing heart, willing it to slow down to at least warp speed. Taking a deep breath, she swung open the door. And stared.

Nick stood there in pleated khaki pants and a snow white Oxford shirt. His throat and face looked enticingly tanned in contrast, his eyes so sparkly and blue. The man was positively edible.

Worse, in his hands he held a bouquet of long-stemmed pink baby roses. Her favorites.

He smiled and held them out. "If I remember correctly, these are your favorites."

The man *would* have to remember that.

"I . . . well, thank you. You shouldn't have."

"Why not?"

Good question. "Well . . . umm . . . it's all too much."

"What's all too much? There are only six of them."

"I'm talking about the music box."

His smile could have made a nun swoon. "Oh, good, you got it."

"Yes. But I can't keep it, Nick."

His smile vanished. "Why not?" he asked again.

"Because . . . because . . . well, I don't collect music boxes any longer."

Now he frowned. "You don't?"

"No."

"Why? You *love* music boxes."

"Yes, well, times and tastes change."

He searched her eyes, and it took everything in her not to burst out crying for the loss of her precious music boxes so long ago. It was ridiculous to feel in mourning for inanimate objects that had been gone for almost fifteen years. But suddenly standing here before her was the first and foremost thing she'd lost back then, to be swiftly followed by everything and everyone else she'd cherished.

It was just . . . suddenly . . . too . . . much.

And she just . . . suddenly . . . began . . . began . . . weeping.

"Rachel?"

Mortified, she swiped at the tears, trying to conjure icy calm. She couldn't. Not when Nick set down the flowers and grabbed her shoulders, his expression part deep concern and part horror. "Rachel, what's wrong?"

She gulped. "No . . . nothing."

"Right, I can see that." He pulled her into his arms, and God help her, it felt so good. Fifteen years of never being able to rely on anyone had obviously taken their toll, and here she was reveling in the strength of his arms, the use of his shoulder. But instead of calming her, she just cried harder. She was losing it, in front of the last person she'd *ever* want to witness her fall from sanity.

"Shhh . . . shhh, sweetheart. Whatever it is, let's talk about it."

"I don't think I can," she said, realizing she was soaking the front of his pristine shirt.

"Sure you can. Open mouth, let words spill."

He gently guided her to her living room couch and pressed down on her shoulders until she sat. He immediately plunked down beside her and pulled her back in his arms. "Doctor Nick is open for business. Tell me what's got you so upset."

"You."

He pulled back. "Me?"

"Among other things."

He studied her for a long time, then used the pads of his thumbs to wipe the tears from her cheeks. "I can guess why you have a problem with me. I was hoping tonight would go a long way toward fixing that part. And as you've already so eloquently pointed out, whatever happened in the past is past, so it certainly can't be that. What else is wrong, Rachel?"

"It's just . . . just . . ." She swallowed some more. "You just symbolize the worst time in my life."

The hurt that crossed his features sliced right into her. "Oh, God, Rachel. I'm so sorry," he said quietly.

As much as she'd like to make him shoulder all the blame, her sense of justice wouldn't allow that. "It wasn't just you, Nick. You were just the beginning. That summer . . . so many things fell apart."

"What kind of things?"

She hesitated. Did she really want to dredge this up? Did she really want to dump it on him? Did he deserve to be served ancient history that should have stopped hurting long ago?

"Rachel, it obviously still hurts, or you wouldn't be sitting here breaking my heart with those big, wet, beautiful gray eyes of yours. Maybe talking about it will help."

Uncanny. Just like that semester in college, the man could practically read her mind. "You don't really want to hear this," she said quietly, blinking back any remaining tear drops. Strange, this man had shredded her soul years ago, but the thought of upsetting him now was distressing, to put it mildly.

"I really do," he said. "How can I hope to fix any part of my culpability if you won't tell me everything?"

"Don't we have dinner reservations or something?" she asked, in a last ditch effort to avoid this conversation.

He glanced at his watch. "We do, but I can change them. Antonio is a good friend of mine. I designed his restaurant."

"You designed Antonio's?" she asked, momentarily distracted.

"I did."

"That restaurant is *beautiful!*" That was no exaggeration. The food there was fabulous, but Antonio's was almost more famous for the atmosphere, which was created in large part by the layout. It was known locally as the most romantic restaurant in Georgia. In fact, legend had it that Antonio's averaged approximately three marriage proposals per night, and that dozens of women had refused their boyfriends' requests for their hand in marriage, because they hadn't had enough romance in them to ask at Antonio's.

"I'm glad you like it," he said. "Because that's where we're going."

Okay, a music box, her favorite roses, and now the most romantic restaurant in town. The guy was either the most considerate man or the biggest con artist on the planet. She had a sinking feeling it was the former. "Oh, Nick," she whispered, her throat clogging with all kinds of new and ancient emotions.

He stroked her cheek. "I'll tell you what. How about you make us a cocktail while I call Antonio and ask him to give us an hour."

She jumped at the reprieve, no matter how temporary. It at least gave her a few precious moments to decide if she *really* wanted to spill her guts to this man, who still had the power to conjure too many deep emotions in her.

"Sounds like a plan," she said, as cheerfully as she could. She surged to her feet. "What can I get you?"

"Do you have tonic?"

"Yes."

"How about a vodka tonic?"

That made her smile inside. That was her favorite alcoholic drink, too. Of course, considering how much she drank, that meant that she indulged about four times a year. But if she was going to screw up the nerve to tell him what he wanted to know, a little liquid courage couldn't hurt, right?

She pointed. "There's the phone. Be right back." She headed toward the kitchen, although she kept an ear tuned to Nick's voice. She heard him greet someone as if they were very old friends. Since she doubted Antonio answered his own phone, she had to figure Nick was familiar with a lot of the staff. Which meant he frequented the restaurant often.

With women?

While she fixed their drinks, she shook off the question. First, because it was none of her business, and second, because thinking about it caused a yucky feeling in the pit of her stomach she didn't care for.

She returned to the living room with their drinks, and Nick stood at her approach, smiling and twinkling and generally looking sexy as sin. He still had a wet spot on his shirt from where she'd sobbed into his chest. After handing over the drink, she touched the spot and said, "I'm so sorry about that."

"Nothing to be sorry about, darlin'. We all need a good leaky faucet session now and then."

She doubted this man had ever cried in his life. He was one of those people who seemed to have an overabundance of guardian angels. The golden boy. The gifted athlete. The intelligent, driven, successful, outrageously handsome man.

"I don't know what got into me," she murmured, wondering why she wasn't as mortified as she'd expect. She sat down and took a healthy sip of her drink. She'd made it exceedingly weak, but still the alcohol warmed her insides as it glided its way down her throat.

He sat beside her. "I think it's more a function of what you need to get off your chest." He sipped, too, then pulled a coaster toward him and set down his glass. "So tell me, Rachel."

"I don't even know where to begin."

"At the beginning?"

She stared down into the bubbles in her drink. "The beginning." Taking a deep breath, she said, "I guess that would be when I realized you'd taken off without saying goodbye."

"Ouch." She heard him take a noisy breath, but she still couldn't look up at him. After a pause he said, "I didn't lie to you, Rachel. I really did have a family emergency."

"I know. Paige pretty much confirmed that."

"She did?" The amazement in his voice had her looking up. He sucked down more of his cocktail, which made his eyes water adorably. "Did she . . . tell you the nature of the emergency?"

"I didn't ask. She just said that your sudden disappearance was her fault."

"Not a chance. It wasn't her fault at all. But it *did* have to do with her. She was my little sister. I *had* to go support her, Rachel."

"I know."

"I'm just so sorry that I wasn't even thinking how it would look to you. I was too damn upset about her."

"Believe it or not, Nick, I admire that. *Now.* At the time I jumped to a totally different conclusion, however."

"Wham, bam, see you next semester, ma'am?"

She couldn't help it. She laughed, although the

Join the Love Spell Romance Book Club
and **GET 2 FREE* BOOKS NOW—
An $11.98 value!**
Mail the Free* Book Certificate
Today!

Yes! I want to subscribe to the Love Spell Romance Book Club.

Please send me my **2 FREE* BOOKS**. I have enclosed $2.00 for shipping/handling. Every other month I'll receive the four newest Love Spell Romance selections to preview for 10 days. If I decide to keep them, I will pay the Special Members Only discounted price of just $4.49 each, a total of $17.96, plus $2.00 shipping/handling ($20.75 US in Canada). This is a **SAVINGS OF $6.00** off the bookstore price. There is no minimum number of books I must buy and I may cancel the program at any time. In any case, the **2 FREE* BOOKS** are mine to keep.

*In Canada, add $5.00 shipping and handling per order for the first shipment. For all future shipments to Canada, the cost of membership is $20.75 US, which includes shipping and handling. (All payments must be made in US dollars.)

NAME: _____

ADDRESS: _____

CITY: _____ **STATE:** _____

COUNTRY: _____ **ZIP:** _____

TELEPHONE: _____

E-MAIL: _____

SIGNATURE: _____

If under 18, Parent or Guardian must sign. Terms, prices, and conditions subject to change. Subscription subject to acceptance. Dorchester Publishing reserves the right to reject any order or cancel any subscription.

The Best in Love Spell Romance!
Get Two Books Totally FREE*!

An $11.98 Value! FREE!

PLEASE RUSH
MY TWO FREE
BOOKS TO ME
RIGHT AWAY!

Enclose this card with $2.00
in an envelope and send to:

Love Spell Romance Book Club
P.O. Box 6640
Wayne, PA 19087-8640

sound still came out a little soggy. "Something like that."

"I promise you it was *nothing* like that." He set down his glass again, then took hers from her hands and did the same. Then he intertwined his fingers with hers. "What happened next?"

"Well, for about a month I guess I was in denial. I kept waiting for you to call and tell me you'd been kidnapped and had just escaped and fought your way out of the jungles of Borneo to come back to me."

He made a face, part grin, part grimace. "Nothing so exciting, I'm afraid."

"Then I finally faced the truth. I was just beginning to congratulate myself on growing up and learning a life lesson the hard way, and surviving it, when the phone did"—her voice hitched—"ring."

His fingers tightened on hers, but he remained silent and patient.

Rachel swallowed hard. "It was an old family friend. Doc Wilburn. He . . . he called to tell me he was coming to see me. He wouldn't say why, but I knew it had to be bad news."

"Uh-oh."

She nodded, wishing her hair were longer like it had been in college, so she could hide her face with it. "He showed up with a sheriff. And I knew, just from his expression."

"One of your folks was hurt?" he asked, and his tone was almost hopeful, which led her to the conclusion that he was expecting worse, but hoping for the lesser of all tragedies.

She glanced up and met his gaze, shaking her head. "Both. Dead. A . . . a plane crash."

"Oh, God." He grabbed her shoulders and yanked her into his arms. "I'm so incredibly sorry, Rachel," he murmured into her hair.

She inhaled deeply, filling up with his scent. It was still so familiar, although more layered these days, considering a hint of sandalwood had been added to the mix. Yet in all these years, she'd never forgotten his unique and oh, so alluring masculine aroma. "Yeah, so am I."

"That must have been devastating."

"Ye . . . yes."

His body went stiff. "I should have been there for you, dammit."

Her laughter was a little choked. "You had no way of knowing."

He lifted her chin until she faced him again. "That's what sucks. I *should* have known. I should have done whatever I had to to keep in touch with you."

" 'Should-haves' are futile, Nick."

He stared at her for a moment, then shook his head. "No wonder you just about hate my guts."

"I don't hate your guts," she said, and meant it. No matter how much anger she'd harbored for this man over the years, she couldn't hate him now. Not when she was positive that his regret was genuine and heartfelt. Not when she now realized that it was his riding to his sister's rescue in whatever crisis she'd been embroiled in that had driven him from school in a mindless panic.

"You have every right," he said softly.

"It's too much trouble."

He stared some more, then smiled grimly. "I can guarantee this: I'm going to make it up to you. I don't know how, I don't know how long it will take, but I'm making it up to you."

"That's not necessary."

"Oh, it most definitely is." He ran his fingers through her hair. "Why'd you cut it so short?" he asked. "It used to be incredibly long."

"The military," she managed, even while she felt like moaning at the sensation of his fingers on her face and scalp. Without her consent, her body was responding to the man. She should be upset about that. Why she wasn't was one of life's great mysteries.

"Which reminds me. Whatever made you join the military in the first place?"

She took a shaky breath and spilled the truth. "Because I desperately wanted to be a doctor."

"You were well on your way at Tech."

Rachel pulled back and lifted her glass, rubbing at the condensation. "My folks died deep in debt, Nick. Shockingly deep in debt."

"Damn."

"Doc Wilburn had to break that news to me too. He was the executor of their wills."

"But how about scholarships? You were so

smart, I can't believe you couldn't qualify."

She shook her head. "By the time the estate was settled, and the government and the banks got through with us, I still owed money. I couldn't justify getting in even deeper." She puffed a bang out of her eye. "Doc Wilburn even offered to loan me the money. I couldn't do that to him, either. And then he mentioned in passing that the army had paid for his education. It was like a lightbulb going off. Since the government had come in and looted everything my parents had, why not let them pay for my medical school?"

"There *is* some kind of poetic justice in that, I suppose."

She grinned. "I thought so."

"Can I ask you something, even if I *am* a little worried about the answer?"

"You can ask."

"Did you sell your music boxes?"

She had to swallow hard a couple of times before answering. "They were a luxury I couldn't afford."

Nick touched her cheek. "God, Rachel. I'm so sorry."

Now, suddenly, she was embarrassed. She felt her cheeks heating up right beneath his fingertips. She tried to duck her head, but he wasn't having it. Sighing, she added, "Anyway, I've been pretty much on my own since then. And tonight . . . seeing you . . . I don't know. It just triggered something I hadn't even known was still inside me."

"I'm glad you trusted me with it. And you're never going to be alone again."

It was Rachel's turn to stare at him. "Meaning what?"

"Meaning I'm here now, and I'm not going anywhere."

"Too many years—"

"Wasted. You're right about that. We have a lot to make up for."

"Nick—"

He covered her mouth with his big hand. "I'm going to tell you something now that I should have made certain to say fifteen years ago. You can choose to believe me, or not. But I'm going to say it, and you're going to sit there quietly and listen. All right?"

After a moment, she nodded.

He nodded back at her, then dropped his hand from her face. Lacing their fingers together again, he took a deep breath, then began. "Fifteen years ago I met a young woman who just blew me away. She was so intelligent and funny, so shy but also playful. She was patient and kind and she gave of herself in every way."

"No kidding."

"No interrupting."

She pressed her lips together.

"The more I got to know her, the more I was attracted to her. Not just as a friend or tutor, but as a woman. By the end of the semester I literally ached, I wanted her so bad. But she was sweet and I was pretty certain not very experienced."

She opened her mouth but shut it again when he shot her a dark, warning look.

"That last night, Rachel, didn't happen because I was *grateful* to you for your help in biology. It didn't happen for any reason but that I couldn't stop myself from kissing you, and when you responded, I was lost. I was in awe that you were handing me that honor. And you know what? Making love has never been that good. Before or since. No other woman comes close to the memory I have of that night. Of you. Of us. It was amazing."

"Oh, Nick!" she said, and felt tears popping up again, so she pressed her head to his chest.

"My family is always asking me when I'm going to settle down. I keep saying I will when I find the right woman. But maybe I have. Maybe I found her and lost her years ago. But by some lucky stroke of fate, she dropped back into my life. And I'd never forgive myself if I didn't do everything in my power to keep her here. Or at least explore what could be."

And she came full circle, sobbing into his shirt once more. And he held her quietly, not trying to stop her, but letting her get it all out.

She didn't know how long they sat there, but when her cries had settled down to the occasional hiccup, he rubbed her back and whispered. "Want to wash up before Antonio's?"

She shook her head.

"Okay, are you ready to go?"

She shook her head.

His body went stiff again. "Please tell me you're not kicking me out."

She shook her head.

"Then, what, Rachel? What do you want?"

She'd already practically ruined his shirt, so she wiped her eyes dry on it before lifting her head. "I want you to make love to me."

He gaped for about five seconds. Then he disengaged, and she felt the lack of heat and strength immediately. Was he going to reject her again? After all those beautiful words? Sentiments?

"Excuse me one second, darlin'," he drawled, then picked up her cordless. Punching a number into it, he waited, then said into the phone while he gazed into her eyes. "Bobby? Nick Hart again. Tell Antonio I'm sorry, but I'm going to have to cancel altogether."

Over the ten nights that followed, baseball wasn't the only game Paige and Ross played. One night he taught her all about football. Making those first downs was a lot of fun, even if they could never score a touchdown.

The following evening she showed him the ins and outs of tennis, and he seemed particularly fond of the drop shot. They won games, sets, but never a match.

Learning hockey had been particularly . . . athletic.

She'd never again watch a basketball player make a three-point shot without thinking of a particular talent Ross possessed. Of course, that night they'd almost fouled out when Ross forgot himself for a moment, and tried to stuff the . . . net.

Paige was quickly becoming a sports fan. Yet, as fun as it all was, as much as she yearned for nights to arrive, something was missing. She couldn't put her finger on it, exactly. Well, she probably could, but hated thinking about the implications.

But if she wasn't honest with herself now, she was in for heartbreak later. And coward that she was, she couldn't face heartbreak again.

Ross didn't love her. He'd made that clear, the last few nights. Not in words, per se. It wasn't like he said, "Paige, honey, I don't love you, but let's fool around anyway. How about a game of squash?" But she'd be really dumb to interpret their lust for anything other than what it was. Slaking needs out of their control.

After all, he knew nothing about her, outside of this hospital room. Well, technically that wasn't quite true, because they'd spent many hours talking about themselves, exploring their thoughts, beliefs, views on life. Still, they'd never had a date, never visited each other outside of work.

And in all the nights of passion and pleasure,

he'd never once mentioned the "L" word. Even her creep college professor had spoken words of undying love in the throes of passion. Or what had passed for passion. She was quickly learning that Professor Drew Stengal hadn't had a clue what true passion was.

Ross, on the other hand, was passion incarnate. He just didn't need love to muddy the waters. He might like her, and he certainly desired her. But even that much was artificial, thanks to this stinking virus. Once it ran its course, once they were released, he'd be back to dating his cover models. This would have been an unpleasant memory that he'd made the most of by whiling away some hours as pleasantly as he could.

For her to interpret their time together as anything more than that would be the second most foolish thing she'd done in her life. So as much as she hated the thought of their . . . liaison coming to an end, come to an end it must. With luck, once the disease had run its course, the memory of her nights with Ross would be nothing more than an enjoyable moment in time for her, as well. And she'd get on with her life, a little wiser, a lot more confident in her sexual awareness, and with her heart intact.

Once they were released, a perfectly clean break was the best way to go.

Paige didn't care for the niggling desire bouncing around in her head. The one that hoped the disease lived a long and happy life inside them.

Chapter Thirteen

On the morning of their fourteenth day in captivity, Paige stared in awe when Dr. Turner entered their room in nothing but blue scrubs, sans contamination equipment.

"Good morning!" the doctor said cheerfully, her gray eyes dancing with humor.

"Good morning," Paige and Ross said automatically. Then Paige chanced a glance at Ross, and noticed he looked about as dazed as she felt.

Dazed, and something else. Something that couldn't possibly be disappointment. Although it sure felt a *lot* like disappointment.

Which was absolutely ridiculous. She *should* feel ecstatic. She was *determined* to feel ecstatic.

"Might as well start packing up, folks. You are free to go."

"Are you serious?" Ross asked, his voice not exactly joyous.

"Perfectly. The CDC cleared you for readmission into the outside world."

"That's . . . great," Paige managed.

"Yeah . . . great," Ross chimed in.

The doctor crossed her arms and then looked back and forth between them, her eyes narrowing shrewdly. "If I weren't mistaken, I'd say you aren't exactly jumping up and down for joy." She waved both hands in their faces. "Hello? Is your hearing all right? I'm telling you that you can both go home. Leave. Blow this pop stand."

Paige blinked. "Oh, of course. Yes, it's wonderful news!"

"Fantastic," Ross agreed.

Which sort of aggravated Paige, because she wasn't exactly feeling fantastic. For some dumb reason a knot formed in the pit of her stomach. Not that she didn't *want* to go home. Of course she did. Nobody would wish this situation on their worst enemy. Fourteen long days stuck in a single room without much of a view.

At least, not much of a view of Atlanta out the window. The view inside the room had begun to grow on her. Which was pretty darn stupid. They both knew this was going to end eventually. They'd be released and they'd return to their lives and that would be that.

And that's exactly how she wanted it to be. She wanted to get back to the bustle of her practice, instead of wasting away watching TV or playing Monopoly. Her days would be full and busy and productive.

But the nights.

She shook her head and tried to banish all thought of what her nights would become once again. She'd had no problems with her nights before this mess began. So, okay, they were lonely at times, but for the most part she preferred the solitude her condo offered. She enjoyed the independence of doing whatever she felt like, without having to get permission from someone else. Even if Ross had been amazingly cooperative in agreeing to whatever she felt like pursuing, she'd still had to answer to another human being.

No, this was definitely a good thing. A fabulous thing.

That was her attitude, and she silently vowed to stick to it.

". . . you can take *all* of your possessions with you," she heard vaguely, and realized she'd been so busy convincing herself she was happy, she'd missed out on some of the ongoing conversation.

"But, I thought you said some things that came in couldn't go out," Ross replied.

"That was only in case you'd actually been infected, Mr. Bennett."

"We were never infected," Paige said faintly. How could that be? For the last ten nights they'd feverishly tried to relieve each other's symptoms. If it wasn't the virus . . .

"Not according to the CDC. You're both squeaky clean."

They glanced at each other, but Ross kept his expression inscrutable. "So we can go anytime?"

"Anytime you like."

"Great," Paige said.

"Really great," Ross elaborated.

"Wonderful."

"Fantastic."

Paige crossed her arms. "Best news I've heard in two weeks."

"In years."

Okay, she was going to clobber him. Just as soon as the doctor took her leave.

Ross stuck out his hand to the doctor. "Thanks for everything, doc."

The woman laughed. "Oh, yes, I'm sure you're just thrilled with me."

Paige studied the doctor. Now granted, they hadn't seen her up close without all that equipment on before, but still, there seemed to be something different about her. What, Paige couldn't say. Maybe the woman was just happy she was finally able to give them the good news that they were being released from this torture chamber.

Although she'd been utterly surprised by them about a week ago, when she'd come to give them the good news that rooms had opened up, and they could now have that much-coveted privacy they'd been clamoring for from the beginning. Both Paige and Ross had hemmed and hawed and finally told her they'd just be magnanimous and stick it out here, seeing as they were settled and all.

Right then Nick entered the anteroom and waved. The doctor moved to the glass partition and hit the intercom button. "Good morning, Mr. Hart."

"Good morning, Dr. Turner," he responded, his tone and expression oddly solemn in contrast to his sparkling blue eyes. "How are your patients this morning?"

"Why don't you come in and find out for yourself?"

"All clear?"

"All clear."

Nick grinned and barrelled through the door, striding straight to Paige and wrapping her in a bear hug. "Hiya, sis! Ready to go home?"

Paige leaned back and looked up at him. "How'd you know I was being released today?"

"I . . . well, it's fourteen days today, so, I . . . err, uhmm—" Was she seeing things, or did her brother's already ruddy skin flush a shade or two darker?

"Called in this morning to get the final results," the doctor finished for him.

Nick was *err, uhm*ing again. This spelled trouble, but she couldn't quite figure out why. She was a

222

little too busy trying to drum up some ecstasy at the news that she was about to leave all this—and Ross—behind.

Nick released her, then said, "Need help packing up? I brought the truck so we could do it all in one trip."

"That would be great," she said for about the tenth time since the doctor entered the room. And with as much enthusiasm.

Luckily, the doctor chimed in, distracting Nick enough that he didn't notice. "Well, I'll leave you all to it," she said. "I've got rounds to make."

She began to walk away, but Nick stopped her with a hand to her arm. "Wait." He then dropped her arm and held out his hand to her. "I just want to thank you for everything you've done for my sister."

The doctor hesitated, then shook hands. "You're welcome. Although I did little more than drain the two of them of blood."

The handshake lasted a little longer than seemed polite, and Paige was about ready to kick Nick in the shin if he didn't stop pushing himself at the poor woman, who obviously didn't want the attention.

The doctor sailed out rather quickly after that, leaving Nick standing as a buffer between Paige and Ross and all the emotions swirling around them. Well, at least swirling inside *her*. She didn't have a clue what Ross was thinking, seeing as he

Trish Jensen

had casually turned and began packing a duffel,
whistling tunelessly.

With a silent huff, she went about gathering her
own belongings, answering Nick in monosyllables
whenever he posed a question. Once her suitcase
was packed, she dropped it to the floor, handed
her brother the laptop and told him to start loading up while she continued to collect her things.

She kept working, even as she heard the door
whoosh shut behind her brother. But within seconds, Ross touched her arm, and she jumped
about a half-mile.

Slapping a hand over her heart, she turned to
him. "What?"

"Looks like this is it."

"Looks like."

"Good news, huh?"

"The best."

"Then how come you're scowling at me?"

"I'm not."

"You are."

She tried her best to slap a smile on her face.
She had the feeling it was a pitiful attempt at best.
"Why would I be scowling at you? I'm so *happy* for
you, seeing as this is the *best* thing that's happened
to you in *years*." Her voice was horridly shrill, but
she couldn't seem to help it.

"Hey, I wasn't the only one pontificating on the
joys of this momentous occasion."

She couldn't argue that. Especially when her
throat was all but blocked and she felt ridiculously

224

close to tears. For ten nights she and this man had shared almost every intimacy the world had known, and many she'd had no idea were possible—much less that much fun. She'd happily attributed her lack of inhibitions to the presence of the disease. She'd assumed that no two people could fool around as long and often as the two of them had without being infected with *some* kind of aphrodisiacal agent coursing through their blood.

What did that say if this attraction hadn't been artificially induced? She didn't want to think about it.

"What do you think?" Ross asked. "So we weren't infected after all."

"Yes, we were," she said stubbornly. "We had to be."

"Are you saying the scientists at the CDC are lying?"

"Maybe. Or maybe they just haven't developed the proper test to determine infection for that particular virus."

He looked at her skeptically. "That's preferable for you to think than to force yourself to admit that we're just plain attracted to each other?"

"Yes."

He was silent for a long, contemplative moment. Paige almost began squirming. "Okay," he finally drawled. "We'll go right ahead and posit that theory. Taking it to its natural conclusion, then, I'm assuming that once we're out of each other's way, we'll forget all about what's happened here."

One could only hope. Except Paige had the feeling she'd need a full frontal lobotomy to forget Ross Bennett and what had taken place between them.

"It could be," he added with a shrug, "if we're still infected, that we'll start enjoying the company of whomever we're with."

She did *not* like the idea of him being *with* anyone else. Idiot that she was.

"Or it could be that the virus has run its course, and we'll enjoy our return to celibacy."

She pounced on that one. "Yes!" she said, pointing at his nose. "That's what's going to happen. Once we're out of here, life returns to normal." Which suddenly sounded pretty darn dreary.

He grasped her hand and pulled her pointing finger to his lips, sucking the tip and licking the pad. Paige almost groaned with unbearable pleasure.

"How about," he said, glancing up at her, but not releasing her hand, "we give it a few days to settle back into our old routines, catch up on work, then grab a bite together, just so we can laugh at all this in hindsight."

Because the suggestion sounded too tempting, she shook her head. "I don't think that would be a good idea. What if we have a relapse?"

"There's always that possibility."

As far as she was concerned, it was more a probability than a possibility. Face-to-face he was pure temptation. No, to purge him she had to avoid him in any kind of personal setting. "I don't think so."

"If you say so."

"I do." *Whether I agree with me, or not.*

When he finally dropped her hand, he smiled. A heartbreaking smile she'd never, ever forget. "I wish you sweet dreams, Paige Hart. Tonight and every night of your life."

"You look like hell," Paige's office manager, Betty Niles, stated bluntly, the moment Paige walked through the door to her suite the next morning.

"And it's a pleasure to see you, too, Betty."

Betty waved an unconcerned and bejeweled hand in the air. "I would think that two weeks of relaxation would have been good for you. But you don't look like you've slept a wink during your entire vacation."

Betty was *way* too perceptive. Although Paige might have been slightly sleep-deprived during her quarantine, she'd still felt utterly rejuvenated every single morning. No, the reason she looked like death warmed over was from *last night.*

Sweet dreams, my fanny. She hadn't been able to close her eyes, much less fall asleep. In fact, she'd been so restless, she hadn't even been able to lie down for any length of time. She'd paced her condo, she'd tried to catch up on mail, some of her workload, dusting, scrubbing, watching *The*

Three Stooges. Nothing had worked, not even the thousand-piece jigsaw puzzle of an Amish farm and wheat field.

At four this morning she'd had to sit herself down with a cup of chamomile and face some hard truths. Okay, so a few short nights in Ross's bed and she'd become somewhat addicted. Well, okay, very addicted. Not to him, of course, but to the intimacy.

She'd never known what it would be like to fall asleep in a man's arms. Her scumball professor had never let her stay all night, of course. He claimed it was because he snored, and didn't want to ruin her sleep. She'd learned, too late, it was more a function of him not wanting to ruin his wife's sleep by bringing in a third party.

But waking up with Ross's strong, warm arms wrapped tightly around her had felt so damn good. She could easily and happily get used to that.

And then there was another truth she had to confront. No matter how much Ross had seen to her pleasure—over and over and over—she'd still felt a certain emptiness whenever they'd fall into an exhausted sleep. She couldn't quite place the cause. All she could come up with was that it went against her nature to be so openly sexual with a man she didn't love.

"The spaceship has landed," she heard through the erotic heat beating through her head. And her entire body, for that matter.

"Huh?"

At some point Betty had stood and rounded her desk, tapping Paige's temple. "Time to visit planet Earth, boss."

Paige made a bumpy landing, but she touched down without crashing and burning. So far. Running a hand over her brow she said, "I'm back."

"Where were you?"

"Probably falling asleep on my feet," she prevaricated, figuring the qualifier in that sentence absolved her of lying.

"Why don't you take a day or two to recoup? Go home. Make yourself a nice big pitcher of mint juleps and order a whole new wardrobe from Saks. It always works for me."

The mint juleps part sounded promising. Only she'd leave out the mint and the juleps and replace them with vodka and vermouth. "How many appointments today?"

"None. Not being certain when you'd be released, I scheduled nothing for the next two days. But I'm betting your cousin Jasmine will be barging through that door..." Betty said, hiking a thumb over her shoulder, "...in three... two..."

The glass door flew open, and Jasmine came storming through in a cloud of Obsession. "Paiaige!"

Paige sighed. "Hi, cuz."

"We just absolutely *have* to talk, Paige."

Betty sniffed. "I'm sorry. I don't remember scheduling an appointment."

To anyone else, Jasmine might have retorted, but this was Betty Niles, a reigning matriarch in Atlanta's high society. Even Jasmine—who as Mrs. Carl Peyton had a certain cache herself—knew enough not to butt heads with Betty.

"Oh . . . yes, of course," Jasmine stammered, over the rustle of silk and the jangling of bracelets. Her auburn hair was held away from her face with barrettes that—if Paige wasn't mistaken—were encrusted with diamonds. "May I have the earliest appointment, please?"

Betty made a show of leafing through her appointment book. "Ah, yes. How about next Wednesday? Two o'clock?"

"Pai-aige!" Jasmine moaned.

Paige resisted the urge to grin at Betty. Her assistant, although initially taking the job as a lark, now viewed her duties quite seriously. And one of her primary duties, in Betty's esteemed opinion, was acting as a buffer between Paige and her demanding family. And she did an excellent job of it, too.

Paige checked her watch. "I think I can squeeze you in right now, Jasmine, if it won't take too long. I have a lot of work to catch up on."

"It'll be quick."

"Let me get some coffee. Do you want some?"

"Caffeine's bad for your skin, Paige," Jasmine opined.

"I'll use extra moisturizer. Go on in and have a seat."

Paige hiked the shoulder straps on her brief-case and laptop higher on her shoulder as Jasmine glided into Paige's office. Finally she allowed herself to smile at Betty. "Ah, yes, it's good to be back."

Ross wasn't a happy guy. Never in a million years would he be sorry he was no longer trapped in a hospital room. But right now—one day after his release—freedom held little appeal.

What was wrong with him? Well, that was probably a dumb question. He knew exactly what was wrong with him. The idea that he'd never see Paige again, save for in a professional capacity. He hadn't actually expected Paige to agree to see him once they were released from quarantine, so that hadn't come as much of a surprise. What *did* surprise him was the level of disappointment he'd felt. And in the last twenty or so hours since they'd left the hospital, the disappointment had grown by leaps and bounds.

Suddenly his king-size four poster didn't look or feel inviting. It felt large and cold. Empty. Sort of like the pit of his stomach. He hadn't fallen madly in love with Paige in those two weeks. He didn't think so, at any rate.

Oh, he'd enjoyed her, enjoyed sparring with her, and definitely making love to her. But love? No.

Ross sat up straight as a thought occurred to him. Technically, they'd never made love. They'd pleasured one another, certainly. But here, today, Ross was as clueless as he'd been two weeks ago about how it felt to be joined with her, inside her, filling her.

Maybe that was it. Maybe he felt like they had unfinished business or something. He'd always been a stickler for seeing a job through to its conclusion. It made sense that the dissatisfaction he was experiencing now would be due, in part, to the knowledge that he hadn't "concluded" with Paige, so to speak.

Of course, little chance of him finding closure with the woman now. He had a feeling that if he mentioned to her that he wouldn't be satisfied until they hit a home run, she'd pretty much laugh in his face. Or slap him.

Considering how enthusiastic and passionate she'd been in the hospital, he was at a loss as to why she wanted to make such a clean, quick break. Unless she was embarrassed, in hindsight, over what had happened between them. Which wasn't exactly good for his ego.

Ross tapped his pen on the desk and tried to come up with a plan of action. It really *was* in both of their best interests to complete the assignment. But much as he prided himself on his cleverness, no solutions were presenting themselves. Showing up at her door and saying, "Let's do it," would probably not work. Asking her out had already failed. Kidnapping was an option, except Paige was a lawyer, and a good one. She'd have his butt tossed in jail faster than he could say, "tort reform."

"Damn," he muttered aloud. He jumped to his feet and began pacing. If he just ignored the gnawing in his gut, would it eventually fade? Disappear completely? Should he begin an affair with another, more willing woman?

That was definitely an option, but not a real exciting one. *Paige* was the woman he had unfinished business with. It would only be right that she be the woman to help him finish it.

His intercom buzzed, and he felt some small relief at the distraction. He strode to his desk and depressed the button. "Yes, Mrs. Whipple?"

"Paige Hart is on line two for you."

A minor explosion blasted through his chest. Some distraction. "Thank you." He took a deep breath and punched line two, then picked up the receiver. "Why, Ms. Hart," he drawled, going for casual and cocky before he found himself pleading with her to get naked, "Miss me already?"

"In your dreams, Bennett."

That was the problem. He hadn't had any dreams, seeing as he'd gotten maybe ten minutes of sleep, tops. "What can I do for you?" *Besides what I'm dying to do for you.*

"Your client is at it again."

Seeing as he and Paige weren't adversaries in

any other divorce cases, he didn't have to ask who she meant. "What did he do now?"

"He put the Buckhead mansion up for sale."

"So? The mansion's his as part of the settlement. He's allowed to do anything he wants with it."

"He promised Jasmine six months."

"He promised she had six months to vacate. That doesn't mean he can't market it, as long as the home doesn't change hands until she's out."

"Do you know how inconvenient it is for realtors to be showing up at all times of the day and night?"

Ross sighed. He didn't pass judgment on too many people. Mostly parents who neglected their children, and cheating spouses. But Jasmine was stretching his limits of fair-mindedness. It wasn't like she didn't have the money to buy the mansion out from under her husband, if she wanted to. It wasn't like she'd be homeless. For the most part Ross had found Paige's family delightful, including Paige herself. In fact, he'd bet that if it were Paige in Jasmine's shoes, she wouldn't utter a peep of protest. Then again, Paige wasn't a self-centered, pampered brat.

"How about this?" he said. "How about if I get Carl to agree to make certain any realtors who want to show the house have to give Jasmine twenty-four-hour notice?"

There was silence on her end that almost screamed *stunned*. Why, Ross didn't have a clue.

It seemed a simple enough solution to him.

"May I put you on hold for a moment while I call Jasmine's cell phone and run that by her?"

There was nothing more irritating to Ross than being put on hold. "Sure. Go ahead."

While he waited for her to return, Ross made some notes about stuff he had to accomplish for some of Paige's other relatives. He was bound and determined to do the best by them that he could. Not that he didn't give his all for *every* client, but he sure as hell didn't want her believing if she'd done the work herself, her relatives would have been better off.

"Ross?"

Back to a first-name basis. That was good. "Yes?"

"It took a bit of persuasion, but Jasmine's agreed to that."

"Good. I'll get in touch with Carl. If he has any problems with it, I'll call you back."

"Okay," she said, and he could swear her voice had lowered half an octave, and had a smoky quality to it that conjured up so many images from the last couple of weeks, Ross immediately became rock hard. He glared down at his betraying body, trying to quell the erotic memories.

"Ross?"

He had to have the woman. Just once. Was that asking too much?

"Ross?"

He was almost certain that if they made love one time, they'd both be free to get on with their lives. Separately and happily. Closure. They needed closure.

"Ross?"

Oops. He had the feeling she'd said his name more than once. "I'm sorry, what?"

"We need to set up an appointment for Carl and Jasmine to meet, to turn over Doodle."

Meet. Okay, so it *would* be in a professional setting. But at least they'd be face-to-face, and Ross would get a better handle on Paige's state of mind. Her eyes and face were so expressive, she wasn't hard to read at all.

"All right," he said, much more calmly than he felt. He was in big trouble if he was so damn excited about an appointment that would probably prove more aggravating than anything else. "What days are good for you this week?"

"Actually, the sooner the better, since Betty has been keeping my calendar clear until she was certain I would be back to work."

Mrs. Whipple had done the same thing. "How's tomorrow for you?" he asked. "That'll give us a day to catch up." And give him a day to plan strategy.

"Tomorrow's good for me. And Jasmine's schedule is . . . flexible."

No doubt. "I'll call Carl and set it up."

"Good."

There was another long silence. Ross was loath to hang up the phone and lose the connection. Okay, that was pretty understandable. After all, they'd been cooped up together for fourteen days. It made sense that they'd come to depend on one another for companionship. In fact, after they got the making love part out of the way, maybe they'd end up being great friends. He'd like that. A lot.

Because he liked *her*. A lot. Nothing wrong with that. After all, she was a smart, funny, compassionate—not to mention passionate—woman. And definitely not hard on the eyes.

"Well," she said after a while, "guess I'll get back to it."

"Wait!"

"Yes?"

"Umm . . . how are you doing?"

"What do you mean?"

"Back out in the big, bad world."

She laughed. "Adjusting. Although all this fresh air is a little hard to take."

"Did you . . . sleep all right last night?"

There was a pause. "Sure."

"Oh."

"You?"

"Oh, yeah, sure. Like the dead."

"Oh."

Lying didn't sit well with him. "Actually, that's not exactly true."

"Oh?"

"The adjustment was a little tougher than I expected."

He heard her breath *whoosh* out of her. "Oh, I'm so glad it wasn't just me."

"Really? You had a rough night, too?"

"I finished a thousand-piece jigsaw puzzle."

"I read *Crime and Punishment*. Or tried to."

"Poor baby! As bad as all that?" She chuckled. "I watched *The Three Stooges*."

"Whoa!"

"Try and top that one."

"The Home Shopping Channel."

"Ouch!"

"I almost ordered a can opener."

"Good thing you rallied the strength to resist."

"Considering I already own two . . ."

She laughed again, and his pulse leapt at the sound. Twenty-four hours and he already missed her laughter. This situation might be more troublesome than he'd originally estimated.

"We'll settle back in," she said.

"Sure we will," he replied, with little conviction.

Another pause. "Well," she finally said. "Let me know what time tomorrow."

"Will do. And Paige?"

"Yes?"

"Sweet dreams."

"Right. You, too."

As he hung up, Ross calculated the odds of getting any sleep tonight. Then he reminded himself that he already owned two toasters, too.

Chapter Fourteen

"Where's Doodle?" Jasmine practically screeched, when Carl Peyton entered Paige's conference room the next morning—alone.

Ross resisted the urge to gulp down more aspirin, as her voice bounced painfully between his temples.

And that outfit. It was a bright purple filmy cocktail type dress that bared a whole bunch of cleavage. Appropriate for a hooker convention, maybe, but somewhat out of place in Paige's subdued office. Jasmine was a pretty woman, but she had lousy taste in clothes. And makeup. And hair styles. Dye one of Dolly Parton's wigs red, and you had Jasmine hair.

Carl, on the other hand, reminded Ross of a

younger, slimmer Colonel Sanders, in his white suit and string tie. The epitome of the Southern gentleman, and strangely enough, he carried the look well.

Paige jumped to her feet, probably to ward off a full frontal attack from her client to his. "It's all right, Jasmine. I told Carl to leave Doodle with Betty until the meeting's over." She glanced over at Carl. "You *did* bring him, right?"

"I did," Carl responded. "I, for one, keep my promises."

"What's *that* supposed to mean?" Jasmine snapped. "If you—"

"Hold on," Ross said, standing as well. He was so bone-tired, he was almost surprised that his legs cooperated and held him up. He moved around the large conference table and shook Carl's hand. "Good to see you again, Carl. Now how about the four of us have a seat and get this over quickly and civilly? We're almost there."

"Can I get you some coffee, Carl?" Paige asked.

"I'd love some, darlin'," he said, then grabbed her hand and pulled Paige close, kissing her cheek. "It's a pleasure to see you again. You're looking mighty fetching this morning."

Paige smiled, a genuine expression of affection crossing her features. So, she actually was fond of Ross's client. That hadn't stopped her from fighting tooth and nail for every little thing on her cousin's behalf, but she clearly held no personal animosity toward her cousin-in-law.

She moved to the sideboard and poured a cup of coffee, adding cream and a healthy dose of sugar without even asking. The woman even knew how Carl took his coffee.

While Ross watched the way she moved, admired her legs and body underneath a royal blue tailored suit, he couldn't help but undress her in his mind. He knew every inch of Paige Hart's body intimately. Well, almost every inch. And he appreciated every inch. Immensely.

And man, he loved the way she walked. She had the grace of a dancer and the body of a stripper. It was a painfully lethal combination. Especially when she was now off-limits.

Paige handed Carl his coffee, then returned to her seat at the head of the table. Carl and Jasmine sat across from one another, Jasmine studiously avoiding Carl's eyes, while Carl looked directly at his soon-to-be ex-wife, an "I know you better than you know yourself" smile on his face.

Paige nodded at Ross, then sipped her own coffee. He took a moment to note that she had dark smudges under her eyes, belying another sleepless night. Ross would take great satisfaction in that, if he wasn't slightly worried about her. The woman needed her sleep. Not her beauty sleep, for sure. Even appearing exhausted, Paige was gorgeous. Still, she needed her sleep or she was going to up and collapse one of these days.

That thought alarmed him. Too much.

He dragged his gaze from her and addressed

Carl. "Okay, now we know that Jasmine has been upset by the number of folks traipsing through the Buckhead place without warning. It's agreed that from now on all realtors are given the twenty-four-hour notice instruction, correct?"

"Already done," Carl said.

"I don't see why you're so eager to get rid of the place," Jasmine griped, but oddly enough there seemed to be a tinge of hurt in her brown eyes. "That was our home. Is it that distasteful to you now?"

"It's that painful, darlin'." He leaned forward. "And I don't see why you want to stay so all-fired badly. I'd think you'd hightail it out of there and get yourself a nice, cozy bachelorette pad."

"How can you say that? I *love* that house! We built it together." She waved. "Well, Nicky designed and built it, but you know what I mean."

"You sure didn't fight to keep it," Carl pointed out. "Everything else, yes. That house, no."

"I was trying to be fair."

Ross almost snorted out loud at that one. Paige's narrowed glance stopped him. "Okay," he chimed in, "so it's agreed about the realtors."

"Agreed," Carl said.

Jasmine huffed, so Paige jumped in with, "Agreed."

Ross nodded and pulled four copies of the one-page amendment to the separation agreement. "If you'll both sign these."

Jasmine, who'd been staring morosely at the

hands in her lap, looked up and finally met Carl's gaze. "How's Doodle been?" she asked softly.

"Finer than a sunflower on a clear blue day. But he misses you something awful."

She smiled slightly, but then squelched it. "You haven't been spoiling him, have you?"

"Rotten," he said, nodding. Then he winked.

Jasmine blushed. She actually blushed. "Oh, great. Now he's going to be impossible to deal with."

Ross glanced at Paige, whose eyebrows were raised quizzically as she watched the exchange. Then she met Ross's gaze, eyes wide in question.

Ross shrugged. He'd always known Carl was an easygoing man, a caring man, who wanted to make certain his ex-wife would be more than comfortable. Pretty darn noble, considering he'd been shocked and hurt by her sudden and surprising demand for a divorce. But after a few encounters with the woman, Ross had sort of felt the man was fortunate to be severing this tie.

"You know what he did the other day?" Carl asked, leaning forward toward Jasmine with a wicked grin on his face.

She smiled back at him, and also leaned forward. "What?"

"Well, you know how bad Mrs. Tuttle's eyesight's gettin'."

"Oh, yes."

"Well, when she was packing up for me, she must have mistaken one of your blue scarves for one of my hankies, so she packed that on up, too."

"The blue one with gold threads through it?" Jasmine asked.

"That's the one."

"I was wondering where that had gotten to! Why didn't you send it back?"

Carl flushed a little. This was getting more interesting—not to mention alarming—by the moment.

"Call me sentimental, darlin'. It still smelled like that wonderful perfume you're always wearin'. I thought it couldn't hurt to keep one little item."

Now Jasmine flushed, clear down to her cleavage. Ross noticed that both he and Paige were watching this exchange as if it were a volley in a tennis match.

"I guess it couldn't hurt," Jasmine conceded. "I have others."

Ross could imagine. She probably had an entire closet devoted to scarves.

Carl beamed. "Thank you, darlin'. Anyway, gettin' dressed one morning, I forgot to close the drawer."

"Oh, you!" Jasmine said. "You're always doing that."

"I know, it's a real fault of mine."

"I never minded, really."

"I know. You were real forgiving about that.

Anyway, Doodle got into that drawer, and what do you think he went straight for?"

"My scarf?" Jasmine asked, with all the hope of a personal injury lawyer, spotting a siren-screaming ambulance.

"That's right. He pilfered that scarf so fast, you'd think it was a steak bone. He dragged it to his bed, and he hasn't given it up, since. He sleeps with that thing."

"Really?"

"Swear to God. I'm thinking he misses you something fierce."

Jasmine's smile was so bright and joyous, you'd think a thousand lights just blazed on. Ross's jaw nearly dropped. He'd seen Jasmine spitting mad. He'd seen her sulky. He'd seen her snooty. Not once had he ever seen her happy.

"Oh, I've missed him too!" she said.

Paige and Ross again exchanged glances. This time they both shrugged. Paige leaned forward and pressed a button on the phone in front of her. "Betty? Why don't you bring in Doodle?"

A moment later the door opened, and Betty led in a white poodle wearing a rhinestone collar.

"Doodle! My baby!" Jasmine jumped up and lunged for the dog, who began squirming and yipping, obviously happy to see the woman.

Ross revised his estimate of Jasmine yet again. She really *did* love this animal, and possibly wasn't fighting over him just out of spite.

Carl sported an ear-splitting grin as he rose and

moved around the table. Together he and Jasmine petted and cooed and generally lavished the dog with love. Their hands met on the animal's back, and both went still, slowly raising their eyes to one another. Then both straightened, Doodle momentarily forgotten.

"Darlin'," Carl said, his voice now husky, "would you do me the honor of taking lunch with me this afternoon?"

Jasmine's eyelashes batted frantically for a moment. "Well, I . . . I suppose that would be okay."

Carl turned back to Ross. "I'll be in touch." He turned and nodded at Paige. "Thank you for everything, sweetheart."

"Wait," Ross said. "You haven't signed the papers."

Carl waved. "We'll take care of that some other time." And with that, Carl, Jasmine, Doodle and Betty departed, leaving the two of them to stare at each other in astonishment.

"What just happened here?" Paige finally asked.

Ross was more than a little afraid he knew exactly what had happened. It was far-fetched. Seemingly impossible. But not completely out of the realm, considering the day he'd had so far.

"Have dinner with me tonight, Paige."

"I don't think—"

"It's important. I've got a theory, and I think we need to discuss it." He held up a supplicating hand. "Strictly business, I swear."

She stared at him a moment, then said, "Okay. Where and when?"

"Strictly business, and you bring me to Antonio's?" Paige asked dryly, as soon as the maitre d' departed.

Ross shrugged. "It's the best food in Atlanta, and besides, I wanted as much privacy as possible."

Paige stared at him, hoping she didn't look pathetically happy to be here with him. Even if it was strictly for business. Honesty had her admitting that she'd missed him like crazy the past couple of days. Not one-tenth as much as she'd missed him at night, however.

She just hoped that the gnawing emptiness would fade, eventually. Because it was beginning to drive her loony.

Ross still wore the slate gray suit and maroon and gray tie from earlier that day. Having gotten so used to seeing him walking around in shorts and T-shirts, she'd completely forgotten how luscious the man looked in business attire. When he'd walked into her office this morning, she'd nearly spit out the coffee she'd been sipping. He'd appeared so suave and successful, and she knew what he looked like sans cuff links. Sans everything, for that matter.

"What are you staring at?" he asked.

"Nothing," she replied quickly. She snapped open the leatherbound menu and pretended to peruse it, although the only thing behind her eyeballs was Ross's smile, Ross's eyes, Ross's dimples. "What are you having?"

"Caesar salad and the salmon," he said, without opening his menu. Instead, he reached for the wine list, also bound in leather.

Paige eeny-meany-miny-mo'd and came up with langostino alfredo.

Their waiter arrived, and Ross ordered a bottle of wine. At least she thought so. She was so lost in her fantasies, her brain was in deep-freeze. Well, no, not freeze. Maybe it was on fire.

Ross seemed content with the silence as they waited for their wine to be poured, then ordered their meals. Once the waiter retreated again, he lifted his glass in a toast. "To Carl and Jasmine's reconciliation."

Paige's goblet stilled midway to his. "You actually think they'll get back together?"

"I'd place a big chunk of my savings on it." He touched her glass, then sipped his wine.

Which brought Paige's attention right to his lips. She glugged down a healthy amount of wine, not tasting a molecule of it. Her eyes watered, and she blinked.

"Easy there, honey," Ross said, his dimples making an adorable appearance. "You keep that up and I'll be carrying you out of here. Not that I'd object."

Neither would she. She took another sip, only

daintier this time. "So what makes you say that about Carl and Jasmine?"

"Because I think we're starting an epidemic."

Paige choked. "A . . . what?"

"I know this is going to sound like something out of a *Twilight Zone* episode, but for some reason, I think the CDC missed something. I think we're infected, and I think we're infecting others."

"Oh. My. God. You can't be serious."

Setting down his goblet, he held up his hands and began ticking. "I had an eight o'clock this morning with Mr. and soon-to-be-former Mrs. Loughlin. Of all the couples I'm handling together, these two were the closest to being destined to murder one another. One hour later they left my office, not at all sure they really wanted that divorce after all."

"Coincidence."

"Ditto Mr. and Mrs. Smythe."

"An unusual day," Paige retorted, waving a dismissive hand.

"Then Carl and Jasmine. You were there. You saw it. Hostility hung in the air at the beginning of that meeting. Slowly but surely it evaporated, and by the time they hauled off for lunch, there were so many lustful vibes swirling around, I wouldn't be surprised if they were naked in the back of the limo before they reached the end of the block."

Paige held out her hand for a refill. Ross

obliged. She swallowed a good third before patting her lips and returning her cloth napkin to her lap. "It can't be. Can it?"

"Two more clients put their divorce actions on hold this afternoon. By the time the Wembleys showed up, I took them in my office, put their hands together and said, 'Now are you sure you want to continue with this divorce?' At first they were adamant. So I said okay and we got on with the negotiating process. By the time they were done, they were practically begging each other to take all their worldly possessions. My guess is they'll be calling tomorrow to have me rip up the papers."

She stared at him. "I . . . I can't believe it. How . . . how would we be infecting them?"

"We touch them."

"Excuse me?"

"Don't tell me you didn't give Jasmine a hug."

"Of course. She's my cousin."

"And I shook Carl's hand."

She polished off her wine. "This is preposterous."

"Seems that way, doesn't it? But I think we definitely have to consider the possibility."

"But . . . just touching them? Even the doctor told us in the hospital that it takes time for the virus to take hold."

"How soon after you woke up in the hospital did you start . . . feeling a little hot under the collar for me?"

Paige would have liked to burst his little egotistical bubble, but that would have entailed telling a big fat lie. She rolled her eyes anyway, just for good measure, but then admitted, "Almost right away. But you have to remember you look pretty hot in a hospital gown."

He dimpled at her again, the slug. "Right back atcha, sweetheart." Then his smile faded. "Now think about this. Not one of my clients I spoke with on the phone miraculously reconciled. Only those who came to my office."

Paige thought back on the day, but her only client appointment was with Carl and Jasmine, so she had no frame of reference . . . except—"Oh, my God."

"What?"

"Betty."

"What about Betty?"

"The UPS man."

"Huh? Paige, honey, I think you better slow down on that wine."

"No. I'm not tipsy! But before you showed up this morning, Betty was in my office and we were coordinating schedules. Since no one was out at the front desk, the UPS man came in with a delivery. He handed it across the desk, and Betty and I reached for it at the same time. All three of our hands collided."

"And?" Ross said, leaning forward, his eyes narrowed intently.

"Betty followed him out the door. I got busy, so

I didn't think twice about it. But then I wanted more coffee, and when I walked out of my office, the UPS guy was still there, and Betty was all flushed.

"Betty and he have been clashing for years, trading insults. So I just figured that they were sparring again. But then when he saw me he turned to leave. The last thing he said to Betty was, 'Eight o'clock?' "

"Oh, boy."

Their salads arrived, but neither touched them. They just stared at each other for long, stunned moments.

From over Ross's shoulder, Paige heard an unfamiliar woman's voice raised in anger. "This is just so typical of you!"

"Keep your voice down," a man answered her gruffly.

"Why should I? The world should know what a rat you are!"

"Trouble in paradise?" Ross asked, cocking his head toward the feuding couple without turning around.

"Sounds like it," Paige answered, then sipped more wine, trying not to eavesdrop. Which was a little hard, considering the woman was on a tear. If Paige understood her ranting correctly, the man with her was responsible for all the ills besetting the Earth, including famine, pestilence and the cost of gasoline.

"Want to experiment?" Ross asked.

"Excuse me?"

"Just watch," he said, then tossed his napkin on the table and stood. "I need to run to the men's room, love. I'll be right back." Then he leaned over the table and gave her a quick kiss, nothing more than a peck, but it instantly set her lips to tingling. In case she looked as dazed as she felt, she brought the wine glass to her mouth and took a slug.

Ross turned and began walking toward the front of the restaurant. When he got to the booth of the quarreling couple, he nodded, then did something of a double take and stopped short.

"Wow, that's a beautiful bracelet," he said to the woman.

Paige couldn't watch the lady's reaction, seeing as Ross blocked her view, but she heard the woman titter, then say, "Why, thank you. Yes, I love it, too."

Ross leaned over slightly. "May I ask where you got it?" He hiked a thumb over his shoulder in Paige's direction and spoke in a whisper that could be heard in Savannah. "Our anniversary's coming up and I've been racking my brain trying to decide what to give her."

Paige was pretty sure she should be outraged at the bold lie, but she couldn't come up with a reason why. Not to mention, it was a rather nice fantasy. What would it be like to share anniversaries and birthdays and holidays with a man like him?

Would he really be thoughtful in the gifts he'd choose for her?

She snorted into her goblet. Obviously, the wine was going to her head.

Ross introduced himself to the woman and her companion, made more appropriate noises, then bid them a wonderful meal and ambled on his way.

Paige gave him points for not pulling out a business card and offering his services, should the feuding couple need them.

She tried to eavesdrop on the couple's bickering some more, but they'd lowered their voices and she couldn't make out the words.

Ross returned a few minutes later, smiling at the couple as he passed. Paige made a valiant effort to keep her pulse from kicking up at the mere sight of him, but realized she'd lost the battle. So instead she just surreptitiously enjoyed the swagger in his step that was sexy as sin. Hot, lust-inducing sin.

Ross winked at her, then slipped gracefully into his seat.

"What's the verdict?" Paige asked.

"Well, they're no longer yelling at each other."

"That's not proof."

"Nope, you're right."

She sipped more wine, wondering whether Ross had lost his mind. Or if they both had. So deep in thought, she didn't see the two strangers approach until they were standing beside the table.

"We just wanted to thank you," the woman gushed, touching the sleeve of Ross's suit.

"Okay," Ross said. "For what?"

The woman held up her wrist, revealing one of the gaudiest, ugliest pieces of jewelry Paige had ever seen. Ross was thinking of buying her something like *that?* But then she shook her head when she remembered Ross wouldn't be buying her anything because they didn't even have an anniversary pending. Unless they began counting the days since they were forced into quarantine together.

The woman dropped her hand. "You reminded us how and when George bought this for me. It was the most romantic vacation of our lives."

"I'm glad," Ross said, and seemed to genuinely mean it. Which was unusual for an attorney whose livelihood depended on fast trains to Splitsville.

"Thanks again," the woman's husband said, then led his wife away, a protective arm around her ample waist.

Alone again, Paige said, "We're starting an epidemic."

"I'm afraid, as ridiculous as that sounds, it might be true."

"What are we going to do?" Paige grabbed the wine and refilled both of their glasses, draining the bottle.

Ross took it from her and held it up for the waiter, signaling their need for another one. "First of all, let's not panic."

"Not panic?" she squeaked. "We're wreaking havoc on Atlanta!"

"Well, it's not like we're passing on a flesh-eating disease. There are worse things than being infected with TCV."

"Think of the implications!"

"Business is going to come to a screeching halt," Ross mused with a small smile, "as couples all over the city will be running home to make love."

"They might not even bother to run home," Paige mused, thinking the nearly floor-length tablecloths Antonio used would hide a wealth of wicked activities.

Ross shrugged. "Atlanta will be the happiest city in the world. Paris will have nothing on us."

Paige's head was growing just a little fuzzy. She giggled. "And you'll be out of business."

Ross's grin vanished. "True."

Paige patted his hand. "There, there. I'm sure there's something else you could do. Personally, I think you'd make a great sports announcer."

His smile reappeared. "Yeah?"

"Definitely," she said, nodding adamantly. "Did you know that we never played polo?"

"That's true. You just say the word and I'll be happy to show you my mallet."

"Now that's just plain crude," she said, ignoring the acceleration of her heartbeat. She was having a harder and harder time remembering why they couldn't get involved again.

"Sorry," he said, but his grin wasn't all that apologetic. "Actually, the smart thing to do might be to start up a dating service."

She giggled again. "Now there's the entrepreneurial spirit."

"I could call it, the Home Run Dating Service. The slogan could be, 'We cover all the bases.'"

"Now, now, truth in advertising," she said, then almost bit off her tongue. Did she really need to remind him that *they* hadn't covered all the bases?

"Don't remind me," he said, wincing dramatically.

Good idea. She searched for a way to steer them off that train of thought. Offering him a bright smile, she said, "You could even have incentives."

"Yeah? Like what?"

"Oh, I don't know. Something like half-price for writing up the prenups?"

He laughed at that, a rich, deep laugh that vibrated throughout her insides. "Great idea. At least I know I have something to fall back on."

Their waiter arrived carrying a large tray. He served their entrees, then opened the second bottle of wine. "Can I get you anything else?"

"No, thank you," Ross responded. "This looks wonderful."

Paige squinted at her plate to see if she could say the same. "It smells wonderful," she commented instead.

"Can I get you anything else?"

"No, thank you," Ross said.

"Enjoy your meal."

Paige wasn't sure how enjoyable the meal would be when she was rapidly forgetting how to hold a fork. But she gamely gave it a shot.

Just as she was about to pop a bite into her mouth, she glanced up and saw through the window that someone who looked remarkably like her brother was approaching the entrance, hand in hand with a woman Paige couldn't identify, since she was walking on the other side.

She set down her fork and waved down their waiter. "Do you know Nick Hart?"

"Yes ma'am. Great tipper."

"Could you go check to see if that's him about to enter, and if so, tell him I'm here?"

"Umm, yes ma'am," the waiter said, but looked a little panicked at the thought. Why, Paige couldn't begin to imagine.

Ross chimed in. "She's his sister."

The waiter nearly collapsed with relief. "Oh, yes, then of course."

Paige frowned at Ross. "What was his problem?"

"He was probably worried you were a girlfriend or something, and that a scene was about to ensue."

"Ohhhhh . . . yes, with Nick that's a definite threat."

Their cozy booth could only fit two, so they couldn't offer for him and his date to join them. Which was just as well, seeing as they were discussing the destruction of the world as they knew it.

"Eat up, sweetheart," Ross said, picking up her fork and placing it in her hand. "You need some food in your belly to soak up some of that wine."

Paige dug into her langostino and pasta. It was scrumptious. Was that a word? Scrumptious? If not, it should be. It was a good word. A little hard to pronounce out loud at the moment, but still a marvelous word.

She wiped her mouth then glanced up. And nearly fell out of her chair when she saw her brother approaching their table, his hand tightly intertwined with . . . their doctor? The one who despised him for whatever he'd done to her years ago?

"You're not going to believe this," she stage-whispered to Ross.

"What?"

She nodded. "Incoming."

Ross twisted around, did a double take, then turned back to her. "Oh, Lord. Is that who I think it is?"

"The very same."

"They're looking rather . . . cozy, don't you think?"

"Yes. Oh, boy, what have we done?"

Nick and Dr. Turner arrived, both looking blissfully happy. "Hey, sis. Bennett. Fancy meeting you two here."

Ross stood and shook Nick's hand but was looking at Nick's date like she'd grown horns. "Doc. How are you?"

She smiled. "Fine. And it's just Rachel now, okay?"

"We touched you," Paige said.

"Excuse me?" Rachel said.

Ross shot Paige a look, but she couldn't quite interpret its meaning. "In the hospital that last day. We touched you."

Nick peered at her closely. "You're snockered!"

"Not yet, but it's the current plan."

Glaring at Ross, Nick growled, "What are you doing to my sister?"

"Nothing!" Paige said, trying to ward off trouble. The two men were fairly evenly matched, height-wise, so if they came to blows they'd probably beat each other to a pulp. "He didn't do anything, Nick." She sighed. "It's what we did to you."

"What did you do to us?" her brother asked, his eyes puzzled.

"Paige, I don't think—" Ross began.

"We infected you."

"Let me get this straight," Nick said, two hours later, sitting down beside Rachel on Paige's living room couch. "You think that you gave us that virus you were exposed to."

"I'm almost positive," Paige said, downing some aspirin and following it up with coffee. She wasn't tipsy any longer, but she figured the aspirin was good preventive medicine.

Rachel sat forward. "Paige, that's just impossible. The tests showed the two of you weren't even infected, much less capable of passing the virus on."

"We think maybe the tests were wrong," Ross said. "Or defective or something. Because weird things are definitely happening."

"Such as?"

"Well, take you two for example," Paige said. "I could swear you despised my brother. And now, here you two are looking happy as clams. And all of this right after you were exposed to us."

Rachel blushed and opened her mouth, but not a word came out. Nick came riding to the rescue. "First of all, sis, Rachel never despised me. She was just a little angry because of my stupid behavior back in college. But we straightened that out."

"Second of all," Rachel piped in, "we straightened out all the misunderstandings before you touched us without the protective equipment."

"Well, I mean I'm sure you talked it out, but . . ." Paige waved vaguely at Nick's hand, possessively tracing circles on Rachel's bare shoulder. The doctor looked stunning in a midnight blue sheath with spaghetti straps. The dress did remarkably more for the woman than hospital scrubs, although she'd look pretty in a burlap sack, Paige suspected.

"Not that it's any of your business, little sister,

but we straightened *that* part out before your release, too."

"Oh." She looked to Ross. He didn't appear convinced.

"What other weird things are happening?" Rachel asked, the shrewd light in her eyes was the clinical doctor type.

They listed off all the sudden reunions between couples who seemed to make up upon physical contact with one or both of them. Paige told them about Betty, and then about Carl and Jasmine.

"Really?" Nick said. "They're getting back together?"

"At least temporarily," Ross said. "I don't know what will happen when the virus runs its course." He glanced at Rachel. "About how long is that supposed to be, Doc?"

"Actually, from the onset of symptoms, only a couple of days. It's a very short term disease."

"Impossible," Ross scoffed. "I think your scientists at the CDC missed the boat on this one."

"Why do you say that?"

"Well, it's been sixteen days here," he said, wagging a finger back and forth between Paige and himself. "It's not going away."

"It's not?" Rachel asked, but the clinical expression was gone, and Paige could swear the woman's lips twitched.

"It's not," Ross said, all indignant. "In fact, it's getting worse."

Paige perked right up at that.

"How is that?" Rachel asked, and Paige could have kissed the woman for posing the question. She was going to make a fine sister-in-law.

Ross started pacing, agitation written in every taut line of his body. He'd taken off his suit jacket, so she got a fine and mouth-watering view of his butt every time he swiveled and marched in the other direction. Finally he stopped and pointed at Paige's nose. "I can't get her out of my mind."

"Your mind is not the part the virus is supposed to affect," Rachel pointed out.

Ross loosened his tie. "Well, you know what I mean."

Nick rose to his feet slowly, his ears practically smoking. "*I* know what you mean, and let me tell you, you sonofa—"

"Nicky, stop it!" Paige said, hopping to her feet as well. "I'm not a little kid any longer."

"You're still my little sister, and this guy's talking about you like—"

"Like he's attracted to her?" Rachel intervened sweetly, standing and using the guise of a loving touch to hang onto Nick's arm for dear life. Paige was really beginning to love this woman.

"I'm *addicted* to her," Ross complained. "Not attracted. *Addicted.* And I want an antidote."

Paige couldn't decide whether to be elated or insulted.

She didn't have time to think about it, though, because Rachel addressed her next. "Are you experiencing the same symptoms?"

Trish Jensen

"Worse. I'm addicted *and* attracted."

"Really?" Ross asked, suddenly not so sour-faced.

"I'm not pleased about it," she retorted, not wanting him to get a big head or anything. "You're not my type, so it's obvious this is some kind of awful illness."

"I don't like this at all," Nick said.

"You have to go to the bathroom," Rachel told Nick, shoving him toward the powder room.

"No, I don't."

"Yes, you do. Either to the bathroom now, or I might have to ask you to run to the store to pick me up some tampons or something."

Nick's tan disappeared faster than an ice cube on an Atlanta sidewalk, which was a pretty amazing sight to behold. "Bathroom, right."

As soon as Nick disappeared behind the bathroom door, Rachel plunked her hands on her hips and faced the two of them. "Okay, this is Dr. Turner talking now, all right?"

That tone brooked no argument, and Ross and Paige nodded rapidly.

She nodded back at them. "My initial opinion stands. You two aren't physically infected. But from all you've told me tonight, I'm going to have to believe that what you're saying is medically possible, and I'm going to report these findings first thing tomorrow to my contacts at the CDC, and we'll begin working on it."

"It's about time," Ross muttered, running a

264

hand through his scrumptious hair. Having sobered some, Paige had decided "scrumptious" was definitely a word, and it managed to convey just the right descriptive lusciousness concerning many things about the man.

"So what do we do until we get an answer?" Paige asked.

"Have sex."

"I'm sorry?" Ross said.

"This is not a professional opinion, mind you," Rachel said. "The medical hat is off. It's more common sense. You're two perfectly healthy adults, obviously with a bug to do just that. What are you waiting for?"

"It won't intensify the virus, will it?" Paige asked.

"No."

"Because that would be unacceptable. I'm not falling in love with a snake."

"Hey!"

"Who said anything about love? This is all about appeasing lust, right?"

"Are you sure you're a doctor?" Ross said.

Rachel shrugged. "Just a second opinion."

Paige was having a really hard time not jumping on Rachel's advice. After all, she was the medical professional in this crowd, right? "We never got a first opinion."

"Yes, you did. Your two opinions. Which were rather unanimous."

"Let me just see if I have this right," Ross said. "You're advising us to go for it."

"Right."

"For the sake of our physical well-being?"

"Isn't it what you both stated you wanted?"

"It's what the virus wants."

Paige gaped at Ross, wondering if he'd lost his mind, or if he'd sipped more wine than she'd noticed.

"Then give the virus what it wants," Rachel replied. "Why fight it?"

"Because the cure might be worse than the disease?" Paige opined.

Rachel practically growled her impatience. "Look, you two do what you want. But you've both admitted it's driving you nuts. You can either continue to grit it out, or you can try to appease it. Your choice. But personally I think you're fools for letting this virus get the best of you. Beat it back, so to speak. Don't let it eat at you."

"What did you say to them?" Nick asked, after Rachel hustled him out of Paige's condo.

"I just gave them some medical advice." *Sort of.*

"Will they follow it?"

"If they're smart."

"Do you think she knows what she's talking about?" Ross asked.

"Well, she's a medical professional. But she was talking off the record."

"We're both lawyers. Do you think she'd risk giving *us* bad advice?"

"True." Paige looked away and fidgeted with her coffee cup. "So what do you think she meant?"

He chuckled softly. "She meant what she said. Go for it."

"Go for what?"

"The home run, darlin'. The home run."

Chapter Fifteen

"I just don't know if the Babe Ruth routine is a good idea, Ross. No matter what Rachel says."

"Why not?"

Paige sighed. "I'm just afraid we'd be doing it for all the wrong reasons."

"What wrong reasons would those be?"

Getting up from the couch, she hugged herself, avoiding his gaze. "Well, first, it would be out of pure lust."

"And that's a bad thing?"

"I was *not* brought up to fall into bed with any sexy man who comes along."

He stepped in front of her and lifted her chin. His smile was sexy all right. And his touch was electrifying. Just a finger under her chin and she felt like bolts of lightning were striking randomly and rampantly throughout her body.

"I'm not just any man, you know. Although I like that sexy part."

"Don't let it go to your head."

"Nope, that's not where it's going at all."

Paige stifled a smile, but she couldn't help glancing southward. Yes, indeed, it wasn't going to his head.

Knowing she could affect him that way made her almost giddy. It was a powerful thing, unleashing a man's desire. Realizing that he was here, with her, and it was Paige he wanted. But would that happen to him with any woman? Was she just convenient at the moment?

"Have you . . . been on any dates since you've been home?"

He shot her a startled look, then burst out laughing. "Paige, honey, we've been home two days. Believe it or not, I don't have a little black book, I don't have a stable of females just waiting to get at my bod. No, I haven't been on a date— unless you count tonight with you. Furthermore, I have no desire to *go* on a date with anyone *but* you at the moment. These raging hots are for you, and you alone."

He kissed her lightly, almost impersonally, and yet Paige's knees almost buckled on her. Her head started swimming, and not from the residual affects of alcohol. She tried to hold on to her thoughts, tried to remember she had several good arguments against taking this next and final step, but her gray matter wasn't cooperating.

"May I ask you something?" Ross whispered right above her lips.

"Yes."

"The last few days, have you felt kind of empty," he placed his hand over her lower belly, "right about here?"

That shook her out of her Ross-induced lethargy. She pulled back. "Yes! How did you know that?"

"I've been feeling it, too."

"What is it, do you know?"

"It's unfulfillment."

"What?"

"It comes from not having made love."

"But . . . we did. Didn't we?"

"No. We pleasured each other, but we didn't make love."

"Are you saying . . ." she laid her hand over his on her belly, ". . . this isn't going away until we do?"

"Well, I don't proclaim to be an expert, but I suspect that's what we're facing here."

Although his hand on her tummy was thrilling, as was her hand laid over his, Paige wasn't so far gone not to be at least a little suspicious. "Are you sure this isn't a ploy just to get me in the sack?"

Ross winced. "I've always hated that expression. It's so impersonal."

If he was faking sensitivity, he was doing a darn fine job of it. "Well?"

His hand whispered up and down her belly, and with each stroke she could almost feel him stroking inside of her. Small fires began erupting in just about every erogenous zone she possessed. She had to stifle a moan.

"I didn't make you feel this emptiness, Paige."

"I thought maybe it was because I was feeling bad about being so intimate with an almost total stranger."

Ross shook his head slowly. "If that were the case, the emptiness would be here," he said, tapping her chest, right above her left breast. "And here," he added, tapping her temple. "Here," he said, back at her tummy, "is unfulfilled desire."

It made sense. But did that mean it was sensible?

"Will just once do it?" she asked him.

"Get rid of the ache?"

"Yes."

"Only one way to find out."

"What if it's a big mistake?"

Ross forked fingers through his hair. "The only big mistake I see here is living my life never knowing what it's like to be inside you."

That inside part of her quivered at the thought. "Oh, Ross," she whispered.

"Do you want that, too?"

"God help me, yes. But we don't love each other."

She thought she detected an instant stab of hurt in his eyes, but it disappeared too fast to take any stock in it.

"We like each other. At least, I like you."

"You do?"

"A lot. Not only that, I respect you."

"You do?"

"A lot. This isn't a one-night stand, Paige. This is the culmination of many nights together. And though I know that your past experience has left you a little wary, just know this: I'd never make love to a woman I didn't respect, just for the sake of . . . hopping into the sack."

She believed him. She didn't know why. He was a shyster lawyer . . . well, not a shyster, but still. He was a man. Weren't they incapable of sincerity? And no matter what Rachel said, he was infected with a virus that made him need sex.

Then again, so was she. And as he'd admitted openly earlier, she seemed to only need it with him.

"What are you thinking, Paige?"

She swallowed. "If this is going to be a big mistake, make it the best one of my life, okay?"

He grinned, grabbed her face and kissed her. Lifting his head he said, "I'll give it the old college try."

Now that she'd committed to it, her hormones started humming at an alarming rate. She was about to make love to the most handsome man she'd ever met in her life. And he wanted her.

Her. And no one else. Somehow she believed that, too.

She wondered where he'd take her. Right here? In the bedroom? On the dining room table? Wherever he decided was just fine by her. She only hoped he wouldn't torture her too much, but get right to the good stuff.

But then a horrid thought occurred to her. "Oh, my God! I *still* don't have any birth control!"

"You don't keep any around?" he asked, frowning.

"Why would I? I've been celibate since I was in college." She flushed. "Well, almost celibate."

He kissed her cheek, inhaling deeply against her skin. "God, you smell good." Then he brushed his thumb along her jaw. "Now don't get mad, okay?"

"Mad about what?"

"I brought some with me."

"Some what?"

"Birth control."

"Oh, my God! You were so sure, you came prepared?"

"I was so hopeful, I came prepared. I never *expected* a thing. But if we got this far, I sure as hell didn't want to have to waste time running to the store."

Paige wanted to be angry at his presumptuousness. She really did. She even worked on drumming it up. Not a chance. Not when he was looking at her with a truly worried frown. She grabbed his tie and pulled him close. "Good call, counselor. I bet you were a Boy Scout, weren't you?"

The frown disappeared, and a smile that could jump-start dead batteries bloomed. "I'd like to earn a badge making you beg for S'Mor."

Paige chuckled. "Earn it, *darlin'*."

He chose the living room. At least, he began undressing her right there and then. He took his good old time about it, too. In the most delicious, torturous way.

He started with her pumps. Placing her hands on his shoulders, he lifted first one leg, then the other; hooking a hand under one knee, and removing the shoe. Before dropping each leg he ran fingers up and down her calves, then higher, up her thigh. The feel of his fingers whispering up her stockings made her shiver and quiver.

"Ross?"

"Mm-hmm?"

"This isn't . . . this isn't a home run."

"Oh, darlin', haven't I taught you anything about baseball? Even when you hit a home run, you still have to run all the bases."

"You do?" she breathed, as he slipped her suit jacket off her shoulders and let it drop to the floor.

"Most definitely."

"Then I think you need to proceed to first base."

"Oh, but this is naked baseball."

"It is?"

He began unbuttoning her blouse, one agonizing step at a time. Agonizing, because he occasionally brushed his knuckles over exposed skin, but seemingly in an innocent fashion, although the sensations he evoked felt anything but harmless. "It is. I don't hit the ball until you're completely naked."

"Oh, no, you don't, counselor," she said, around a gasp, as his hand grazed her ribs. "You need to bone up on the law, so to speak. There *is* such a thing as mutual discovery." She began attacking his tie.

"But it's my turn at bat," he retorted, trying to stop her groping hands.

"This is naked, all-bets-are-off baseball."

He sighed dramatically, rolling his eyes. "I'd expect you to fight me all the way on this."

Then he unbuttoned the cuffs of her shirtsleeves, and before she could cry, "Beyond the scope of interrogation, Your Honor!" he pushed her arms behind her back, and somehow locked the sleeve cuffs together, effectively rendering her hands useless and trapped.

He smiled at her as she sputtered her indignation, then flicked open her front-clasping bra without even looking down. Brushing the cups of the bra from over her breasts, he bent and began suckling her.

"Ross," she gasped. "This is . . . you missed . . . Oh, God . . . first base."

"Stop squirming, baby. If this is all-bets-are-off baseball, I get to run the bases in any order I want."

Her attempts to unbutton the two cuffs from one another were half-hearted at best. Sex maniac that she was quickly becoming, she loved being helpless under his sensual assault.

Somehow he managed to drop her skirt before she even realized he'd found the zipper. "Oh, God," he whispered, looking down.

"What?"

"A garter belt?"

She looked down, too. "Something . . . wrong with that?" she managed to choke out.

"No, oh, no. Damn, woman, you are *so* sexy." His fingertips strayed down her belly, then traced the lacy edges of her garter at her hip. "This is the best damn baseball uniform I've ever seen."

His finger slid across her panty line to below her belly button, then slipped under the panties.

"Oh! I . . . can't keep standing," she croaked, as her knees began buckling on her.

"No problem, baby." He unbuttoned her shirt cuffs, freeing her hands, then bent slightly, and before she knew it, she was cradled in his arms. "Where's your bedroom?"

She waved vaguely down the hall. "Last door on . . . the right or left."

"You're not sure which one?"

"At the moment, no. At the moment, I'm not sure where I am."

"You're with me, baby. Exactly where you should be."

Paige laid her head on his shoulder, inhaling the faint remnants of aftershave, mingled with his unique and heady scent. Two days away, and she'd missed his smell, his touch.

She had a sinking feeling that taking this step would no more vanquish this aching need than a single aspirin would cure a migraine. But she couldn't deny she needed this, needed him, in the most elemental way.

"Paige?"

"Hmm?"

"Could you maybe just point me in the right direction?"

Without lifting her head, she pointed. Through a fog she heard him kick open the door. "Did I get it right?" she asked.

"Oh, yeah, babe. This room is definitely you. It even smells like you."

"Is that a good or bad thing?"

"Good. Very, very good."

He laid her down on the bed, then quickly followed, covering her body with his. "I've been waiting for this all my life."

Paige wanted to ask what he meant by that, considering Ross wasn't born two weeks ago, but all thought flew away when he pushed aside her shirt and settled his mouth over her breast. "Ohhhhhhh . . ."

Needing skin on skin, Paige began feverishly unbuttoning Ross's shirt. He lifted his head and smiled. "Patience, love."

"Not a chance. I want you naked."

He chuckled, gave her a quick, hard kiss, then rolled off her and stood. Shrugging out of his shirt, he asked, "Feel like a game? Bowling, maybe?"

"No games," she breathed, admiring his smooth, tanned chest and hard, rigid abdomen. The guy could model for romance novels.

She sat up and removed her blouse and bra, then went for her garter.

"No!" Ross said, as he pulled several condom packages from his pants pocket. "Please, leave them on."

She stopped, staring at the pile of prophylactics. "Are you serious?"

"Oh, absolutely. They're sexy as hell, babe."

"No." She pointed at the mound of foil packages. "About all those?"

"Former Boy Scout, remember?"

"I thought . . . once."

"One night, right."

"You're changing the rules on me."

"Nope," he said, kicking off his shoes, and tearing off his socks. "If once is enough for you, we stop at once." He dropped his slacks.

Paige drank in the sight of him in his Calvins.

The man was already aroused. As much as she'd explored his body, she hadn't, until this moment, considered the logistics. She sure hoped she could accommodate him.

Without removing his briefs, he climbed back on the bed beside her. Touching her face gently, he smiled. "You're calling the shots, pretty lady."

Oh, the power. Now if she just knew what to do with it. She laid back on the pillow. "Kiss me."

"Where?"

"All over."

And he did, starting with her mouth.

Paige let sensation take over. Wrapping her arms around his neck, she plunged fingers into his hair, holding him to her, demanding, wanting. Simply kissing a man had never felt like this before. Nerves all over her came to life, crying out for his touch, his invasion.

He lifted his head, smiled again, then kissed his way down her throat to her collarbone. She gasped at the erotic response such an innocent gesture could evoke in her. Grabbing his hand, she placed it over her breast. "Here. Kiss me here."

His mouth glided down her chest, and she cried out as he took her breast, his tongue flickering over her nipple in exquisite torture. His fingers whispered down her abdomen, to her panty line, then underneath the silk as he touched her right where she needed him most.

Paige cried out and arched up into his hand.

"Yes. Please," she begged, gasping for breath.

He released her breast and slid down her body, as his fingers continued working their magic. Then suddenly he stopped and her eyes flew open. He knelt between her legs, pushing them further apart. Then he pulled the crotch of her panties aside. She might have been embarrassed to be so blatantly exposed, so blatantly wet and needy, if she weren't so crazy for him to touch her.

"God, Paige," he whispered, then ran his knuckle lightly up and down her, over and over until she thought she'd go mad.

His finger slipped inside her, and she splintered apart, sobbing with joy at the amazing explosion. Ross didn't stop stimulating her, but wrung every wrenching jolt from her body.

"God, baby, you are so responsive," he said.

When she finally caught her breath, she looked up at him. "But . . . you."

"Oh, we have plenty of time for me."

For several minutes he ran his fingers over her body, almost like a blind man, memorizing her curves and hollows, letting her float back to earth at her own speed. She tried to reach for him, to give him that same exquisite pleasure, to stroke and suckle him until he was mindless, too.

"Not yet, baby," he said, his voice husky. "I have much more of you to kiss, first."

"I don't think I can stand it," she gasped.

"Sure you can."

He sat back on his heels, then put a hand under her left knee and lifted her leg. Through the silk of her stocking, he began at the sole of her foot, kissing his way up her ankle, calf, knee and thigh.

The pressure began building between her legs all over again. Before she knew what was happening, she was desperate for him to relieve it.

"Oh, Ross, now!"

"Okay, baby," he said, then kissed her *there*, overtop her panties.

Paige almost screamed. Her hands clutched at his shoulders, fingernails digging into his flesh.

Again he pulled aside her panties and there was nothing between his mouth and her womanhood.

She came almost immediately, crying out his name as convulsions rocked through her, sending her soaring to a place she'd never before visited.

The rest was a blur. Somehow Ross disposed of his briefs, her garter and panties. He managed to roll a condom into place, even while she grasped for him, begging in whimpers for him to take her.

He primed her again with the tip of his penis, stroking, teasing, driving her mad with desire. "You want me, baby?"

"Yes! Oh, please, now."

"Inside you?"

"Yes!"

"Part of you?"

Paige grabbed his face, pulling him down until they were nose-to-nose. "Counselor, if you don't finish your closing argument, you are *not* going to like the verdict."

He laughed, then kissed her, then plunged inside her. Paige gasped into his mouth. He went still. "Am I hurting you?"

"In the . . . the best possible way." She wrapped her legs around his waist and arched up, driving him deeper.

His eyes slammed shut. "Oh, baby. You feel so damn good." Setting a slow, deep rhythm, he brought her alive once more, this time from the inside out.

Suddenly he rolled over onto his back, their bodies still joined. "Make love to *me*, love."

She braced her hands on his chest, not quite certain how to proceed. It wasn't like she didn't know about this way of making love. She wasn't that naive. She'd just never actually done this.

He must have seen something in her expression, because he cupped her hips. "Just do what feels good, babe."

She wiggled a little, which caused him to emit a low groan. She liked that. So she raised up a little, then wiggled her way back down, taking him deep. He whispered an expletive, but in an awe-struck sort of way.

Paige was really beginning to enjoy this. Not only did it feel wonderful, she was making him feel that way, too.

Teasing him with her body proved a double-edged sword, however. Before she knew it, she was reaching for that starburst right along with him. His breath rasped and he urged her on with groans of pleasure, murmured words. His hips bucked upward, as he spread her knees further apart, driving deeper and deeper into her.

"Come with me, baby," he whispered, then reached down between them and laid his thumb on her. Paige threw her head back and cried out, exploding around him, her muscles contracting around his hard and pulsing shaft. And together they fell over the edge.

Ross stroked his fingers up and down Paige's back, loving how she'd just up and collapsed on his chest. They were still joined, and with the least encouragement from her, he would be more than ready to make love with her again. And again. And again.

So much for getting her out of his system. He'd badly miscalculated on that score. The woman was so beautiful, so responsive, so damn sexy, he had the feeling he'd crave her for the rest of his life.

Which wouldn't be bad, if it weren't for the fact that he had the feeling she didn't want to share his bed for another night, much less decades.

She lifted her head from his chest and looked at him in a way that had him instantly hardening inside her. Her eyes sparkled, but were heavy-lidded from contented exhaustion.

"Hi," she said.

"Hello, sweetheart."

She practically purred into his chest. "That feels so good."

"*You* feel so good."

She crossed her arms over his chest and rested her chin on them. "Well, that worked."

That's what he was afraid of. "It did?"

"Oh, yes. I'm . . . practically dead."

"Well, that wasn't exactly the goal."

She laughed softly, then kissed his chest. "You know what I mean."

He took a deep breath. "Does this mean . . . you want me to leave now?"

The alarm that flared in her eyes was heartening. "I thought you said one night."

He ran his fingers through her hair, memorizing the texture. "Well, *I* wanted one entire night. But if you're practically dead . . ."

She pushed herself up. "Are you . . . cured?"

"Not by a long shot, baby."

"Then I think you need to stay the whole night."

He almost whooped his relief. "If you think that's best."

Chapter Sixteen

"Face it, buddy, it's not the disease," Ross muttered to himself the next morning. He slammed a fist on his desk, then rubbed his forehead. He was in deep, deep trouble.

He and Paige had made love all night. Over and over. And each time just seemed to intensify his need to make love to her again. Being inside her felt like being home. Right where he belonged.

No, indeed, this was not a disease. At least not one he contracted on his trip to the hospital.

Yet Paige had happily declared the two of them cured this morning, right before she'd sailed into the shower. Ross had almost been irritated enough to stick around and confront her when she emerged from the bathroom, but wasn't quite sure what he'd say.

So he'd slipped out of her condo quietly, vowing to give it some thought before he informed her that they weren't over—not by a long shot.

Well, informing her might not be the most brilliant approach. Convincing her would work better. Except he wasn't quite sure how to go about that.

His phone buzzed. "Yes, Mrs. Whipple?"

"Your tux just arrived from the cleaners."

"Oh. Okay, thank you." He'd forgotten all about the charity function he was scheduled to attend Friday night. Which was pretty stupid, considering it was for Children's Legal Advocacy and he was on their board of directors. He even felt a little guilty about the speech he'd have to deliver, considering he was going to be given accolades that rightfully should be going to Mrs. Whipple, who'd had to step in and handle many of the organizing decisions while he'd been in the hospital.

Speaking of hospitals, he was suddenly missing one. Which was more than halfway insane.

His phone buzzed again, and he shook his head. He wouldn't get *anything* accomplished if he didn't stop obsessing over Paige for at least a minute at a time. "Yes, Mrs. Whipple?"

"There is a Nick Hart here to see you."

Whoa! If Ross had a Kevlar jacket handy, he was pretty sure he'd be donning it right about now.

"Okay," he said slowly. "He's not armed, is he?"

"Not that I can see. Should I frisk him?"

"I guess that's not necessary."

"Really, I wouldn't mind."

"Mrs. Whipple! What would Mr. Whipple say?"

"Who's going to tell him?"

Ross laughed. "Send him back." He stood and fidgeted with his tie as he waited for Paige's brother to storm in and beat the hell out of him. Or try to, at any rate.

A moment later Mrs. Whipple opened his office door and waved in Nick Hart. Nick didn't look like a man storming in to defend his sister's honor, which was a good sign, Ross decided. But if this wasn't about Paige, Ross couldn't even begin to guess what Nick was doing here.

"Thanks for seeing me without an appointment," Nick said, striding to the desk and holding out his hand.

Ross took it, then waved him into a guest chair. "Coffee? Soda?"

"No, thank you."

Returning to his desk, Ross sat. "What can I do for you?"

"I need some legal advice."

Ross had to clench his jaw to keep it from dropping. "From me?"

"Yes."

"Why not go to Paige?"

"This isn't her forte. Besides, I really don't want

Paige or anyone else in the family to know about it."

"I was under the impression that you're not married."

"I'm not."

"Dr. Turner?"

"Nope, she's not married, either. Not yet, at any rate."

"Okay . . ." Ross pulled his ever-present legal pad closer, and picked up his pen. "What kind of legal advice are you looking for?"

"This is confidential, right?"

"Absolutely. Do I hear wedding bells between you and the pretty doctor?" Although Nick Hart didn't seem like the prenup sort to Ross. In fact, Ross wasn't too keen on prenup agreements in general. To him it was a symbol that the couples were already setting themselves up for failure.

"Not if Pamela Jones has anything to say about it," Nick grumbled.

"Who's Pamela Jones?"

"She's the wife of Freeman Jones."

"The media guy?"

"That's the one. I designed their new house."

"So what's going on with Freeman Jones's wife?" Ross asked, biting down a sick feeling in his gut. He'd *hate* to learn that Nick Hart had had an affair with a married woman. Paige would be so disappointed in her brother.

"Apparently a whole lot. She got caught fooling

around on her husband with a much younger man."

Ross held up a hand. "Before you go any further, Nick, I have to tell you right now that I don't represent adulterers. I'm not condemning you or anything, it's just one of my personal rules."

Nick's eyes widened. "You think . . . you wouldn't . . . it's not me!"

Ross suppressed a smile of relief, surprised at how relieved he was to hear that. "Then I'm not quite sure why you need me."

"Because she's claiming it's me. How she pulled my name out of a hat, I have no idea. But Mr. Jones came storming into my studio this morning, roaring about lawsuits and screaming phrases like 'alienation of affection.' It took me a good ten minutes to calm him down enough to understand his problem."

"Why would she name you if it's *not* you?"

Nick scowled and ran a hand through his hair. "Your guess is as good as mine. I can barely tolerate the woman."

"So I take it she didn't actually get caught in flagrante delicto."

"From what I could gather, she flung it in his face after she got mad at him for putting her on an allowance."

"Not the brightest bulb in the lamp, is she?"

"A few watts shy of a flicker, if you ask me."

"And you have no idea why she'd pick you to be her paramour?" Although Ross was pretty certain he could answer that question himself. Nick Hart was a handsome man, if he was any judge of such things. And Ross guessed most women would probably pay good money to spend time with him. No doubt Nick had inspired a few fantasies in Mrs. Whipple.

"I don't have a clue. Except that we've been spending a lot of time together, going over plans for the new house. Jones had pretty much given her carte blanche, and she's taken full advantage of it. Now that I think about it, I just sent Mr. Jones a revised estimate with all the work order changes on the construction, and believe me, the cost has more than tripled since she got her hands on it. Maybe that's where the allowance thing fits in."

"You absolutely swear there's not even a speck of truth to her allegations?"

"I swear."

"No motel bills that might pop up? No jewelry store receipts? No cell-phone bills?"

"Well, we've certainly talked on my cell phone. But it was strictly business."

"Okay, you're seeking legal advice, why?"

"Because the guy's threatened to sue me. Not only that, he's threatened to refuse to pay for the work order changes to the house. I have a lot of capital tied up in that project. I can't afford for him to default."

"When you denied all of this to him, did he believe you?"

"No."

"Okay, here's what we're going to do. First, we're going to prove that you have never been with his wife intimately. Second, we're going to prove that she authorized all of those work order changes . . . she did, didn't she?"

Nick nodded. "I even had her sign for them. The paperwork is all in order."

"She had the power to sign those papers?"

"Of course. Freeman Jones wanted his 'Pookie' to have anything her little larcenous heart desired."

"Then he doesn't have a leg to stand on, so to speak. Except the one between his legs, which is probably not doing a good job of holding him up at the moment. No problem."

"How are we going to get him to back off? He could ruin me in the press."

"First, I get her to give me dates, times and places where these supposed trysts took place."

"She could always make up some bull about us fooling around at the job site. We were there together plenty."

"Alone?"

"No, the entire . . . oh, yeah! The crew can vouch that we never disappeared alone together. And we certainly weren't putting on any peep shows."

"Right. Second, do you have any . . . distinguishing marks on your body? Anything that only a woman who'd seen you intimately would know?"

291

Nick thought about that. "No birthmarks or anything. No moles, either."

"How about scars?"

"Yes! I have a scar on my shoulder from an old biking accident."

"Visible?"

"Yes." He pointed to his left shoulder. "Right here. It's about two inches long."

Ross made some notes. "Perfect. As for the media angle, we'll make it abundantly clear that if he tries anything like that, he's in for a lawsuit or two of his own, not to mention public embarrassment."

"So what do we do?"

"You don't need to do a thing. I'll take care of it."

"What are *you* going to do, then?"

"I'm going to give Mr. Jones—or his lawyer if he so desires—a wake-up call. If he proceeds with a suit, I'm going to depose Mrs. Jones. When she gets trapped in lies, they are going to be looking at countersuits of defamation of character, loss of income, frivolous suits, breach of contract, and probably a few more I'll remember along the way."

Nick sat silent for a moment. "You're good."

"I hate to tell you, but this is cakewalk stuff."

"Will it work?"

"I don't see why not. But I tell you, if she describes that scar, I'm going to be pretty damn ticked."

"She will not know about the scar."

"Good." Ross shook his head. "Men can really lose it when it comes to women." Unfortunately, he wasn't thinking just about Freeman Jones at the moment.

"No kidding." Nick rolled his shoulders. "Thanks so much."

"No problem."

"You won't tell Paige about this."

He sincerely doubted, even if he *wanted* to violate the attorney-client privilege, he'd have a *chance* to tell Paige about this or anything else. The woman had seemed so eager to see him gone this morning, he didn't think she'd be calling him anytime soon. "I won't tell Paige about this. But I don't see why you can't. You haven't done anything wrong."

"I don't want it getting back to Rachel, somehow."

"Again, if you're innocent, why not?"

Nick pursed his lips, then finally answered. "As it is, I'm still on shaky ground with her. I don't want even an inkling of doubt making it shakier."

Shaky ground. Ross could relate. "Can I ask you something, Hart?"

"You're about to save my butt. I guess you're entitled," the man said with a slight grin.

"Is Paige . . . over what happened to her in college?"

Nick frowned. "How do you know about what happened to Paige in college?"

"She told me."

"She told you? About . . . the professor?"

"Yes."

"Wow. I'd say that's a pretty good sign. I don't think she's ever told anyone about that, besides the family of course."

Ross sat forward, eager for some insight into Paige's psyche. "Actually, I think she told me out of pure boredom. There wasn't much more to do in there but swap old war stories." *Well, except at night.*

"Maybe."

"So . . . has it left permanent scars?"

"I don't know about scars. It still ticks her off."

"I think it still affects her, though. And I don't know what to do about it."

"What do you mean?"

Ross hesitated, then spilled. "She doesn't seem to want to think about the future, you know?"

It was Nick's turn to sit up. "You, too?"

"Oh, boy. Same with Rachel?"

"Yes! Why is it that women never want to commit?"

Ross shook his head. "I don't know. I mean, I try to make Paige happy, but she just won't even consider the long haul."

"Same here! And what's worse, Rachel won't even give me a good reason why."

"I know exactly what you mean. Why can't women learn to communicate?"

"Rachel doesn't *even want* to get into personal stuff between us."

"Sometimes I feel I'm only good for one thing," Ross complained.

"I hear that one," Nick agreed, nodding.

"Do you ever get the feeling that their jobs are more important than we are?"

"Definitely. Rachel lives and breathes that hospital."

"Paige says she's so busy, she doesn't even have time to think about getting involved in a relationship."

"Why are women so difficult? It's not like I'm trying to monopolize Rachel's time."

"And just think how they'd laugh if we even hinted we'd like them to date us exclusively."

"Oh, Rachel would howl, for sure," Nick said.

"Could you imagine what Paige would say if I brought up the subject of marriage?"

That stopped Nick. "Are you *thinking* about marriage?"

"I'm not holding my breath. I can't even get her to date me."

Nick gaped. "But . . . I thought . . . you two . . . were . . . you know . . . getting pretty close."

"Oh, sure. When she gets her hormones in an uproar. But emotions? Forget it." He scowled. "You know . . . and not to get too personal, but we had a pretty intense night. Has she called me today? *No.*"

Nick pointed at Ross's nose. "Rachel has probably 'accidentally lost' my phone number. Even though I wrote it on her bathroom mirror with her lipstick."

"Hey, that's kind of romantic," Ross said.

"My bet is Rachel doesn't think so. Do you know I spent hours the other day cooking her a gourmet meal? Did she show up in time? No. She got sidetracked at the hospital and forgot all about it."

"Women!" Ross said in disgust.

"Women!" Nick agreed.

"Betty!" Paige practically screamed. "I can't find Aunt Alicia's file!" It was Friday morning, but she felt none of the relief she usually associated with the anticipation of a weekend.

Betty showed up at her threshold a few seconds later. As usual she was dressed in a designer outfit that would probably cost Paige a month's income. "A lady doesn't screech, my dear, unless she's being paid obscene amounts of money to do so by Twentieth Century Fox."

Paige cringed, realizing she was fast becoming the shrillest female in Atlanta. "I'm sorry. But why can't I find anything anymore?"

"If you remember correctly, you asked me to have several files copied and couriered over to Ross Bennett's office. My guess is they're still in the To Be Filed pile."

"Oh! Of course."

"Would you like me to go get them?"

Paige ran a hand across her forehead. "No, that's all right. I'll find them."

Betty plunked down in one of Paige's guest chairs. "Okay, then let's talk about you."

"What about me?" Paige asked warily.

"About the alien that has invaded your body."

Moving back to her desk, Paige slumped down in her chair. "I'd like to say I don't know what you mean, but that would be a pretty stupid lie."

"So true. What's wrong, darling?"

"I . . . I'm not sure."

"Take a guess."

Oh, she could guess all right. But she didn't think she could voice her opinion to Betty without dying of embarrassment. How to explain that apparently that one night with Ross hadn't "stuck," so to speak? That while she'd been happily sated the morning after that incredible night, by evening a hole had begun gnawing in the pit of her stomach, and by the time she'd flung herself into bed with a vengeance, the hole had been gaping.

Two nights without him, and she missed him like mad.

"How does one . . . go about figuring out if maybe they have a defect of sorts?"

"See a doctor."

"That's the problem. I've seen a doctor, and she keeps insisting on giving me a clean bill of health."

"And if you're talking about Dr. Turner, she's one of the best St. Catherine's has, Paige."

"I know, but this makes no sense."

"What makes no sense?"

Paige glanced over at Betty. The woman was the cream of the crop of Atlanta society, and yet in her regal way, was pragmatic and fairly open-minded. As long as rules of etiquette were followed, of course. And Paige couldn't decide if discussing her sex life fell within the boundaries, or not.

"Maybe it's all in my head?" Paige opined.

"Maybe what's all in your head?"

"Power of suggestion?"

Betty pounded a fist on Paige's desk. "Spit it out, girl. I can't help if you keep skirting the problem."

"I think I'm a sex maniac," Paige blurted.

Betty stared at her for long, uncomfortable seconds before bursting out in genteel laughter. "And this is a problem how?" she finally asked.

"I'm not that type of girl," Paige reminded her. "At least I didn't used to be. Now it seems to be all I think about."

"Lucky you."

"Oh, no," Paige disagreed, shaking her head rapidly. "It stinks. How am I going to get my normal life back, when all I can think about is that snake, Ross Bennett?"

"Maybe you care about him more than you want to admit."

"Impossible."

"Why?"

"He's a snake! He's a divorce attorney! He's a . . . he's a . . ."

"Darn handsome man, who has a secretary who thinks he walks on water."

"Well, she would. He pays her to think that."

"Mary Lou Whipple needs her salary about as much as I do. She works for him out of devotion, not to feed her family."

Paige stared at Betty. "How do you know so much about Ross's secretary?"

"Darling, she's a friend. We shark lawyer secretaries must stick together," she added, with a regal sniff, followed by a slight smile.

"Still—"

"Have you ever heard of Children's Legal Advocacy?"

"The nonprofit that recovers child support from deadbeat dads?"

"Yes."

"A wonderful organization, from everything I've heard," Paige commented.

"They are holding a fundraiser tonight."

"That's nice, but I'm not sure how that's relevant to our discussion."

"Guess who's one of the founding members, and sits prominently on the board?"

"Uh-oh. Not Ross."

"Yes, Ross."

Paige laid her head on the desk. Did she need this? How was she going to fight her attraction to the man if he kept doing things she considered admirable?

A memory niggled at her. One day in the hospital, when the doctor had come into their room, she'd handed Ross a file folder. The tab on the folder had sported three bold letters. C.L.A. Children's Legal Advocacy. In the next few days she'd seen him working with that file, but had assumed those were the initials of a client. And he hadn't bothered to inform her otherwise.

So the man didn't boast about his charity work. Great. Another reason to resent him. If he'd bragged, she could hold it against him.

"Why are you fighting this?" Betty asked softly. "I say, go with the flow, Paige. Allow yourself some happiness."

Good question. Why *was* she fighting it? After all, even if she'd held a grudge against all divorce attorneys at one point, Ross had proven over and over that he was an anomaly. An *ethical* divorce attorney. A kind and generous man. And, dangit, about the most giving and sexy lover in the world. Not that she had much experience, but if their nights together were any indication, she'd been blessed to have him for her second lover. To learn what true lovemaking was.

"What if he doesn't feel the same way? What if he's already forgotten me?"

"Only one way to find out. Contact him."

"Oh, I couldn't! I wouldn't know what to say."

"How about, 'Hi, Ross, want to go out with me?' "

"No way, I couldn't."

"Well, there is another way."

Paige knew her eyes were gleaming with hope, but she didn't even try to mask it. "How?"

"That fundraiser tonight?"

"Yes?"

"I just happen to have an extra ticket. My . . . gentleman friend had to cancel at the last minute."

Paige perked up at that. "Gentleman friend?"

"Don't go getting that matchmaking look in your eyes." Betty waved and her bracelets jangled. "It's really nothing."

"Who is it?"

"I'm sure you don't know him."

"It's not Harvey, the UPS guy, is it?"

Betty flushed. "Why in the world would I want to spend time with that . . . that . . . utterly aggravating man?"

Paige was just a little worried she knew *exactly* why Betty had suddenly found the man attractive, Rachel's denial aside. "Because he doesn't take your guff?"

Sniffing, Betty said, "I don't *do* guff. Really, Paige."

"Then who's the gentleman friend?"

Betty glanced away. "Harvey, the UPS guy," she mumbled.

Oh, boy. "If he's so aggravating, why are you . . . umm . . . dating him?"

301

"It's *not* dating, Paige, dear." At the sight of Paige's widened gaze, she shrugged. "I may be older, but I'm not ready to be pushing up daisies quite yet."

Paige didn't want to hear this. Betty, society maven, having an illicit affair. With Harvey, the UPS guy. She felt a mammoth headache coming on.

"But enough about me. Back to you. Come to the fundraiser tonight."

Oh, it was tempting. "I couldn't."

Betty sighed her exasperation. "Again, why not?"

"Doesn't it feel a little like chasing him?"

"No, it feels like attending an event for a very worthy cause."

"But—"

"We'll go together. It'll look like I dragged you along."

"I don't know."

"And guess what? The man doesn't know it yet, but one of the auction items is a date with him."

That news speared right through her. If she didn't attend, some other woman was going to pay good money to get Ross alone with her. He'd be at a stranger's mercy. In all good conscience, Paige couldn't do that to him.

She stood up abruptly and grabbed her purse.

"Where are you going?" Betty asked.

"Shopping. I don't have a thing to wear."

Betty sniffed again, but her lips twitched. "My limo will be at your place at eight."

Chapter Seventeen

"You look marvelous," Betty said that night, promptly at eight, when Paige slid into the limo.

"What? This old thing?" Paige said dryly. She'd combed Atlanta for three hours that afternoon before finally finding the perfect dress. It was a cream silk ankle-length gown, with a scarflike shoulder strap that crossed over to her left shoulder, and trailed down her back.

She'd curled her hair slightly, leaving it loose, but for two gold barrettes that pulled it back from her face. She hadn't wanted to look *too* eager by running to her hairdresser to put it up in an elaborate coif.

And the truth was, she wasn't all that eager. More anxious than anything. How would Ross act toward her? Polite? Distant? Or, heaven forbid, indifferent?

How should she act toward him? Friendly? Happy to see him? Or, heaven forbid, would she faint at his feet?

She happily accepted the flute of champagne Betty offered her, but remembering the way she'd embarrassed herself the other night, she merely took a sip, then held it with both hands, mostly to keep them from shaking.

"Relax," Betty said. "You are going to be a smash."

Paige sincerely doubted that, but offered Betty a grateful smile just the same. "Have I mentioned lately how much I adore you?" she asked.

"No," Betty said, patting her thigh. "You've been sorely neglectful in that regard."

"My apologies."

"You're forgiven. Now tell me, what in the world kind of business would Nick have with Ross? Do you have any idea?"

Paige blinked. "Nick? My Nick?"

"The one and only."

"What do you mean?"

"You didn't know he went to Ross's office a couple of days ago?"

"No!"

Betty nodded. "Indeed."

"How did *you* know that?"

"I had lunch with Mary Lou Whipple. She mentioned what a handsome cuss your brother is."

"Did she say what it was about?"

"Of course not! We might like a bit of gossip as much as the rest of them, but really, Paige, it wouldn't do to discuss business."

Business? Nick? With *Ross?* That made no sense whatsoever. If Nick ever decided to tie the knot, Paige was pretty sure she'd be invited to the wedding.

A horrible thought occurred to her. "Mrs. Whipple didn't mention any . . . shouting or anything, did she? She didn't hear any punches being thrown, or furniture overturning?"

"If she saw or heard anything like that, she didn't mention it."

Paige had a horrible vision of seeing Ross tonight sporting a black eye. Or worse. She was going to kill her brother next time she saw him.

"This is not a good thing," Paige murmured.

"I'm sure it will be fine," Betty said. "Did you bring your checkbook?"

The ballroom of the Marriott was crowded, and glittered with gowns and chandeliers and crystal flutes of champagne. Although there were a few tables scattered in corners of the great room, for the most part people strolled around, mingling. Waiters circulated, offering canapés and refreshments.

A string quartet played classical music that drifted over the room in soothing tones. A podium was set up toward the back, the dais currently dark and empty.

Paige recognized a few acquaintances, spotted local celebrities, but for the most part she knew almost no one. This room sported the crème de la crème of Atlanta society. She could imagine how much a single ticket had cost.

Ross was nowhere to be found, and Paige started worrying that if he and Nick had really gotten into it, Ross might have had to cancel his appearance.

Betty was being a doll at sticking close to Paige, or dragging her along from one group of guests to another, always making certain to introduce her as if she were royalty.

Paige did her best to pay attention and attempt to memorize names, but she couldn't help but scan the crowd in search of a familiar body, familiar brown hair.

But with practically every man there decked out in a black tux, it wasn't an easy task. Only her knowledge that she had some sort of radar where Ross was concerned assured her—albeit not in a good way—that he wasn't close by.

At least not physically. But wherever she and Betty went, Ross was almost invariably the topic of conversation. At first she'd had a hard time associating words like philanthropist, young genius, tireless defender of the downtrodden, and other such praise with the man she knew. But as the night wore on, something akin to pride began blooming inside her, and she realized that Ross was indeed all of those things. And more. Much more.

One group they'd mingled with included another lawyer who donated his time to the CLA, and from him she and the rest of those standing nearby were made privy to the fact that Ross was receiving an award tonight, and he wasn't aware of it. Also, the man confirmed what Betty had told her earlier. One of the auction items was Ross himself. And he didn't know about that, either.

Paige thought that in some ways these people were ambushing the poor man. She was doing him a favor by rescuing him. He'd better appreciate it.

After a little over an hour the quartet suddenly ceased playing, and lights blared on, spotlighting the dais. Conversation became muted, and everyone turned to face the podium.

A tall, distinguished black man climbed the steps, and Paige squinted, knowing he looked familiar, but—

"Is that the mayor?" she whispered to Betty.

"His honor himself," Betty agreed.

Paige was impressed.

Mayor Pullman greeted the crowd to enthusiastic applause. He was one of those politicians who was loved by all, the poor, the middle class, and obviously the wealthy. He had a way of writing innovative policy that contained something for everyone, without stiffing any segment of his town's population.

And this man, arguably the most respected in Atlanta's history, was standing at a podium ticking off all the reasons he admired Ross Bennett.

And the list was impressive. No, it was actually mind-boggling. Paige had spent two entire weeks in Ross's company. Had he ever bothered to mention that he'd once saved two young boys' lives? According to the mayor, Ross had talked a distraught father—who'd kidnapped his children—into agreeing to exchange the kids for himself. Ross had ended up being held hostage another twenty-four hours, before successfully convincing the guy to give himself up.

Had Ross ever mentioned that he'd bullied city officials and rich philanthropists alike into building two very unique shelters for abused mothers and children?

Had he ever noted that at those very same shelters he volunteered his time giving lectures to those mothers on the law, how to use it to their benefit, how to protect themselves and their children?

Did he once talk about the scholarships he sponsored for kids with hard work ethics, where he matched their paychecks from whatever jobs they worked, depositing the donations in college trust funds?

Never.

Instead, he'd sat there and let her call him all

kinds of names. He allowed her to pass judgment, without defending himself.

Paige wanted to cry. Why would a man like that even *want* to get involved with a shrew like her? There was no way she'd bid on his date now. He deserved better.

Swallowing a painful lump, she tuned back in as Mayor Pullman wrapped up his introduction of the man of the hour.

"We're very lucky that Mr. Bennett was even able to be with us tonight, after having the misfortune to be caught in the courthouse bombing, and then finding himself in the nearly unbearable position of being quarantined for weeks."

Unbearable? Was that Ross's assessment, or the mayor's? It hurt terribly to think that Ross looked back on that time as practically torture, but she supposed she couldn't quite blame him.

"Without further ado, please help me welcome Ross Bennett."

This time the applause was thunderous. Paige scanned the room desperately, wondering how it had been possible not to spot him earlier. But then her eyes landed on him, near the bottom of the stairs, shaking hands and smiling with a small group of well-wishers. One of which was a stunning blonde. A stunning blonde who didn't let him go before planting a lingering kiss on his cheek, then intimately wiping away any trace of lipstick she might have left behind.

Paige's heart cracked. Of course he'd bring a

date. Why hadn't she even considered that?

Suddenly she felt like such a fool. An idiot. Whatever arrogant part of her that had harbored hopes that his single-minded interest in her wouldn't just disappear was squashed like a bug right there in that ballroom. She almost felt like falling to her knees. Or running from the ballroom.

Running was the more preferable—if cowardly—option.

"Betty, I think I need to leave," she whispered.

"Nonsense."

"No, really."

"One does not walk out the moment the guest of honor takes the spotlight. It's impolite, dear."

Right now she wasn't sure she didn't want to go ahead and risk the wrath of Miss Manners. She didn't think she could stand it.

On the other hand, this might be the last time she could stare at him without appearing rude or pathetic.

And boy, was he easy to stare at. It didn't surprise her that he looked good in a tux. More than good. Stunning, would be a better word. Mouthwatering would be apt, too.

Camera flashes bounced all over him, but other than squinting a little, he accepted the onslaught with an easy grace, waiting for the commotion to die down. When it threatened to continue, he held up a hand. "The longer you keep that up, the more I'll begin to believe I deserve it."

The crowd laughed, but settled down.

"Seriously, I can't thank y'all enough for your generosity and enthusiasm for a cause that means a lot to me. But before I bore you to death with some of the ways your generous contributions will be used in the coming year, I'd like to clear up one misperception.

"Mayor Pullman gave the impression that my recent forced incarceration in Saint Catherine's was an ordeal. While I wouldn't have wished that situation on anyone, it was far from painful. The staff at the hospital was wonderful, and I couldn't have asked for a more entertaining cellmate. Believe me, it wasn't torture."

Betty reached over and squeezed Paige's hand. "See?"

"Did you tell him I'd be here?"

"No."

Paige was torn between being delighted he'd mentioned her, and agonized that if she'd been that entertaining, why he hadn't invited her to this shindig?

Then again, why would he? She certainly hadn't left him with the impression that she wanted to see him again, in any capacity. But he sure didn't waste any time finding another woman to accompany him tonight.

Another thing. Why hadn't she sensed his presence earlier? In the hospital, in the restaurant, in her condo, she felt a tingling just under her skin whenever he'd been in the same room. It wasn't an unpleasant feeling, except at the beginning when she'd resented his presence in her life, her room. In fact, by the time they'd begun sharing a bed at night, she'd not only gotten used to it, she'd come to crave it.

But it seemed to be gone now. Could it be that their final night together had really and truly cured them?

But if that were the case, why did she *still* crave it, crave him? Could it be that because the attraction was no longer reciprocated that buzzing awareness had disappeared? Had he given off vibes when he'd wanted her, but now that he'd moved on, he no longer did?

It was a thoroughly depressing thought.

Applause rang in her ear, and Paige suddenly realized she'd just missed Ross's entire speech, as she looked up to see him stepping back from the dais. He waved, then began heading for the steps, but the mayor met him halfway, and forced him to turn around. The surprise on Ross's face was obvious.

Paige listened in growing astonishment as the mayor presented him with a plaque for Atlanta Humanitarian of the Year. She'd known he was receiving an award, she hadn't known he'd be receiving *that* one.

Ross's encore acceptance speech was practically speechless. He'd been stunned into silence, which Paige noted for posterity. She hadn't been able to get him to shut up for fourteen days. Even when she'd been ravishing his body, he'd talked incessantly.

Then the mayor introduced the female auctioneer for the night, still holding on to a bewildered Ross's arm, trapping him.

As the auctioneer explained that the bidding was about to begin, she explained that one item had not been included in the roster.

"Since our most esteemed honoree tonight is a handsome, single, eligible bachelor, we were certain he wouldn't mind the first fund-raising item on the block tonight to be a romantic date with him."

Even several feet from the mike, Ross's, "What?" could be heard ringing throughout the ballroom.

"Come on," Betty said, tugging on Paige's arm. "We should get right up front."

"I don't think—"

"You certainly don't sometimes."

"Betty, stop! I can't do it."

"Of course you can."

Before Paige could gather her wits, she found herself bulldozed right up to the front of the podium.

"It's for a good cause," the auctioneer said cheerfully.

"I sincerely doubt—" Ross began

"One thousand dollars!" a woman called out.

The auctioneer peered out into the crowd. "Now, Mrs. Pemberton, don't you think we should confine this bidding to the single women?"

"Well, shoot," the woman grumbled.

"But I think that's a good starting bid, ladies. One thousand dollars for a night on the town with our handsome Humanitarian of the Year. Who wants to open the bid?"

Betty elbowed Paige in the ribs, but before Paige could even open her mouth to say Ouch, another woman called out.

The floodgates opened. Paige stopped trying to keep up with which females in the crowd were vying for a date with Ross, but she had to wonder if every single unmarried woman in Atlanta had shown up for the event. Before a minute was up the bid had risen to twenty-seven hundred dollars.

"Bid already!" Betty growled.

"I can't afford this!"

"I'll pay for it. Just bid."

"I can't let you—"

"Bid!"

"Three thousand dollars!" Paige said weakly.

"Excuse me?" the auctioneer said, cupping her ear. "I didn't hear you."

If Paige could disappear in a puff of smoke, she'd do it right there and then. "I said three thousand dollars," she repeated.

Ross, who'd been staring at his Bruno Maglis, suddenly glanced up. He squinted into the crowd, and when his gaze landed on her, his face split in a wide and dimpled grin. He stepped forward, grabbed the gavel from the auctioneer and said,

"Going, going, gone, to the sexy blonde in the front row." The bang reverberated throughout the room like a gunshot.

"Hi."

"Hi."

"You look gorgeous," Ross said, and meant it. He couldn't believe how incredibly happy he'd been to discover Paige in the crowd. The night had seemed so hollow, no matter how gratifying the unexpected award had been. He hadn't quite pinpointed why until he'd heard her soft voice. And then it hit him like a hammer to the head. The award, the fund-raiser, didn't mean what they should if he couldn't share them with *her*.

And the thought of being auctioned off like a piece of furniture to someone else had horrified him. But he couldn't embarrass the well-meaning event organizers, so he'd stood there, feeling like an idiot.

"Thank you," she said quietly. "You, too."

"I'm so glad you came." Ross snagged two flutes of champagne from a passing waiter, and handed her one.

"I . . . guess I better go. I don't want this to be awkward for you."

"Huh?"

"Well, for your date."

"My date?"

"The blonde."

"What blonde?"

"The one who kissed you before you went up to make your speech."

He wracked his brain. "Oh, her."

"She didn't look all that forgettable to me."

"Oh, I doubt she's forgettable. Especially to my law school buddy, seeing as she's his wife."

Her delighted smile sank right through him, warming his entire body. "Really?"

"Really."

"Oh."

The relief on her face was adorable. "You weren't jealous, were you?"

"Of course n— Well, maybe a little."

That concession was a big one, and he decided it needed to be rewarded with one of his own. "I've missed you."

She hesitated while rowdy bidding swirled around them. "Oh, heck, I've sort of missed you, too."

He took her hand. "Come on, let's go someplace quiet."

"Don't you need to—"

"No."

He tugged her into a small sitting room off the ballroom, glad to see it empty. They sat on a green couch, and for a few moments Ross allowed himself to absorb her presence, her beauty, her perfume. Then he asked, "Why'd you come, Paige?"

She took intense interest in the bubbles in her glass. "I . . . well, I've been something of a bear to work with lately, and I was afraid if I didn't come with Betty, she'd quit on me."

"Mrs. Whipple hasn't exactly had it easy, either."

Glancing up, she searched his face for he didn't know what. "Ross?"

"Yes?"

"I don't think that closure thing worked."

"I *know* it didn't. At least not for me."

"So what are we going to do about it?"

"Keep trying?"

She laughed, but then sobered instantly. "I don't deserve you."

"Excuse me?"

"I stood there and listened to all the things you've done, and all I could think of was how rude I was to you. How much I misjudged you. How unfair—"

"Shh," he said, with a finger to her lips. "You had good reason, sweetheart."

"No," she retorted, shaking her head. "I've let an event that happened fifteen years ago turn me into a judgmental shrew. I was *so* ready to condemn you without a shred of evidence, except what you do for a living."

"You know what? If I were into psychobabble, I'd probably say something like, 'It was a self-defense mechanism. You were so afraid of being attracted to a man who symbolized everything you despised. Perfectly understandable.' "

"Do you have to be so . . . reasonable?"

"It's one of my biggest faults. I was always getting grounded for it as a kid." He wrapped a curly strand of her hair around his finger. "You'd rather I'd be a real jerk?"

She sniffed. "It would make my own behavior a little easier to swallow. How can you forgive me so easily?"

He shrugged. "Sweetheart, I think the only one here who needs to forgive you is you. But if it makes you feel better, I'll tell you how it would be so easy for me to, if I felt the need." He brushed his thumb over her petal soft cheek. "Because there are so many wonderful qualities about you."

She ducked her head. "This from the Humanitarian of the Year."

"Paige, look at me," he said softly, lifting her chin. "You know how easy it is to write a check? To sit in on board meetings every few months?"

"You do more than that," she whispered, then ducked her head again.

Ross sighed dramatically. "Maybe a little. But I have nothing on you. Paige, you're a humanitarian every day of your life."

"You're kidding, right?"

"Not a chance. Don't forget, babe, I've seen you in action. You are a brilliant attorney, and you look out for your clients with a zealousness that is awesome. You look out for your family. You see injustice and you fight it. Every single day. It

318

makes me tired just *thinking* about all you do for others."

When she looked up, he was horrified to see tears in her eyes. Her laughter was hitchy. "Oh, yes, Wonder Woman has nothing on me."

"Don't you dare cry on me. I mean it."

She sniffled and blinked and smiled a wobbly smile. "You're a sucker for a woman's tears, huh?"

He wouldn't admit to that for all the retainers in the world. "Nope. I've seen too many. They don't move me at all."

"Right."

"Really! In fact, I laugh in the face of a crying woman. So dry those up right away," he said, waving frantically in front of her eyes. "You don't want me to lose what little respect you think I have for you right this minute, do you?"

She swallowed convulsively for a few moments, then croaked out, "No. I'd hate to offend your bad-ass self."

"Now you're catching on."

"Ross?"

"Yes?"

"Kiss me now, or find your bad ass in a sling."

Paige managed to pull herself out of her fog of lust—and what she worried was something much more meaningful—long enough to do the right thing and allow Ross to return to his fundraiser. She'd had to make a major pit stop at the women's room to fix her face and hair, both of which came away from his kisses looking like she'd just been mauled by a bear.

"You look like you've just been mauled by a bear," Betty informed her. "Or maybe a particularly amorous humanitarian."

"Help me," Paige said desperately.

"On you, darling, it looks good." Betty scrutinized her further. "Did you fix what wasn't broken?"

"I think so," Paige said, still frantically working through her hair. "At least he did."

"So, is Mary Lou right? Does the man really walk on water?"

"I wouldn't go that far," Paige said, although she had the feeling she had an embarrassingly moony look on her face. "But he's a really good swimmer."

"Good swimming skills are important."

Paige gave up on her hair and turned, wrapping Betty in an impulsive hug. "Thank you so much."

"Land sakes, child! What for?"

"For being such a good friend, for making me come here tonight, for the swift kick in the butt."

Betty sniffed. "I would never do such a vulgar thing. But you're welcome just the same. Maybe now you'll finally give me a raise."

Paige stepped back, laughing. "I'll give you a raise the day you actually start cashing your paychecks."

* * *

Ross wasn't enjoying this event as much as he should. First, he was getting more than a little embarrassed by all the accolades being heaped on him, as if he'd just brought about peace in the Middle East.

Second, Paige insisted on staying in the background, when he'd just as soon have her by his side. He was so busy checking on her whereabouts, and scowling whenever he saw some man drooling over her, he had the feeling he'd insulted more than a few of Atlanta's elite.

She looked amazing in that filmy dress that managed to outline her body in stunning detail. Nothing like walking around shaking hands and accepting congratulations with more than half a hard-on.

He was almost sorry that Paige had shown up. If she weren't here, he'd be working the room and coaxing folks to whip out their checkbooks. Then again, if she hadn't shown up, he'd have been roped into a date with some other woman. The idea held no appeal whatsoever.

He'd never been a one-woman man before. Not that the notion worried him. Quite the contrary. Fidelity was a trait he highly respected, even had yearned for, although he hadn't realized it before meeting Paige. Well, he'd always been a fan of total commitment—which in his line of work was probably pretty pathetic—but mostly in the abstract. It had never quite applied to him before now.

Paige might be the one. Now he just had to make her see that they at least owed it to themselves to pursue this *thing* between them.

Ross made some noises he hoped would pass for a response to yet another congratulatory comment, then glanced around the room, looking for the woman in question.

When he found her, he was not overjoyed to see that Freeman Jones had her cornered near the entrance. *Uh-oh.* "Please excuse me," he said to a woman, interrupting her in mid-gush.

Paige spotted Ross across the ballroom, and had to stifle a smile at the way he kept nodding and smiling at some woman who had his arm in a stranglehold. But even as he listened to what was probably gushing, his eyes scanned the room, and she was pretty certain he was searching for her. It gave her a kind of gooey feeling inside, knowing that man was thinking of her, even in the midst of accolades raining down over his head. But if she'd been expecting him to start blowing her kisses or something when their eyes finally connected, she was sadly mistaken. To her bemusement, he frowned instead, then disengaged from his conversation partner and began barreling toward her. What had she done? It wasn't like she was flirting with this nice old man.

"Have you ever done any modeling?" the nice old man asked.

Paige dragged her gaze from Ross's scowl. "No, no I haven't."

"Television?"

"I'm sorry, no."

"What a waste of bone structure," he commented. "Say, you wouldn't be interested in auditioning for an anchor spot down at the station, would you? We have a position opening up."

She didn't know what station he was referring to, but since he was talking as if he assumed she knew who he was, she decided not to inquire. "I'm afraid I'm not qualified . . ." Would calling him "sir" be an insult? Why didn't Ross make everyone wear name tags? "I'm a lawyer." Brilliance struck. She held out her hand. "Paige Hart."

He took her hand, and if she wasn't mistaken, caressed her palm with his thumb. He bent low and kissed her knuckles. "Such a lovely name to go with a lovely creature."

Okay, this nice old man seemed to be turning into a lech right before her very eyes. But then he straightened abruptly. "Hart, did you say?"

"Yes," she said slowly, suddenly wary. Which of her relatives had he encountered?

"Are you any relation to Nick Hart, the architect?" the man asked.

Okay, this couldn't be too bad. Nick was about the most benign liability in the Hart clan. Unless of course the man had a daughter Nick's age. "Yes, I am," she said, smiling.

Instead of returning the smile, the guy's lips actually puckered. "You know how close I came to putting that boy's head in a noose?"

Definitely, this man had a daughter. "Nick?" she said, but refrained from asking why. She didn't think she really wanted to know.

The man opened his mouth, but just then Ross reached them, slapping the older gentleman on the shoulder a little harder than Paige felt was necessary. Or prudent, for that matter, seeing as the guy nearly keeled over.

"Well, hello there, Mr. Jones!" Ross said heartily. "So glad you could make it!"

"Considering you practically blackmai—"

"It's such a worthy cause, don't you agree?" Ross interrupted.

"Yes, it appears so," Mr. Jones said, his tone suddenly grumpy. "I was just telling Ms. Hart, here, that—"

"She's about the most beautiful woman in the room?"

Paige would get gooey all over again, if she weren't beginning to suspect that Ross was attempting to divert the conversation, and he was appealing to her vanity to get it done. Which was almost as aggravating as the knowledge that it was sort of working.

"That too," the man said, then shot Paige a thoroughly lecherous once-over, which, she noted, Ross intercepted and didn't particularly enjoy. The older man held up his hands in a square and trained his eyes directly at her chest. "She was born to be in front of a camera."

"Yes, well she's a little shy," Ross said in something of a growl, then threw an arm around her shoulders and pulled her against him, ruining Mr. Jones's fake camera shot.

Mr. Jones dropped his hands, scowling at Ross. "We were also discussing her bro—"

"Probably not a real good idea," Ross interrupted again.

The two men exchanged a long look, before Mr. Jones gave a curt nod, then slid his gaze back her way. "If you'll excuse me."

"By all means," Ross answered, joviality restored somehow.

Mr. Jones turned away, then swung back to Paige, hiking his thumb at Ross. "You can thank this guy for getting your brother's keister out of the sling."

Paige's jaw dropped open as the man stalked away. Mouth hanging, she turned to Ross. "And what, exactly, did he mean by that?"

"Who knows?" Ross said, shrugging. Then he pointed a finger at his temple and drew circles. "I think the guy's a little touched, if you get my drift."

"Who is he?"

"You don't know?"

"No. But obviously you do, if you blackmailed him into attending tonight."

"Blackmail? Me?" Eyes wide with innocence that

would have made a used car salesman proud, he laid a hand over his heart. "I'm shocked you'd think such a thing."

Paige crossed her arms over her chest, her own eyes narrowing. "Who is he and how does he know Nick?"

"Freeman Jones."

"The media mogul?"

"The one and only."

"How does he know Nick, and why was Nick's butt almost in a sling?"

"I don't know how he met your brother. Maybe Nick designed a building for him?" He braced his hands against the wall at her back and leaned into her. "Enough about that. When do I get my date?"

His aftershave scented the air around her in the most delicious way. He smelled and looked so good, Paige almost forgot to continue grilling him. "Are you trying to distract me from this conversation?"

"Let's just say I'm trying to steer it in a much more interesting and potentially fun direction. So when's my date?"

With his hazel eyes all smoky and his lips so close, Paige decided to let him steer. For now. "When do you want your date?"

"Right now?"

Disappointment formed a knot in her belly. "Here? You want the fundraiser to be our date?"

"No, I want this hotel to be our date. How about we get a room and order some dinner?"

"That sounds decadent."

"Absolutely."

"And illicit."

"Yup."

"I think you're trying to seduce me."

"What was your first clue?"

Her heart was accelerating to dangerous speeds. "I suppose I have to honor the commitment."

"It would be the gracious thing to do."

"Lord knows I wouldn't want to do anything disgraceful."

"Oh, lady, I hope that you do. I *really* hope that you do."

Chapter Eighteen

The tub was filled with water, bubbles, Ross and Paige. The water and the bubbles were going strong. Ross and Paige were about to drop into comas. She lay with her back against his chest, his arms wrapped around her, experimenting lazily with bubble formations on her body.

"What's this one look like to you?" he murmured, his voice hoarse.

She glanced down at her breast. "A blob of bubbles."

"You have no imagination. That's Pike's Peak."

"Of course. How could I have missed it?"

He laughed, pushing her hair aside and kissing the crook of her neck. "Have I mentioned I can't get enough of you?"

She tilted her head to give him more room to work with. "Yeah? Think it's the disease still at work?"

"If it is, may it be as unending as civil litigation."

Paige chuckled, so content, so *happy* it was hard to comprehend. Even when she'd thought she'd been in love with her professor, she'd never felt like this. She never wanted it to end. She never wanted *them* to end. Which was terrifying and thrilling at one and the same time.

It had to be the middle of the night, and they'd never quite gotten around to ordering food, but she wasn't hungry at all. Exhausted, yes. Contented, yes. Dizzily sated, yes. Yet she was totally certain that given a few minutes, she'd be as ready now as she'd ever been in the hospital to make love with the man.

"Paige?" he said softly, tracing circles on her shoulder.

"Hmmm?"

"Can I run something past you?"

"Of course."

"I've been thinking." He hesitated. "Maybe it's time to get out of divorce law."

She slopped a gallon or so of water over the side of the tub twisting around to face him. "What?"

He smiled and peeled hair from her cheek. "Maybe a change of direction would be good for me. For us."

Her heart just about exploded. "How can you

say that? *Why* would you say that? You're just about the best divorce lawyer in the universe."

He stared, then burst out laughing. "Darlin', you're sometimes hard to figure. I thought you'd be happy at that news."

She rose to her knees, between his thighs. "Well, you thought wrong."

Ross was having a difficult time concentrating on the conversation. "Damn, woman, you're gorgeous," he said, not even pretending not to ogle.

She grabbed his chin and forced his gaze northward. "Stop ogling and talk to me. This is important."

Reluctantly, he stopped ogling. But he made a mental note to not let her get away with a command like that too often.

"You can't do it, Ross."

"Why not?"

"The work you do is too important."

"Knock-knock," he said, tapping her forehead lightly with his knuckles. "I divorce people."

She frowned, and crossed her arms over her breasts, which was a real shame. "But you do it *equitably.* You make sure the underdog gets his or her due. You don't take scumbags." She shook her head. "Nope, you can't quit."

To say he was mildly shocked would be a gross under-exaggeration. He didn't know what had made her have such a drastic change of heart. To hope that she was beginning to care for him just a little might be setting himself up for a hard fall.

That knowledge in and of itself was worrisome. To admit she had the power to wreak havoc on his heart was to realize just how much she'd come to mean to him. He'd traveled way beyond physical attraction.

"Ross? What's wrong?"

"Huh?" he said, shaking his head.

"You look funny."

"I was . . . just thinking."

"Please tell me you aren't going to quit your practice," she said, spreading her hands over his shoulders, which felt really, really good. If she kept that up, she could probably get him to agree to commit hari-kari. "Okay, I won't give up the divorce work. But I'm definitely expanding into other work. The way things are going now, I could single-handedly bring the divorce rate in Atlanta down to near zero."

Paige sat back on her heels and peered at him. "You're still getting couples reconciling?"

Ross nodded, grinning. "Give me a bow, an arrow and a diaper, and call me Cupid."

Surprisingly, Paige's forehead creased and her eyes went cloudy. "Oh."

Ross's heart zinged at the look on her face. "What? What's wrong?"

She surged out of the tub and grabbed a towel, wrapping it around her in a sudden flash of modesty. "I better go."

"Oh, no, you don't," Ross countered, flipping

331

the switch to drain the tub, then standing himself. "Tell me what's wrong."

Her chin was practically hitting her chest, so he cupped it and raised her head. To his dismay, he saw moisture swimming in her eyes. "Paige?" He stepped out of the tub. "What is it?"

She waved toward the main room. "None of this is real, is it? It's all the damn disease."

"I don't believe that. I'm going to have to side with Rachel here. All those couples getting back together is merely a coincidence."

"Not when Betty's doing Harvey the UPS guy."

"Excuse me?"

"Never mind." He tried to pull her into his arms, but she resisted. "I thought . . . I thought . . . maybe . . ."

"Maybe what?" He tugged her to him again, and this time she let him, burying her face against his neck. "Tell me," he said, figuring it might be easier for her to voice her thoughts if she could direct them toward his throat instead of having to look at him head-on.

"I thought," she started, then hiccuped and took a deep breath. "I thought maybe you actually liked *me*."

"I *do* actually like you. A whole, whole lot." He ran his hands up and down her slender back, loving the feel of her. "Paige, however this started, where we are now is *way* past the merely hot for each other stage."

"What stage are we in now?"

Okay, dangerous territory. "What stage would you like us to be in?"

She flung her head back and looked up at him, her eyes still damp but now gleaming mischievously. "Typical lawyer. Are we now engaging in serious negotiations?"

"I think so. So tell me what you have to bring to the table."

Her devilish smile faded. "That's just the problem. I don't know if I have anything to offer."

If she'd taken a sledgehammer to his chest, it couldn't have hurt worse. "God, baby, how can you even say that?" He grabbed her shoulders and squeezed. "Being around you makes me . . . happy. Excited. And I don't just mean sexually. You stimulate my mind as much as my body. I love that about you."

"You do?"

"Very much."

She swiped the back of her hand across her nose. "Okay, that's what I'm bringing to the table then. What have you got?"

He laughed and wrapped her in a quick, fierce hug. "I'm cute?"

"So's Brad Pitt, but he doesn't do a thing for me."

"Loveable?"

"As are dogs."

He grinned. "Smart?"

"I hear Hitler was a genius."

"I don't suppose being well-endowed is a ne-gotiating point?"

She glanced down, appearing to ponder. "It could be . . . but . . ."

"Hey!"

She looked up and smiled. "I guess you'll do."

Ross took a deep breath, then took the plunge. "So . . . where do we go from here?"

"To breakfast? I'm suddenly starving."

He didn't know if she was deliberately misunderstanding him, avoiding the question, or truly didn't realize he was asking about a lot more than their immediate future, but decided not to force the issue. After all, he didn't have any answers, either. He really liked her, might even be in love with her, and he couldn't imagine her not in his life at the moment. He hadn't been kidding when he'd told her in the hospital that he wasn't commitment-shy. He wasn't. He fully planned on settling down one day and living out his life with the woman of his dreams.

Was Paige that woman? It sure felt that way right now. Yet he was acutely aware at how quickly and fiercely their relationship had exploded. He'd handled way too many divorces—most of them bitter and ugly—between couples who'd leapt into marriage in the throes of that initial burning passion, only to find soon enough that they didn't have enough emotional fuel to sustain the fire.

He'd vowed long ago that something like that

would *never* happen to him. When he married, it would be for life. Which was why, he supposed, he still found himself happily single.

It occurred to him in a burst of sudden clarity that he cared about Paige too much to make any kind of promises about the future that he wasn't certain he could keep. Ironically, he liked her enough that he didn't want to hurt her. And considering her past, she was probably much more vulnerable to being hurt than most women.

She was so beautiful, with strands of honey-blond hair plastered to her neck, her lashes spiky, framing eyes soft and sparkling with what he hoped was repletion.

Her lips had that "kissed long and well" look that made him want to kiss her even longer and better. He settled for short and light. "Breakfast it is."

"You disappeared rather abruptly Friday night," Betty noted, as soon as Paige walked in the door of her office.

"Oh! Oh, Betty, I'm so sorry. I . . . I totally forgot. I hope you didn't wait around looking for me."

"I may be getting old, darling, but not dumb. When you and that adorable young man were both notably absent, I made an educated guess that you'd make it home just fine."

Paige worked hard at holding down a blush. She'd made it home all right. Just not that night.

Or the night after. If she hadn't had a full schedule of appointments this morning, she wasn't sure she'd have made it home yesterday.

The funny part was, she and Ross didn't spend the entire time ravishing each other. Oh, they'd made love plenty, but not constantly. Instead they'd talked about practically everything under the sun. Those subjects they hadn't agreed on they'd debated, sometimes hotly, but never stubbornly. She'd even gotten Ross to change his mind on a few topics. Now there was something new. A man who could admit when he was wrong, or not fully informed.

Another thing she'd noticed. Ross never skirted an issue. If she asked, he answered. And not in that man way of trying to put himself in the best light. He owned up to mistakes with a self-deprecating humor she found refreshing, endearing and, if she wanted to be honest with herself, totally sexy.

"My goodness, dear. You have it bad."

"Excuse me?"

"I take it your weekend was an unqualified success?"

"I . . . had fun."

"I'll just bet. I know dreamy when I see it."

Leaning a hip on Betty's desk, Paige said quietly, "Betty, can I ask you something?"

Betty's perfectly shaped brows lifted. "Of course."

"How do you know?"

"Know what?"

"Know . . . you know, if it's the real thing?"

"As opposed to?"

"Well, artificial. How can you tell if what you're feeling is more than just good old-fashioned lust?"

"Never underestimate lust, darling," Betty said with a smile. But then it faded and she chewed thoughtfully on a manicured nail. "Do you enjoy his company even when you're not . . . you know, all hot and bothered?"

"He's a lot of fun, yes. But the problem is, around him I'm *always* hot and bothered."

"I know the feeling," Betty murmured, more to herself than to Paige.

"Meaning what?" Paige prodded.

"Just that . . . well, I have no idea where this attraction to Harvey came from. It was out of the blue. I've known that man for years, couldn't stand him, actually. He was always calling me Betty Blue Blood. As if that's a bad thing. He's uncouth, hardly a gentleman. Nothing like my Joseph was. Then, all of a sudden"—she waved a vague hand—"bam."

Paige's stomach flip-flopped. That's what she was afraid of. What if what she and Ross were feeling was truly artificially induced? What if they woke up one day, side-by-side, looked at each other and wondered what the heck there was between them besides hot sex?

How would they ever be sure? Although Rachel had seemed certain they weren't infected, too many wacky things were happening around them.

She blinked, then cleared her throat. "Well . . ." She checked her watch. "Oh, look. Aunt Delila should be here any second. Would you pull her file for me, please, Betty?" she requested as she sailed past Betty's desk to her office.

"Delila cancelled," Betty informed her, dogging her steps right into the office.

Paige whirled around, almost knocking Betty over. "She did? Does that mean she's decided to just go ahead and pay the parking tickets?"

"No. It means she got another lawyer."

"*What?* Who?"

"She didn't say. She only said that Alicia highly recommended him, and said he's cute; besides."

"Aunt Alicia? But she . . ."

Betty nodded. "Your cousin Jennifer cancelled, too. So did your Uncle Zeke."

Paige moved around her desk and laid her briefcase—none too gently—on top of it. "My entire family is deserting me?"

Betty peered at her. "I thought you'd be happy. You're always moaning about how much time they take out of your schedule."

"Well yes, sure, that's true." And until now it had been. After all, she barely broke even taking care of her relatives' never-ending legal problems. "But Ross is a divorce attorney."

"Apparently he's branching out."

And the conversation from the other night was beginning to make sense. He'd given her fair warning that he wanted to handle cases other than divorce. But did he have to begin by raiding her clientele?

Had his offer in the hospital stemmed from something other than trying to be helpful? Maybe his practice had been in trouble before that, and he saw an opportunity when presented with one. After all, that money he gave away like free candy had to come from somewhere.

No, she wouldn't believed that. She couldn't believe it. He was well aware that she offered her legal services to her relatives at or below cost. However, come to think of it, her relatives weren't actually aware of that, seeing as she didn't itemize her expenses on the bills she presented to them.

Still, after the evidence of his goodwill in so many other areas of his life, could she really jump to a lousy conclusion? After all her false starts believing the worst and finding herself apologizing, over and over, for mistaking his ultimate intentions, she didn't want to do it again.

But she was accustomed to the demands of a huge family. Ross wasn't. As much as he'd said he'd envied her number of relatives, he'd never actually had to deal with them en masse.

When he experienced the Hart clan in all its eccentric glory, would he run, screaming? Screaming from them? Screaming from her?

After the previous weekend, she didn't like that thought one bit. Then again, if what they had wasn't real, wouldn't it be better for them to part ways before one of them got hurt? Namely, her.

She'd learned lately that Ross had a boatload of redeeming qualities over and above his incredible lovemaking. All he knew about her—in spite of his protests to the contrary—was that she was quick to judge, and quick to condemn.

He had no good reason to love her. She, on the other hand, was falling hard. And it was going to be a tough landing if and when he woke up and realized that lust only took them so far.

She glanced up at Betty, guessing her expression had just turned a little desperate. "So my morning has just cleared up?" she asked in a grainy voice.

"Until eleven," Betty said.

"Good." She stood up and began marching toward her office door.

"Where are you going?"

"To confront a snake."

The reception area in Ross's office looked like a Hart family reunion. No less than ten of her relatives were leafing through magazines when Paige stormed through the glass door.

She glanced around and planted her hands on her hips. "Aunt Kitty, Uncle John, Jennifer, Uncle Zeke, Ted—Ted? What are you in for?"

Her cousin turned an interesting shade of puce. "That's between me and my attorney."

"Until recently, *I* was your attorney."

He looked away, his big ears flaming as bright

as his face. "Yeah, well, this is a job for a *male* attorney."

"He peed in public," Aunt Kitty informed her.

"Oh."

The elder woman behind the desk smiled at her, but the smile was strained. "You're not another Hart, are you?"

"I am. And I'm next." Paige remembered her manners. "I'm Paige Hart. You must be Mrs. Whipple."

The woman practically fell over with relief. "Oh! Oh, yes! You're not here for legal advice, are you?"

"I might be," Paige said, glaring down the members of her clan. "I need to know how to divorce deserting family members."

"Now, Paige—"

"Paige, honey—"

"We were trying to help ease your load."

"Alicia said—"

Ross's office door flew open, and Nick emerged, smiling. At his first sighting of Paige, his smile collapsed. "What are *you* doing here?"

"I could ask the same," she said coolly.

Just then the intercom on Mrs. Whipple's desk buzzed, and she heard Ross's voice say, "Next?"

Paige practically ran toward Nick, glancing over her shoulder at poor Mrs. Whipple. "That would be me. And Nick."

"But—"

Before she shoved Nick back through the door

to Ross's office, she looked back at the various members of her family. "This could be a while. You might want to reschedule."

"But—" a bunch of her relatives sputtered at once.

"Have at him, once I'm done," Paige said, then really *did* shove Nick back into Ross's office. "But I get him first."

She marched in and slammed the door shut, rattling the windows in a strangely satisfying way. Then she pointed to a chair and commanded, "Sit, Nick."

"Hello, Paige," Ross drawled. "Nice to see you."

"*You,*" she said, scowling at the gorgeous worm, "I'll deal with in a minute."

She stalked over and planted herself in front of Nick. "You tell me right now why you're going to him instead of me for whatever trouble you've landed in."

"Trouble?" Nick said, sporting the sorriest innocent expression she'd ever seen. "Umm ... erh."

"Spill. Now."

"Nothing major," Nick said, working at the collar of his shirt. "And besides, it's a done deal."

Paige snorted and turned to Ross. "What did he do?"

Ross appeared pained, but shrugged and said, "Attorney-client—"

"Bullhockey. He's my brother. If he's also a

felon, I deserve to know, so I can add his prison address to my Rolodex."

"I'm not a felon!" Nick said, indignant.

"Then why do you need *him?*"

"This was a man-type thing," Nick said.

Paige snorted and growled all at once. "Man-type things are getting real tiresome here."

Nick stood, then sank back into his chair. "Okay, I was accused of . . . misconduct."

"What kind of misconduct?"

Running a finger around his collar, Nick finally croaked out, "The sexual kind."

Paige stared at her brother for a good five seconds before bursting out laughing. "You've been *misconducting* since you were sixteen years old. So what's new?"

"I'm innocent."

"And I'm Gandhi."

"It's true!"

The door to Ross's office flew open, and Rachel stood there, smoking like a tire fire. "You jerk!"

Mrs. Whipple stood behind her, puffing. "I tried to stop her!"

"Right," Ross said. "Come on in, doc, and join the party."

Rachel walked in, her eyes shooting sparks at Nick that scared even Paige. "I found this musk melon on my table this morning. Know anything about it?"

"I might," Nick said.

" 'Marry me' was carved into the sucker."

343

"You could read it. Good."

"You proposed by melon?" Ross asked.

Nick scooted back in his chair. "You like melons," he reminded Rachel.

"As breakfast food, not life-altering requests."

Not that Paige wanted to break in at an inopportune moment, but she was going to anyway. "Rachel?"

"Yes?"

"That's really over-the-top romantic for Nick. Live with it. Now say yes the melon."

Rachel hesitated and then looked at Nick and the transformation from outraged female to lovesick beauty was almost scary. "I'll think about it."

"Good," Paige said, clapping her hands. "That sounds like a yes to me. Done. Out. Both of you."

They left, arguing the entire way. Especially when Nick clapped a hand over Rachel's back end, and she socked him in the gut.

"They're in love," Ross decided.

"But is it real?" Paige asked, her body pounding with lust even as they spoke.

"Why wouldn't it be?"

"We infected them. We were infected. This is dumb."

Ross stared at her for a good long minute. "You're so sure that lust is all we have going for us?"

Taking a deep breath, Paige headed into her speech. "Well, not on my part. I'm . . . pretty sure it's not just . . . superficial lust. You're good-looking, no doubt about it. Very sexy, even. But I can't believe that that's all I'm interested in, because that would make me pretty shallow. And I wasn't brought up that way. Men, on the other hand, have no problem with shallow."

"Wait—" he started.

"I'm not blaming you, really. I have brothers, remember."

"I'm not—"

"So I can live with that and act accordingly, as long as you're honest about it. I'd really appreciate honesty."

"Okay, well—"

"Speaking of honesty," she cut him off, "I'll dish a little of my own, so you know I'm being sincere here, too. You're getting on my nerves taking over all of my family legal stuff."

He stood up and walked around his desk. "I'll take on those issues one at a time. First, I appreciate the sexy part. And I have to say right back atcha. You are one beautiful woman. Just because I think that and enjoy that about you, doesn't automatically brand me as shallow."

"Well, true," she conceded, feeling a little gooey.

"Second, I didn't ask for—"

"Ro-oss!"

They both looked to his office door, and Jasmine stood there, with Mrs. Whipple behind her, ready to kill a whole boatload of Harts, by the look on her face.

"Jasmine has defected to you, too?"

"Not that I know of."

"Then what's she—"

"Jasmine, go away for a moment," Ross suggested, rather strongly. "I'll deal with you in a minute."

He turned back to Paige, and the fierce light in his eyes nearly made her faint right there and then.

"Paige, you decide right now whether we're going to continue seeing each other. Because if we aren't, I need to get over you."

"You need to get over me?"

He waved. "I need to stop thinking up ways to be with you."

"Have sex, you mean."

He frowned at that. "Let me ask you this. Are you so shallow that you believe that's all you're good for?"

Frustration made her blow like Vesuvius. "No! Well, maybe. I don't know." She swallowed before she started screeching like a banshee. "Don't you see? How will we ever know? What happens if we jump in and land on our heads? I'm scared to death of making another huge mistake."

"And I'm scared of making a first one. But if we let the fear overrule everything else, we'll never—"

"Pai-aaaaige!" Jasmine practically screamed. "Carl's here! Make him go away!"

Paige swiped at her eyes and glanced over her

shoulder. "I thought you two got back together?"

"As i-iif. That lasted about one day. That man is impossible!"

Paige and Ross exchanged glances. Apparently the virus hadn't infected Carl and Jasmine as much as it had them.

"Go away, Jasmine," Ross growled, in a tone that worried even Paige.

"Wait outside, Jasmine," Paige said. Then she turned on the man. "How dare you bring them both here?"

"I didn't have a clue either were showing up. Not to mention the rest of your family." He stepped around his desk. "What brought *you* here?"

"I don't know. I guess I just wanted to find out where your head is right now. The not knowing is ruining my life."

"How's that?"

The man actually looked befuddled. Which made her want to invest in a switchblade. "I might be really falling for you," she said. "At least, I think so."

He swallowed. "You came all the way over here to inform me?"

"I thought you ought to know, and it's only polite to deliver this type of news in person."

"Okay."

"That's it? Okay? You have nothing better than that?"

"I'm crazy about you," he said. "You're all I think about. How's that?"

Better than double chocolate fudge ice cream. But she still hadn't heard an "L" word in there anywhere. "How are we supposed to know exactly what this is, Ross? How do you know we aren't just full of virus and lust?"

"We don't. Still, we have a great time together. So why mess with success?"

Paige stalked right up to him and grabbed his lapels. "I wasn't raised to engage in meaningless flings, mister. I need to know that you're not just in lust with me."

She pulled him closer because he smelled so damn good. "Don't get me wrong. Lust is good. I'm really beginning to enjoy it. But it's not a basis on which to build a lasting relationship. Especially if it's temporary. I'm just a little scared here. Tell me there's something more going on."

He hemmed and hawed, which was an answer in itself.

Paige prided herself on not clutching her chest to try to ease the pain. She let go of his suit coat and backed up. "I guess there's nothing more to say."

"Wait! Sure there is. Paige, honey, we have a great time together. Why would you want to give up on that, just because we can't pull out a crystal ball and see into the future?"

She shook her head. "It's not even the future I'm worried about. Can't you see, it's the past. We came together under false pretenses, and that just isn't me."

"However we got together, we're good. Don't give it up." He blew out a noisy breath. "Please."

"You know, Ross, I've had exactly one other important relationship in my life. And that one was built on false premises and promises. You know how that turned out. I just don't want to go through anything like that again."

Now he looked angry. "I am *nothing* like your dweeb professor, Paige."

"I know that. I really do." She was about to cry, and she refused to do it with a roomful of Harts standing outside. "I just . . . don't want to . . . make another mistake."

"I am *not* a mistake. *We* are not a mistake."

He was so darn handsome, even when he was frowning. She wanted so badly to find a flaw she could grab and hang on to, just so she could turn to it again and again in the next lonely days . . . or maybe weeks . . . possibly decades of missing him.

For a moment she wavered. What would it hurt to continue to see him? Well, *seeing* him wasn't a problem at all. In fact, she craved the sight of him.

Problem was, the more she saw, the more she craved. And she couldn't stand another devastating ending.

Then again, she couldn't stand the break now, either. Then again, why deny herself? Now, later, she was going down hard. Why not have fun before the fall?

"Okay, forget ending it," she said, nodding. "Let's just have sex until we both have heart attacks."

Ross's mouth dropped open. "You mean it?" he asked, too happily and excitedly for her taste.

"Sure. I'm going to use you until you drop and I get bored."

"Bored?" He appeared utterly indignant at the idea.

"Yawning," she said. "I'm giving it a month."

"You think you'll be bored with me in a month?"

She swallowed tears and heartache and the desperate need to thrash him until he fell in love with her. "I'm being generous."

Okay, she'd kept her word and given him a month. And what a month it had been. Every spare moment they'd spent together, watching movies, competing fiercely at every board game ever invented, cooking the kookiest meals, consulting about Hart family legal problems—which put the Gotti family to shame—and having sex, sex, sex.

But true to her word, on day thirty Paige Hart had dropped Ross Bennett like a maggot-infested piece of fruit.

He still relived that moment in his nightmares. Earlier that night she'd kicked his keister in Trivial Pursuit—although he *still* believed she'd stacked the cards—drove him crazy making love to him, then got up, got dressed, and left him with an, "And a great time was had by all."

And then she'd disappeared. At least, where he was concerned. She wouldn't take his phone calls, wouldn't answer her doorbell, ignored his e-mails, and worst of all, kept referring her family members to him for legal advice. If he had to litigate one more Hart infraction, he was going straight to the loony bin.

Paige Hart had dumped him. And it wasn't like he didn't understand why. She wanted to be certain that what they had was more than just a fling, driven by a disease no one but them believed they'd contracted.

Then again, if he was honest with himself, he hadn't believed that disease theory for a while now. If he had a disease, it was a Paige Hart disease. She'd wiggled like a nasty, wormy virus into his blood, and she wasn't leaving anytime soon.

Ross was pretty sure Paige wouldn't take kindly to the analogy.

Huffing out a breath in frustration, he called Paige's work number once again.

"Betty? Ross."

"Mr. Bennett, my daddy used to say that there's nothing worse than frogs in heat."

"I'll try real hard not to recognize the relevance, here."

"My daddy was a simple man, of course. My hus-

351

band would have said, 'Time to dump that stock.' "

"I've got a foolproof plan this time," he said.

"Like those flowers, yesterday? She tossed them into the toilet saying something about freshening the bathroom."

Ross winced. "This one will work. But I need your help."

"Tell me the plan, dear heart, and I'll see what I can do."

"I thought Jasmine defected to Ross full time," Paige said, as she glanced at Betty's Daytimer.

"She wants a second opinion," Betty replied, sniffing.

"Couldn't we refer her to someone in, say, Cleveland?"

Betty slammed down her pen. "Last week you were complaining about Ross taking care of your kin. Now you're complaining because one of your own wants your help."

Paige massaged her temples. "I know. I'm sorry. I'm not myself."

"You're not anyone I know, to tell the God's honest truth. Paige, just what is wrong with you?"

Paige almost smiled at Betty's slip from Atlanta diva to plain old Southern girl. But she couldn't quite smile about anything anymore. It had been three weeks since her split with Ross, and she was utterly miserable.

She'd thought that a month of unadulterated

sex would either appease them both, or at least make them tire of each other, or better yet, make him realize they were meant to be together for the long haul. But none of that had happened. Instead, she'd made the toughest decision of her life. To walk away.

And it sucked.

And he sucked.

And life sucked.

But she wasn't about to back down now. Obviously, he wasn't ready for anything more than a never-ending fling. And as much as she'd like to fling with him into eternity, it just wasn't enough any longer.

She'd considered extending her deadline for another month, but all that would have gotten her was another month of happiness.

Okay, she was going insane. She had to keep focused here. Another month of happiness with no guarantees of when it would all come to a crashing halt.

There, that felt better. She finally remembered why she was being stupid. To keep herself from hoping. She'd had hopes a long time ago, and that had been stupid, too. Not that one bad experience made for a pattern, but—

"Pai-aaaaige!"

Paige smiled, more for the relief from her tortured thoughts than from any kind of happiness in dealing with Jasmine. "Hi, cuz. Let's go in my office."

"He wants me to share Doodle, Paige!" Jasmine whined as they headed to Paige's office. "He wants joint custody."

"I thought y'all worked these details out with Ro—Mr. Bennett."

"We did, but then Carl changed the rules."

"And Ross let him?" Paige said, indignant for a couple of reasons. Her cousin was being twisted, and Ross should be hung by a noose. She recognized that number two there didn't actually fit in logically, but it still felt good to visualize.

"Ross thought it was fair," Jasmine said.

"Let's go into—" Paige started, when the door to her suite opened, and Ross strode in, followed by Carl Peyton.

Jasmine squeaked her dismay, and Paige nearly collapsed at the sight of the jerk who didn't love her.

The jerk looked so good, she wanted to throw heavy metal objects at him.

"What do you want?" she asked in a less than friendly tone.

"We need a group meeting."

"Schedule it."

"It's scheduled," Betty piped in. "Did I forget to mention Carl and Mr. Bennett would be in on the meeting?"

Ross wasted no time in grabbing Paige's wrist and dragging her to her own office, herding Carl and Jasmine along.

He wasted no time getting to the point. "Let's all hold hands."

"Excuse me?" all three of them said at once.

"Okay, never mind. Let me just touch all of you."

"Excuse me?" Carl said, while Jasmine got a decidedly happy gleam in her eyes that Paige didn't care for in the least.

While all of them stood, dumbstruck, Ross shook all of their hands, had them shake each other's hands, touched Paige's cheek for good measure and major lust-inducing action, then stood back.

"Okay, you two," he said to Jasmine and Carl. "Work it out."

"Work what out?" Jasmine asked.

"Reunite."

"Reunite?" Carl piped in. "We've been all over this. Much as I adore this li'l filly, we just keep playin' the wedding bell blues."

"Carl's a sweetheart," Jasmine added. "But we just weren't meant to be married. But I *do* want to remain friends, hear?"

"And I'd like to visit in on Doodle, darlin'. All right?"

"Okay, once in a while, I suppose. But no more T-bones."

"A porterhouse now and then?"

"Oh, you!"

Paige rolled her eyes at Ross. Same old, same old, her expression said.

That wasn't good. He was trying to make a point here, and it wasn't working.

"What say you two try to work it out one more time?" he asked desperately—and probably pathetically—crossing his fingers behind his back.

"I want to be friends," Jasmine said again, for the first time making Ross want to hug the stuffing out of the woman.

"Same with me, doll," Carl agreed.

Ross wanted to hug him too, but not as enthusiastically. "Good, good. This will work out well." He shoved the two of them out with little fanfare.

"What was all that about?" Paige asked, stepping back from him as if he was ready to pounce. Smart, smart woman, because he was more than ready.

"Note that Carl and Jasmine didn't get infected by being in contact with us."

"Maybe we don't beam up as effectively, Scotty."

"You still beam me up big time."

She snorted, but still a grin grabbed at her lips and pulled upward. "You're a pervert."

"I know. You love that about me."

"I *like* that about you."

"Okay, what you love about me is that I'm wild about you."

"I like that about you, too."

He gestured toward the door. "Didn't you see? We didn't infect Jasmine and Carl! It *was* coincidence. I've had more divorce cases than I can handle land on my lap. None of them are begging to reconcile at the touch of my hand. We're *not* infected, Paige. Our . . ." he waved a hand, ". . . need to be together is real and natural and if you try to deny them, I'm suing."

She stared at him. "Suing for *what?*"

"Alienation of affection."

"It's still lust," she argued, just to savor the moment longer, and to torture him, because he deserved it for taking so long to figure out how he felt, and mainly because it was her job as a dedicated female.

He banged a fist on her desk and then ran his hand through his hair. "Dammit, Paige, I know I hesitated there for a while about making any permanent kind of commitment, but it was only because I wanted to be so sure. I told you before that I do this once and only once."

"Do what?"

"Fall in love. Get married, the works."

"Whoa! Married?"

"That's right," he said, his jaw set stubbornly. "Forever. And I mean that. So don't go getting any ideas about getting tired of me. When we get married, that's it. You're stuck with me. So you better be pretty damn sure it's what you want, too. It is, isn't it?"

"That's not exactly the most romantic proposal I've ever witnessed."

That stopped him. "And just which ones have you witnessed that were so much better?"

"Nick's musk melon was a pretty inspired idea."

357

He scoffed. "Oh, please, anyone could come up with that one. How many men have you seen who go to such lengths to prove to you that it's you and me and love, and not some ridiculous bug?"

"Love, huh?" she said, proud that her heart didn't bang right out of her chest and into his hands. Although in truth, he'd been holding her heart in his hands almost from the moment they'd been quarantined together. Lucky for her, he was just enough of a dumb male not to realize it.

His fists hit his hips. "If you don't love me, too, just say so."

"I lust you like crazy," she said, moving closer.

He swallowed. Hard. "Lust is good. But I'm sort of looking for something deeper."

She grabbed his tie. "I admire you tremendously."

"That's good, too. I like that you admire me. Really. But what I'm looking for—"

She wrapped the tie around her hand and yanked him closer. "Your sports knowledge is impressive."

"I'm real happy that gave you a thrill, but what matters is if you love—"

"Touchdown, Bennett."

He stared into those deep green eyes for what seemed like hours and wondered at the thrill of being able to look into them forever, and wondered even more about being able to seal the somewhat spoken deal in a beautifully unforgettable way. "What are my chances of going for an extra point?"

Epilogue

"You are a snake."

"And you are a shrew."

Paige would argue that point if it weren't so damnably true. She stepped over the dollhouse Ross had erected, and stalked the builder himself. "Your client is not getting Piddle."

Ross picked up their daughter and wrinkled his nose. "My client's kingdom for a diaper change."

Paige grinned and kissed Taylor's forehead. "My cousin will be so happy to know what great negotiating skills you have, counselor."

She followed him into Taylor's room and stood beside him while he handled the task. The contentment and love she felt almost made her tear up.

"Can my client keep the ski lodge in Tahoe?" Ross asked, as he powdered Taylor's pink butt.

"Anything but the dog," Paige said. "She just wants the dog."

Ross sighed and picked Taylor up, hugging her and inhaling deeply. "Don't tell her I said so," he whispered in her ear, "but your mom is a pain in the butt."

Taylor giggled and gurgled.

"Hey!" Paige protested

"Too bad I can't get her out of my system."

"Kind of like a nasty virus?" Paige asked innocently.

Ross nodded. "Looks like I'm stuck with your mom." He kissed Taylor, then smiled over her head at Paige. "Lucky me."

AGAINST HIS WILL
TRISH JENSEN

Get Ready For . . . The Time of Your Life!

FBI agent Jake Donnelly is not a happy camper. His favorite aunt is gone and he's gained . . . not the childhood retreat he loves, but custody of a bulldog. Worse still, the terms of the will require him and Muffin to spend two weeks at a dog spa owned by a quack canine shrink named LeAnne.

But after one look at the luscious LeAnne, Jake knows the dogs aren't going to be the only ones drooling at the Hound Dog Hotel. At a place where doggie astrologists talk about the Puppy Love dating service and breakfast is eaten at the Chow Chow diner, it is easy for desires to be unleashed. Private therapy sessions with the lovely doctor soon have Jake eating out of her hand and deciding maybe Muffin *is* man's best friend if he can bring his owner and his trainer together for good.

__ 52377-9 $5.99 US/$6.99 CAN

Dorchester Publishing Co., Inc.
P.O. Box 6640
Wayne, PA 19087-8640

Please add $1.75 for shipping and handling for the first book and $.50 for each book thereafter. NY, NYC, and PA residents, please add appropriate sales tax. No cash, stamps, or C.O.D.s. All orders shipped within 6 weeks via postal service book rate. Canadian orders require $2.00 extra postage and must be paid in U.S. dollars through a U.S. banking facility.

Name_____
Address_____
City_____ State_____ Zip _____
I have enclosed $ _____ in payment for the checked book(s).
Payment <u>must</u> accompany all orders. ☐ Please send a free catalog.

Marry Me, Maddie
Rita Herron

Maddie Summers is tired of waiting. To force her fiancé into making a decision, she takes him on a talk show and gives him a choice: Marry me, or move on. The line he gives makes her realize it is time to star in her own life. But stealing the show will require a script change worthy of a Tony. Her supporting cast is composed of two loving but overprotective brothers, her blue-blood ex-boyfriend, and her brothers' best friend: sexy bad-boy Chase Holloway—the only one who seems to recognize that a certain knock-kneed kid sister has grown up to be a knockout lady. And Chase doesn't seem to know how to bow out, even when the competition for her hand heats up. Instead, he promises to perform a song and dance, even ad-lib if necessary to demonstrate he is her true leading man.

___52433-3 $5.50 US/$6.50 CAN

Dorchester Publishing Co., Inc.
P.O. Box 6640
Wayne, PA 19087-8640

Please add $2.50 for shipping and handling for the first book and $.75 for each book thereafter. NY, NYC, and PA residents, please add appropriate sales tax. No cash, stamps, or C.O.D.s. All orders shipped within 6 weeks via postal service book rate. Canadian orders require $2.00 extra postage and must be paid in U.S. dollars through a U.S. banking facility.

Name_____
Address_____
City_____ State_____ Zip_____
I have enclosed $_____in payment for the checked book(s).
Payment <u>must</u> accompany all orders.☐Please send a free catalog.
  CHECK OUT OUR WEBSITE! www.dorchesterpub.com

Aphrodite's Kiss
Julie Kenner

Crazy as it sounds, on her twenty-fifth birthday Zoe has the chance to become a superhero. But x-ray vision and the ability to fly are only two things to consider. There is also her newfound heightened sensitivity. If she can hardly eat a chocolate bar without convulsing in ecstasy, how is she to give herself the birthday gift she's really set her heart on— George Taylor? The handsome P.I.'s dark exterior hides a truly sweet center, and Zoe feels certain that his mere touch will send her spiraling into oblivion. But the man is looking for an average Jane no matter what he claims. He can never love a superhero-to-be—can he? Zoe has to know. With her super powers, she can only see through his clothing; to strip bare the workings of his heart, she'll have to rely on something a little more potent.

___52438-4 $5.99 US/$6.99 CAN

Dorchester Publishing Co., Inc.
P.O. Box 6640
Wayne, PA 19087-8640

Please add $1.75 for shipping and handling for the first book and $.50 for each book thereafter. NY, NYC, and PA residents, please add appropriate sales tax. No cash, stamps, or C.O.D.s. All orders shipped within 6 weeks via postal service book rate. Canadian orders require $2.00 extra postage and must be paid in U.S. dollars through a U.S. banking facility.

Name_____

Address_____

City_____ State_____ Zip_____

I have enclosed $ _____ in payment for the checked book(s).
Payment <u>must</u> accompany all orders. ❏ Please send a free catalog.
CHECK OUT OUR WEBSITE! www.dorchesterpub.com

Bewitching the Baron

Lisa Cach

Valerian has always known before that she will never marry. While the townsfolk of her Yorkshire village are grateful for her abilities, the price of her gift is solitude. But it never bothered her until now. Nathaniel Warrington is the new baron of Ravenall, and he has never wanted anything the way he desires his people's enigmatic healer. Her exotic beauty fans flames in him that feel unnaturally fierce. Their first kiss flares hotter still. Opposed by those who seek to destroy her, compelled by a love that will never die, Nathaniel fights to earn the lone beauty's trust. And Valerian will learn the only thing more dangerous—or heavenly—than bewitching a baron, is being bewitched by one.

___52368-X $5.50 US/$6.50 CAN

Dorchester Publishing Co., Inc.
P.O. Box 6640
Wayne, PA 19087-8640

Please add $1.75 for shipping and handling for the first book and $.50 for each book thereafter. NY, NYC, and PA residents, please add appropriate sales tax. No cash, stamps, or C.O.D.s. All orders shipped within 6 weeks via postal service book rate. Canadian orders require $2.00 extra postage and must be paid in U.S. dollars through a U.S. banking facility.

Name_____
Address_____
City_____State_____Zip_____
I have enclosed $_____ in payment for the checked book(s).
Payment <u>must</u> accompany all orders. ❏ Please send a free catalog.

Virtual Desire

Ann Lawrence

His silver-blond hair blows back from his magnificent face. His black leather breeches hug every inch of his well-muscled thighs. He is every woman's fantasy; he is the virtual reality game hero Vad. And Gwen Marlowe finds him snoring away in her video game shop.

She knows he must be a wacky wargamer out to win the Tolemac warrior look-alike contest. But the passion he ignites in her is all too real. Swept into his world of ice fields and formidable fortresses, Gwen realizes Vad is not playing games. On a quest to clear his name and secure peace in his land, he and Gwen must forge a bond strong enough to straddle two worlds. A union built not on virtual desire, but on true love.

___52393-0 $5.99 US/$6.99 CAN

Dorchester Publishing Co., Inc.
P.O. Box 6640
Wayne, PA 19087-8640

Please add $1.75 for shipping and handling for the first book and $.50 for each book thereafter. NY, NYC, and PA residents, please add appropriate sales tax. No cash, stamps, or C.O.D.s. All orders shipped within 6 weeks via postal service book rate. Canadian orders require $2.00 extra postage and must be paid in U.S. dollars through a U.S. banking facility.

Name_____

Address_____

City_____State_____Zip_____

I have enclosed $_____ in payment for the checked book(s).

Payment __must__ accompany all orders. ☐ Please send a free catalog.

CHECK OUT OUR WEBSITE! www.dorchesterpub.com

Get Ready for . . . The Time of Your Life!

Teresa Phelps has heard of being crazy in love. But Charles Everett seems just plain mad. Her handsome kidnapper unnerves her with his charm and flabbergasts her with his accusations. He acts under the misguided belief that she holds the key to finding buried treasure. But all Tess feels she can unearth is one oddball after another.

While Charles' actions resemble those of a lunatic, his body arouses thoughts of a lover. And while Charles helps to fend off her dastardly and dangerous pursuers, Tess wonders if he has her best interests at heart—or is she just a pawn in his quest for riches? As the madcap misadventures ensue, Tess strives to dig up the truth. Who is the enigmatic Englishman? What is he after? And most important, in the hunt for hidden riches is the ultimate prize true love?

___52371-X $5.99 US/$6.99 CAN

Dorchester Publishing Co., Inc.
P.O. Box 6640
Wayne, PA 19087-8640

Please add $1.75 for shipping and handling for the first book and $.50 for each book thereafter. NY, NYC, and PA residents, please add appropriate sales tax. No cash, stamps, or C.O.D.s. All orders shipped within 6 weeks via postal service book rate. Canadian orders require $2.00 extra postage and must be paid in U.S. dollars through a U.S. banking facility.

Name_____
Address_____
City_____State_____Zip_____
I have enclosed $ _____ in payment for the checked book(s).
Payment <u>must</u> accompany all orders. ❑ Please send a free catalog.

No Strings Attached
Judy Gill

Get Ready . . . For the Time of Your Life!

Lawyer is a dirty word in herbalist Holly O'Mara's estimation; in her view attorneys are logic-driven, fast-talking slime balls. And while her hunky new neighbor has all the right equipment, he is just as misguided as the rest of the breed. Although she has a concoction for almost every ailment, Holly never thinks she'll need one for an attorney with an infectious grin.

The ethereal Holly captures all of Luke Nathan's attention. And as the hard evidence for his attraction mounts, he knows he wants more than just a no-strings-attached affair. For the skeptic has found a creature even more rare than Sasquatch: a woman for whom he will willingly relinquish his free-wheeling bachelor days. Now Luke has only one choice: to make a case for the existence of true love.

___52366-3 $5.99 US/$6.99 CAN

Dorchester Publishing Co., Inc.
P.O. Box 6640
Wayne, PA 19087-8640

Please add $1.75 for shipping and handling for the first book and $.50 for each book thereafter. NY, NYC, and PA residents, please add appropriate sales tax. No cash, stamps, or C.O.D.s. All orders shipped within 6 weeks via postal service book rate. Canadian orders require $2.00 extra postage and must be paid in U.S. dollars through a U.S. banking facility.

Name_____
Address_____
City_____ State_____ Zip_____
I have enclosed $_____ in payment for the checked book(s).
Payment **must** accompany all orders. ❏ Please send a free catalog.

ATTENTION
BOOK LOVERS!

Can't get enough of your favorite **ROMANCE**?

Call **1-800-481-9191** to:

- order books,
- receive a **FREE** catalog,
- join our book clubs to **SAVE 20%!**

Open Mon.-Fri. 10 AM-9 PM EST

Visit **www.dorchesterpub.com**
for special offers and inside
information on the authors you love.

We accept Visa, MasterCard or Discover®.

LEISURE BOOKS ◊ **LOVE SPELL**